The Spirit of Ugly
A Spiritual Warfare Novel

Demon Strongholds Series
Book Three

Eric M. Hill

Published by SunHill Publishers
Atlanta, Georgia 30312

The Spirit of Ugly: A Spiritual Warfare Novel
(The Demon Strongholds Series)
Copyright 2020 by Eric M. Hill
www.ericmhillauthor.com

A Note from the Author

Hello! If this is your first time reading one of my stories, I welcome you and thank you for choosing my book to read among the millions that are available. If you have read at least one of my stories and have returned for more, that says it all! I can't think of a greater compliment and vote of confidence than for someone to read one of my books and ask for more. ☺

Get Free Spiritual Warfare Short Story!

Join my email family and get one of my free short spiritual warfare stories at https://dl.bookfunnel.com/ajx91tx3ku.

Contact Me

Here's my contact info: ericmhillauthor@yahoo.com.

God bless you!

Other Books by the Author

Chapter 1

He looked back at her in the mirror through her eyes, feasting on the tormenting insecurity he felt inside of her. Myra's brokenness enabled him to speak louder in her mind than she had ever heard him before. She looked at her face and grimaced, but dared not let a tear streak her blush and make an already impossible task more impossible.

"There's a monkey out there somewhere missing a butthole, and I know where it is," said the evil spirit.

"I'm so ugly," Myra whined, for the tenth time, echoing the obvious. "Why did I have to come out looking like this?"

"What zoo did you break out of?" the demon said, loving the effect of his words on this daughter of Eve. "You can become a star in one of those animal documentaries."

Myra had already spent the last two hours applying makeup. But it wasn't right. It was never right. No matter how long she spent putting it on, it never turned out right.

"It's impossible, garbage face. There's not enough time in existence or makeup in the world to hide that kind of ugly. Maybe you should try a paint brush."

Myra pushed out a heavy breath of hopelessness. "I can't do it. I...just...can't...do it."

"Yes, you can. Keep trying," said a different voice in her mind. "You haven't tried hard enough."

The demon of ugliness turned around at the new voice. He looked at the intruding demon's face and was thoroughly unimpressed. Everything was wrong with it.

Nose too big, and darkness knows it was too *wide*. Eyes too narrow and not quite even. One clearly protruded more than the other, which now that he looked more closely at the other eye, he saw it was obviously sunken.

What must that do to his depth perception? he thought. He moved his hand forward and backward and watched the demon's eyes. And were those swollen things above and beneath his mouth supposed to be lips? His own eyes narrowed at what he saw dripping down both corners of the unwelcome demon's mouth.

Is that pus?

The other demon gruffly wiped his mouth with a scaly forearm. "I was warned about you. They said you always got something to say about how someone looks. Well, I don't care if that is what demons of ugliness do. I got one thing to say to you before we start working together to oppress this girl. Keep your mouth off of me."

The spirit of ugliness took a slow and contemptuous survey of the demon's wretched body from head to feet. He smirked and looked at that hideous face. "There's not a chance in darkest hell that will ever happen."

"Good. Make sure it doesn't."

"Or else?"

The new demon took three menacing steps and stood toe to toe with his challenger. "Or else I'll..." His words trailed off nervously as he watched with big eyes the demon of ugliness grow another three feet tall and fill out another two hundred pounds—at least!

The demon of ugliness looked down, waiting for the petulant demon to finish his sentence. He didn't. "If you have nothing to say, shut your mouth. You're attracting flies."

The startled demon did just that and took several steps backward. "I didn't know. I was once a great fighter, too. I sometimes forget that I am now cursed with tiredness and no longer have this ability."

"You didn't know what kind of ugly spirit I am? There's a lot you don't know, demon. It's a grave mistake to enter a fight with weapons you no longer have. It's also a grave mistake to underestimate the power of ugliness. Do you know why you're here?"

"Just that I was to report here to work with you."

"To work *with* me? I am the invading spirit here. I have first rights. You don't work with me. You work *for* me. You understand?"

"Yes, my lord."

"Now which one are you? I requested several demons to help me strengthen this stronghold."

"I'm a perfectionist spirit."

The ugliness demon eyed his new help critically. "And what's your specialty?"

"Exhaustion."

"Is that why you're breathing so hard? You look like you're about to pass out. They sent me a sick demon."

"I'm not sick," he said, wheezing as though he had asthma. "It's just the way it is. Lust spirits and their gooey, sticky drippings. Anger spirits and their horrible tempers. Insane spirits and their paranoias. Me," he took a long breath, "I specialize in using perfectionism to exhaust people. What else would that tyrant, God, afflict me with? Pimples? Oh, how I hate Him!"

"Exhaustion," said the ugliness demon, thoughtfully. "Exhaustion."

"The way it works is I convince people to wear themselves out trying to satisfy a standard of perfection that I create. It's a moving target they can never hit."

Ugliness thought on the possibilities. His lips turned up into a snarl of a smile. "I pound it into her head that she's ugly...that nothing she can do can fix how she looks. I destroy her confidence, her self-esteem. You," he bounced his index finger at Exhaustion, "you come along and do the exact opposite. You tell her she *can* fix herself."

"That she *must* fix herself," Exhaustion corrected.

Ugliness continued. "One minute she has no hope. The next minute she's desperately chasing a hope that isn't there. Her whole life becomes one dizzying merry-go-round of trying to undo...me. I like it." Ugliness asked sharply, "But can you do it?"

"My lord, it's what perfectionist spirits like me do. Many of us work with ugliness demons against women. It's not that hard, especially here in America." Exhaustion grew jubilant as he wheezed out, "Tens of billions of dollars are spent every year by cosmetics companies to make women feel inadequate."

He smiled and narrowed his protruding eye. "The more inadequate they feel, the more dough they blow. But there's always another commercial to convince them there's still something they're missing. And then there's always a spirit like me to keep them from ever finding what they're missing." He clapped his hands once. "But I keep them looking. Boy, do I keep them looking!"

The ugliness spirit was warming up to this demon. He wasn't half bad. Maybe he wasn't as—no, he couldn't go that far. He was ugly. But he did like his style. He caught the jubilance of this perfectionist spirit.

"I like commercials myself," he said. "They help me to convince women they're ugly. Oh, I get a few men here and there, but mostly women. Thanks to darling Mother Eve and her attraction to beauty. What's that Scripture in the cursed book? Whatever you obey becomes your master? Or something like that."

He chuckled. "My darkness, most of them are convinced they're ugly long before I come along. And believe it or not, a lot of them are considered beautiful by human standards." His big shoulders bounced as he gurgled a laugh. "Doesn't make a difference how they look on the outside, that curse has got 'em! Mother Eve, oh, Mother Eve.

"They feel her curse deep in their ravaged souls. Sometimes I don't even have to work to get in. They're so convinced they're ugly that I just walk through a wide-open door."

"The red-carpet treatment," said Exhaustion.

He looked approvingly at the exhausted demon. "Yep, they roll out the red carpet for me. Just like in Holly—who's there?" he yelled across Exhaustion.

There was a faint sound of a lot of boots slopping through the of muck of lies in Myra's mind.

"Somebody's out there," said Exhaustion, nervously. When no one answered his lord's inquiry, he stretched out his neck in the direction of the sounds. "I wonder if it's angels."

"It's not angels," said the ugliness demon. "They wouldn't announce their arrival. Besides, she doesn't pray, and no one's praying for her. This ugly thing is on her own." He stepped forward and bellowed, "I said, who's there?"

Out of the darkness came a hideous group of demons of all sorts, shapes, and sizes. They were dressed like pirates and looked like monsters. The ugliness demon examined their features as they came to a stop. Every single one of them was ugly. "So, you're what they sent over," he said.

"Where is she?" demanded one of the demons. "I'm tired of walking through dry places. Take me to—"

"Quiet," yelled the ugliness demon. "I have first rights to this daughter of Eve. You are here because of me. Do you understand?"

No one answered. But their expressions and body language showed their submission to his claim.

"My name is Hideous," he said. "I was the one who saw this opportunity and took it. I brought first darkness. You are here to strengthen *my* grip." He lingered on *my*.

"What's her deal?" asked one of the demons.

"First things first," said Hideous. "Each of you, identify yourself and your specialty."

"Self-Hatred," said a demon with a shrieky voice. "I make people hate themselves."

"Fear, but I manifest as sabotage. I get people to sabotage themselves."

"Eat," said a spirit who shook like he had mild epilepsy. "Eat. Eat. Eat. Eat. Eee—"

"I think we get the point," Hideous interrupted. "Gluttony."

"Eat. Eat. Eat," the shaking demon continued.

Exhaustion looked at Hideous. "Is that thing ever going to shut up?"

"I don't think he can," said Hideous. "He has no self-control. Get his fat butt out of here."

Exhaustion grabbed the trembling demon by the arm and yanked him away, pulling him back into the darkness from where he had come.

"Worry," said a demon.

"Yeah, yeah, yeah. You make her worry," said Hideous. "Next."

"Bulimia. I—"

"We know what you do, Bulimia. You get 'em to eat like a human vacuum cleaner, then they throw it up or crap it out. Did I get that right?" Hideous obviously didn't like this spirit for some reason. "Where's the rest of you? You normally work in a group. Is anorexia nervosa with you?"

"Yes, my lord."

"Well speak up. All of you. Make it brief. We've got work to do."

The bulimia nervosa and anorexia nervosa strongholds started naming themselves.

"Diet. I get them obsessed with dieting."

"Exercise."

"Next," said Hideous.

"Rejection."

"Next."

"Self-Rejection."

"Of course. Next."

"Fear of Rejection."

"Oh darkness," said Hideous, appreciating Myra's growing danger. "What fun we're going to have. Next."

"Food Rituals."

"Whatever," said Hideous, unimpressed. "Next."

"Fear."

"Of what?" asked Hideous.

"Eating in public."

Hideous frowned. "Now just exactly how is that going to help my stronghold. Oh, forget it. Next."

"Cutting."

"Now we're talking," said Hideous.

On and on it went. Nearly a hundred demons assigned to one woman who had given in to the belief that she was physically ugly. There were several demons there that thoroughly underwhelmed Hideous. But overall, he was pleased. He knew not every demon would find deep access to the woman. But the shotgun approach was best. It was always better to have too many demons than not enough demons.

"Can we go at this woman now?" a demon asked.

"Eat. Eat. Eat. Eat." Gluttony was back in the room.

Hideous looked over his work crew. "Let's go get her."

Chapter 2

Myra studied her face as though her life depended upon getting it right. The difficult thing was she didn't know what *it* was. Was it her complexion? Her forehead? Her nose? Her eyes? Lips? Chin? Ears? The shape of her face?

She focused on her complexion. She was noticeably the darkest person in the family. Grandma, Mom, her two sisters and brother. She shook her head in sad resignation. Even her two aunts and two uncles had lighter complexions. Of course, it was silly to make a big deal over skin complexion. Light, dark, what difference did it make? But common sense wasn't enough to shake the stubborn thought or the stinging inadequacy it brought.

Her mind drifted to the dreaded family Thanksgiving photo sitting on Grandma's mantle over the fireplace, and the one they'd take this year. As usual, she'd stick out like a Tootsie Roll pretending to be a Twinkie. She wondered again if it really was crazy to consider the possibility that she had been adopted.

What about her eyes?

Hideous helped her. "You should be frying rice or doing something with an egg roll. You look like a black Chinese." He laughed at his own joke.

Why aren't my eyes large like Tina's? Or just regular like Lauren's? Why am I the only one with Chinese eyes? she thought. Then she thought of her roommate's nationality and felt guilty. Allison's eyes are beautiful, she thought. But I'm not Chinese. I'm black.

"And don't forget about that rhinoceros nose," said Hideous. "It's awful. Your sisters have much smaller noses."

Exhaustion chimed in with his labored breathing. "Why don't you do something about it? You should fix it. Get a nose job. A lot of people with bad noses are getting them fixed. Why not you? You want to fit in, don't you?"

Myra had never thought about getting a nose job before. She turned her face to the left and right in contemplation. Maybe she could get it narrowed a bit.

"It's time, Myra. Get your butt out of that bathroom." This was her roommate, Allison. "It doesn't take all of that. You're going to see a psychiatrist, not a beautiful boy toy."

"Give me a few," said Myra, from behind the locked door.

"You don't have a few, Myra. You've been in there, what, two hours? Get your crazy self out of the bathroom. You're costing me money. Dr. Brown doesn't play. You show up more than fifteen minutes late, she won't see you. And there goes my discount."

Myra swung the door open. "Seriously, Allison? You're making money off of me?"

Allison responded playfully, "Seriously, Myra, you spent two hours putting on makeup and that's the best you could do?"

Allison's words struck the stronghold in Myra like a stick striking a bee hive. Demons swarmed inside her mind, and some that hadn't yet gained access swarmed around her head.

"No, just kidding, girlfriend. You look beautiful. And, yes, I'm profiting off of you. Chinese are into money, too. A hundred-dollar discount off my therapy bill for every person I refer to her. You're number three."

"That's just sick, Allison. Who else have you referred? Anyone I know. Probably Raquel. It's Raquel isn't it?"

Allison pointed Myra out of the bathroom. "None of your business. Now go get some help. You're too pretty to be so depressed and weird."

Weird.

You're weird.

The demons swarmed more.

"Everyone, listen up. Stop what you're doing," ordered Hideous. "Loop those words: 'You're crazy!' 'You spend two hours putting on make-up and come out looking like that!' 'You're weird!' That's all I want her to hear. Nothing about her being pretty. Do you understand? That's all she hears. Negative. Negative. Negative. Nothing. But. Negative."

Myra had to get out of there! The voices. They were so loud. She left the apartment as quickly as she could without looking like she was running from something. It was bad enough that her closest friend thought she was weird. She didn't want her to think she was now paranoid.

Myra turned up the volume to her music as she drove. Maybe she could drown out the voices. But the higher she turned up the music, the more clearly she heard the voices. "I have to get some help," she said. "I hope this lady can help me."

A sinister voice in her mind rose above the rest. "She can't. It's only going to get worse."

Fear tore at Myra's fledgling hope. "But why?" she asked fate. "Why is life so hard?"

Chapter 3

Myra parked her car in the lot and let out a hopeful breath. She looked at the large home and beautiful landscaping and was put at ease that the psychiatrist's office wasn't in an office building.

For sure, this wasn't a social visit to see a friend. She was going to see a psychiatrist. Her life was a royal mess. But somehow going to see someone in a house made her situation seem a little less dire.

The large wooden sign in the yard was planted in a bed of flowers. Four very full and beautifully green and white plantain lilies were planted around the sign, each at a ninety-degree angle, like a small baseball diamond. The sign was simple, yet powerful. It read:

The Hope House
It's time for you to bloom!

That sign was spot on. She thought of how frustrated she was. There were so many things she wanted to accomplish. So many things she wanted to experience. Life was not supposed to be just one long, torturous grind.

Myra studied her deficient face in the car's overhead mirror and was acutely aware of the aimlessness of her soul. She couldn't sit there forever. "Okay, here goes," she said, getting out of the car with equal amounts of hope and hopelessness.

She walked across the lot and stood at the door, looking up and to the right into the face of the camera. According to Allison, Dr. Brown had learned the hard way that it was easier to *keep* the wrong person out of her office than to *get* the wrong person out. So good neighborhood notwithstanding, you had to fill out your paperwork online, complete with photo, and look into the camera when you arrived if you wanted to get past the heavy wooden door.

The door electronically clicked. Myra entered and stepped directly into a spacious and cozy lobby. Comfy furniture. Soft, soothing music. Beautiful plants. The place oozed hope. Maybe Allison was right. A glint of a smile was in her eyes.

She checked in with the receptionist, a really attractive woman who was around her own age. Myra noticed every detail about the woman with the observational skill of a movie spy. She also noticed that as she compared the woman's good looks with her own lesser looks, she didn't hear the cruel, mocking voices in her mind.

What she did not and could not have noticed was the reason the voices had suddenly gone silent.

***

Hideous couldn't believe it. He had just personally inspected every area of the stronghold, not for weaknesses—the woman had no prayer support; so the threat of counterattack was nearly nonexistent—but for opportunities. There were many.

The stronghold certainly wasn't yet strong enough to warrant the greatest certification available as a stronghold. But the walls were relatively thick and high, and his hold on this woman was strong and getting stronger. Her self-esteem was shot. And what little she had managed to hold on to was the residue of empty worldly standards. It wouldn't be long before he'd have her like one of those zombies on *The Walking Dead*. Alive, but really dead.

And now this surprise attack?

"Sound the alarm! Sound the alarm!" he screamed to his surprised subordinates. "Get to your positions! Feed those lies!"

The demons hadn't been together long enough to move with the precision and discipline of practice. Nor had they had the benefit of advance warning of the attack. How many angels were there? What kind? Why were they here? What authority were they claiming?

Hideous had told them the woman had no prayer support, but unless one was fond of the idea of losing a battle and being cast prematurely into the dark prison, the question had to be asked: Was someone praying for this woman? And if so, how much? What quality was it? Was it tearful? Fervent? So many unanswered questions.

Then every one of those questions became dangerously irrelevant.

Hideous and his demons watched anxiously from behind the walls of the stronghold. *If only I had had more time for the other demons to get inner access to the woman,* he thought.

"My lord," said a demon to him with a worried expression followed by a loud gulp, as he looked through binoculars. "There's something bad out there."

"What is it?" demanded Hideous. "Tell me. This isn't a TV game show."

"I don't know, sir. Something's got the eastern sentry guard terrified. He's nearly killing himself running away from whatever it is. He's coming our way and screaming something."

"What? What?"

"I...can't make out, my lord. He's all over the place."

"Give me those things." Hideous snatched the binoculars. He looked through them and saw nothing but a large dull light in the horizon moving toward them.

A few moments later, the terrified demon came up over a small hill, stumbled and fell, and popped up screaming as he ran, "Mercy! Mercy! Mercy angels are coming!"

The inconceivableness of this happening wouldn't let Hideous believe he had heard the demon's faint cries correctly. *Why would mercy angels help this woman?* he thought. *She doesn't serve Him, and no one's praying for her.* "There's no way he said mercy angels," he said aloud. "Did he say mercy angels?"

Hideous looked to his left and right and let out a string of curses when he saw that he was suddenly alone. The cowards had abandoned him. He pulled his sword and hurried down the stone stairs and walked menacingly toward what appeared to be his entire army huddled like a bunch of frightened rabbits. He puffed up to his full stature as he walked. He'd make an example out of one or two of them so the others would know he was serious.

He pointed his sword. "You. Fat boy. Gluttony, come here. I'll show all of you what happens to cowards. Fear of Eating in Public, you, too. I don't know why they sent you anyway. Get over here."

Not a single demon moved one inch.

Mutiny, thought Hideous. *The bunch of them have conspired to take my property.* Hideous bared his teeth, then let out a loud roar.

Even this wasn't enough to move one rebellious demon from standing there like statues. Hideous moved toward the rebels. "I'll teach you—"

A roar such as he had never heard before exploded behind him and seemed to go on forever. When the monstrous sound ended, something instinctively rose up in Hideous that led him to stay perfectly still.

Hideous saw a large figure in his peripheral vision. But it wasn't until the thing came into full view and stood in front of him that he saw just how tall and wide it was. Then another came from the other side. They both had big heads and huge mouths and powerful jaws.

Hideous thought this was like a man standing face to face with a standing polar bear. You could fight, but really, where would that get you? These things hadn't attacked yet. Maybe they wouldn't. The best he and his demons could do was to stand still and hope these polar bears weren't hungry.

The first beast stood before Hideous for what seemed like eternity as the other one walked among his army of petrified demons. Then the second angel did something that could have made Hideous move had he not had the good sense to fight the urge.

The thing walked through several demons as though they weren't solid, as if they were smoke. He stopped at each demon he invaded and lingered, as though examining them. He went to another and before he could examine him, the stupid demon moved.

In a flash, the big mouth of the beast covered the demon's whole head. Large, sharp teeth clamped shut on his neck. The beast's large head jerked side to side and it was over, except for the crunching sound of the demon's head in the mouth of the mercy angel.

Why in all of darkness are these things called mercy angels? thought Hideous.

The mercy angels would remain until Myra left Dr. Brown's office.

Chapter 4

Myra saw Dr. Brown coming down the short, carpeted hall. Her smile appeared professional, but not insincere. She was corporate CEO attractive. *Obvious, but subdued.* Her gait and eyes projected intelligence and confidence. Yet, her features were soft enough to convey approachableness. It was a good combination. Myra felt good about being here.

On top of the therapist's head sat a black and red spider the size of a grapefruit. Its long hairy legs draped over the sides of her face and neck like a sparse mop with two bloodshot eyes. The demon looked at Myra without interest and sank its teeth into the doctor's head. He then began to meticulously wrap her head with demonic silk.

Myra glanced at the large decorative clock directly before her on the opposite wall. Just as Allison had predicted. The clock hit one minute before their appointment when the therapist greeted her and shook her hand. At exactly 11:00 a.m., she was in Dr. Brown's office seated on a fat, comfortable sofa and answering her first question.

"Would you like some water? I also have tea and coffee."

"A water would be fine. Thank you."

Dr. Brown handed her a water and sat across from her on a chair. Next to her was a small table. On it was a laptop, a paper tablet, a pen, and a small recorder. "Thank you for filling out the online questionnaire. That saves a ton of time and helps us to hit the ground running."

"I can see how that helps."

"Would you like to record the session on your phone? Or would you like me to record it for you? It's entirely up to you to have it recorded...or not."

Myra hadn't thought about the possibility of recording it. She pondered.

Dr. Brown smiled. "Tell you what, I'll record it for you. If at any time you want me to turn it off, it's off. If we keep it on and at the end, you'd rather we delete it, I'll delete it. Does that work?"

"Yes. That sounds good."

"It's one of those things you don't think about until you get home and you say, Now what did she say?" They shared a chuckle. "Don't let the size of this little sucker fool you. It's a Zoom. They make some really powerful recorders. So don't worry about projecting your voice. If you speak at a normal tone, trust me, it'll hear you." She pushed the button. "So, Myra, how are you feeling today?"

Right this moment I'm feeling great. I don't hear voices in my head, she thought. Myra pondered the question. She nodded to herself. "Peaceful. I think that's...the word."

"Peaceful. That's a lovely place to be. It's actually the state of being you listed on the questionnaire that you'd like to achieve through our session. Let's define that term to make sure we're speaking of the same thing as we go on. What do you define as a peaceful state of being?"

There's no way I'm telling this lady the first meeting that I hear voices. Myra thought hard on this question.

"Take your time," the therapist encouraged. "I've found that quality of words is better than quantity of words in this field."

"There's no other way to say it, but to just say it, I guess," said Myra. "I feel ugly."

"Inside or out? Or both?"

"Definitely physically. But inside, too."

"On a scale of one to ten, one being the lowest level of intensity, and ten being the highest, where would you say you are?"

Without hesitation, Myra said, "Ten. But not now. Ten is where I'm normally at. But right now I'm..." she considered the odd sense of freedom she had experienced since coming to this office, "...at maybe a four or five. Maybe lower."

She was too afraid to admit at a conscious level that she was actually at zero for fear of making the voices come back.

"So, you're normally at a ten, but you're presently four or five or lower. Tell me some other times this feeling of being ugly has dipped low."

"It doesn't dip low. I live at level ten. I go to sleep. Then I wake up to level ten."

"This *feeling* of being ugly—you are apparently functional, from what you wrote in the questionnaire—how would you describe its effect on you?"

Sadness filled Myra's heart. "I'm not the person I was meant to be."

"Tell me about the person Myra Hansen was meant to be. Use first person affirmative language. For instance, I'm a confident go-getter who is willing to take risks."

"Okay," said Myra. She searched her pains. Her voice was low and unconvincing. "I'm not ugly."

"Use affirmative language, Myra. It's much more powerful to say what you are than to say what you aren't."

Myra's eyes watered. "I'm...beautiful." This brought a tear. She quickly dabbed it. "I've never said that." She pushed forward. "I don't ignore—I mean, I pursue my dreams. I am confident in my relationship with men. I accept compliments. I think good thoughts about myself."

When Myra's gaze into her heart broke and she lifted her eyes, they were met with an assuring smile from Dr. Brown. "Those are wonderful affirmations. I'm proud of you, Myra." The therapist smiled. "Is that all?"

"Yes."

"Then let's explore something else. What is your earliest memory of feeling ugly? This may take a little effort to—"

"I know exactly when it happened. Twice."

"You do?" Dr. Brown was surprised. "Tell me about them."

Myra shared the first time it happened.

"And the other?" asked Dr. Brown.

"I was twelve. It happened when I was watching a commercial about make-up. A woman who wasn't wearing make-up was asked by the invisible narrator: 'You want to be beautiful, don't you?'" Myra relived the moment. "The first time is when I was convinced that I was ugly. That some people thought I was ugly."

"And the second time?"

The second time is when I became convinced that everyone else knew I was ugly. I was stabbed at nine and bled out when I was twelve. I've been dead in this torment since I was a little girl."

"That's quite a graphic description of pain." The therapist shook herself free of the picture. "It's really impressive and possibly helpful, Myra. We aren't all able to pinpoint with such accuracy when our problems began."

Myra looked at her therapist, wondering if she was including herself in that statement.

Dr. Brown saw the question in her patient's expression. "I mean most people have to really search their soul for that kind of recall. And even then..."

The session continued. Near the end, Dr. Brown said something shocking. "I've talked to many women who have acute feelings of ugliness as you do. Several of them have stated that they have negative thoughts so strong that it's almost like a voice is in their head. And others just come out and say they hear voices telling them they're ugly."

Dr. Brown waited, then said softly, "I want you to know that if this ever occurs with you, you don't have to be afraid or ashamed to tell me. This doesn't mean you're crazy. Okay?"

When the session ended, Myra nearly floated back to her car she was so hopeful. She sat with her hands gripped on the steering wheel and her eyes closed. She basked in the relief she felt. "Thank you, Dr. Brown. I'm not crazy."

"But you are still as ugly as ever," shouted Hideous.

Chapter 5

The peace Myra had felt at her first visit to her therapist had proven to be a cruel joke. It had lasted only until she made it back to her car. She truly couldn't tell whether she was worse now than before she saw Dr. Brown.

But, ironically, the relapse from her short-lived peace to the reality of her normal state of torment couldn't totally suppress the fragile seed of hope that one visit to the therapist had planted in her heart. Against the suffocating pressure of thinking her every tomorrow would be a repeat of yesterday's troubles, the seed refused to die. Instead, it kept reaching upward toward a sun that Myra didn't see, but hoped was there, nonetheless.

Something inexplicably good had happened when she visited that therapist.

Thoughts of what she'd have to endure once she arrived at her parents' home for Thanksgiving dinner competed with the fragile hope she entertained that things could get better.

Could.

Would.

How many light years separated could and would? Or fantasy and reality? And was Dr. Brown the bridge to get from one to the other? As she drove closer to the dreaded family gathering and thought more deeply on the matter, Myra concluded that as improbable as it was that she'd ever be totally normal, there was something about Dr. Brown that made it impossible not to believe she would at least get better.

Thanksgiving at the Hansens. What an oxymoron!

She didn't grin, but her face did relax as she told herself she would survive the annual cutting jabs disguised as innocent humor, egotistical posturing disguised as innocent comparisons, and flaunting of achievements disguised as innocent conversation.

Now a wry grin did form. There was nothing innocent about this whole annual charade. Why drive in or fly in from all over the country to gather for Thanksgiving dinner when they spent more time carving one another than Dad spent carving the turkey?

Oh well, I've survived twenty-six Thanksgivings, she thought. What's one more? It's not going to kill me.

Chapter 6

There was probably room to park on her parents' huge cobblestone driveway that led to their four garages. But Myra parked on the street as she did every year to prevent getting blocked in by someone's car. And as she did every year, she'd use this to her advantage and be the first to leave, ignoring the protests of family members who'd regret the early departure of one of their dart boards.

"They're going to have a good time with you," said Hideous. "That dress you're wearing is horrible. It's almost as bad as that thing you call a face."

Exhaustion panted a few times and sat down. "There's really...no excuse...going out in public...looking that bad. You should've...tried harder. You can always...try harder." He released a long, tired breath.

As Myra walked up the hill, she looked down again at her dress, wishing she had worn something else. She wondered what it was about her family that couldn't get enough of beating up one another. It took as much effort to tear people down as it did to build them up. Why not just be kind?

"Hey, girl, get those skinny, Pelican legs up here. Your poor father's been waiting on his newly promoted marketing director daughter all day."

Myra looked up at the familiar voice. Dad was beaming at his youngest child. *So was Hideous...and a host of other wicked spirits.*

***

The mini-mansion was physically bright, but spiritually dark from the cloud of negativity that engulfed it. Inside the home, the atmosphere was thick with the sulfur of criticism and offense. Demons who often only saw one another every Thanksgiving drank in the toxic air and excitedly greeted one another, anticipating another Hansen holiday that would provide them with enough stories to laugh about until the next Thanksgiving massacre.

"Hideous, is that you?" said a demon. "Or did someone forget to dump the garbage?"

Hideous's face tightened into what he would have considered a smile. "Well, if it isn't Repugnant." He studied the demon's terrible complexion and the deep scratches on his face. Repugnant waited in dark delight for the comeback. "Hmm, nothing that a couple of sticks of dynamite can't fix," said Hideous.

Repugnant laughed and slapped him on the shoulder. "That's the Hideous I know. How in darkness have you been?"

Before he could answer, Exhaustion said, "You should try harder...to fix it."

Repugnant looked at the presumptuous demon, wondering if the ugly thing had meant what it sounded like he had said.

"My lord...is right," said Exhaustion. "You should put more effort..." the exhausted spirit placed his hands on his chest and caught his breath, "...into fixing your face."

"This disgusting, tired thing is yours?" asked Repugnant.

"He's a perfectionist spirit. Specializes in wearing people out. I put in a request to get some more demons to strengthen my stronghold. He's actually doing a pretty good job with my girl, Myra, here. She's mentally exhausted trying to satisfy this demon's standards."

"Hmm," said Repugnant, looking disdainfully at the demon. He looked at Hideous. "You mind?"

"What do I care?"

Repugnant's meaty backhand hit flush. He followed this by gripping the mouthy demon's throat with one hand and pounding his face three times with his large fist. The assault was over before Exhaustion knew what had happened. Repugnant let go, and the stunned demon fell to his knees, then fell backwards in an awkward position. His eyes were open, but he was asleep.

Repugnant got on a knee beside him. "Maybe I should put more effort into fixing my face. But you should put more effort into keeping your mouth shut."

The ugliness spirit stood up and looked at Hideous with happy eyes. He draped his arm around his neck and shoulders. "Hideous, my friend, we've got to get inside to the slaughterhouse. I think this is going to be the best year ever. That sister, Lauren, has picked up a pride spirit that is absolutely hilarious."

"Another one?"

"This one's different."

"What's his deal?"

Repugnant couldn't contain his chuckles. "It's something you gotta see for yourself."

***

George bent his lean, but still muscular six-foot-six frame, and tightly hugged his daughter. Myra closed her eyes and smiled. After several seconds, she said, "Okay, Dad, this is getting weird."

He kissed the top of her head and instead of letting her go, he playfully twisted her back and forth in his arms and said, "Weird? Weird is every year parking your car on the street so you can be the first to hightail it out of here. What's with that?"

"Ohh...*bust-ed*," she sang.

He let her go and hugged her shoulder as they walked toward the house. "You know I'm still the best point guard to ever come out of UCLA. The floor *general*. I see everything."

"Dad, you didn't go to UCLA. You went to Princeton."

"And what's your point?"

"If I have to explain it to you..."

"You're such a legalist. You should've been the attorney and Lauren should've been the marketing director." He shook his head. "Goodness knows, she can tell a story."

"She's creative."

"She's a liar. And she's borderline narcissist."

"Daddy," protested Myra.

He laughed. "Don't you daddy me. You know it's true. Everyone knows it's true. They just don't say anything because they're scared to death of her."

"Well, she is tough," Myra conceded.

"Tough? She's vicious. I don't know how Jacques puts up with her."

"Dad, you stop that. He puts up with her because he's her husband and he loves her."

"Don't get me wrong, Myra. I know he loves her. I love her, too. I'd just like her to ease up a bit so that doesn't change. Ken lasted what? A year? And that's why Raphael left her at the altar.

"That Frenchman she married may wake up one day and find out he doesn't have to sit on the toilet to take a leak. Then where will that daughter of mine be?" He looked at the front door. "Uh oh, there's the vicious one now," he whispered to Myra.

Lauren stood in the front door as though she were a beautiful painting and the door's frame was accentuating her beauty. One hand was on her hip; the other lay lightly on the frame. The only thing missing was the fashion photographer looking feverishly into his camera, and saying, *That's it. Yes, yes. Beautiful. The camera loves you. Now, keep your head down and look up. We want to see those lovely eyes.*

Myra always thought Lauren was the most beautiful woman she'd ever seen. And the second most beautiful woman in the world was her other sister, Tina.

"Me and your mother, we can make some beautiful babies, can't we?"

"He's not talking about you, Pelican legs," said Hideous. "Look at her. You'll never look like her or Tina."

Exhaustion chimed in. "But you have to...keep trying. Get that...nose job. Get some boobs. You don't have to be...ugly. You just have to...try harder."

Myra saw Lauren's eyes assessing her as they approached. First, her shoes. *Disapproved.* Next, her legs. *Disapproved.* Dress. *Definitely disapproved.* Neck up. *Disapproved.*

Myra tried unsuccessfully to ignore the strong negative thoughts that assailed her. She also couldn't ignore the strange feeling of being hit in her soul with something like darts.

"You did not wear that dress," Lauren declared in disbelief. "Daddy, I'm hoping this is not the first time she's hearing this. Myra, what were you thinking? And maybe we can do something with your makeup before Mom sees you."

More darts.

"Her dress is fine. Her makeup is fine," said Dad.

Myra did as she always did when her family insulted her. She pretended all was well and absorbed the blow. "Well, happy Thanksgiving to you, too, Lauren," she said, with a smile that was as genuine as possible under the circumstances.

Lauren turned both of her white-gloved palms up in exasperation at both of them.

"Lauren, last time I checked, your little girl's name is not Myra," Dad chided.

"Dad, you can't let—"

"Move out of the way movie star."

Lauren shook her head and let them in. "Don't say I didn't try to help."

Chapter 7

Myra entered her parents' home with all the enthusiasm of a person about to be audited by the IRS. Yet she wore an obligatory smile. One didn't want to face the tax man with a bad face and make him think something was wrong. That would only prompt more questions and make the misery greater than necessary. The same principle applied with her family visits.

"Myra, darling, you've arrived."

This was the cultured voice of Elizabeth Hansen. Former glamour model and present highly-compensated mature model. Former Miss Michigan and Miss America. And...*Mom*.

"Hi, Mom."

Mother was as polished and tactful as Lauren was rough and tactless. A direct insult would've been beneath her and out of character. Yet Myra did notice and feel her mother's quick and anticipated scan. She didn't have to say it. *Disapproved.*

Elizabeth smiled and gave her youngest daughter air kisses on both cheeks. "You look nice."

Nice was everything that beautiful, stunning, and gorgeous were not. It was Elizabeth's garbage word. Myra felt her total being shrink in her mother's presence—again. How was there even anything left to shrink?

"Have you seen your sisters? Your brother hasn't arrived yet. He's bringing someone with him."

Myra bypassed the question about her sisters. "A new girlfriend?"

"Well, you know your brother. I'm sure he does have a new one. But this is an accomplished male friend of his whom he thinks may appreciate your sister, Tina." Mom let out an audible breath. "He says his friend may be too nice for this family. Oh, that Cornelius. Can you believe he'd even articulate such an inappropriate joke? When is he ever going to grow out of this period of rebellion?"

May appreciate your sister, Tina.

Myra knew exactly what that meant.

May appreciate your sister's beauty.

May appreciate your sister's sense of fashion.

May appreciate your sister's accomplishments.

Myra felt bad because she felt bad. She should be happy for her sister, shouldn't she? Tina was all those things and more.

"Good for her," said Myra, sincerely. "She's a good person."

"Good for *him*," said Elizabeth. "Tina's a real treasure. He'd be quite the fortunate guy to interest a woman such as her."

Such as her.

Strangely, there were no voices in her mind echoing her mother's words. Nor were there strong negative thoughts forcing themselves upon her. Instead, she heard and felt only troubles of her own mind and torments of her own soul.

Why didn't Mom see her as a 'such as her' daughter?

***

The assortment of demons frolicking in and around the Hansen home was like a tossed salad of evil spirits. There were a few similarities in appearance of demons within the same categories, but this was the exception. For the most obvious common trait among them was the dissimilarity of their appearance.

Tall and short. Fat and skinny. Powerful and puny. Scaly and smooth. Dry and wet. Dark and light. Basic physical differences. But there were other differences. Differences in behavior, mannerisms, personalities, and attire, although not every demon wore clothes.

Repugnant had introduced Hideous to several new spirits that had joined the stronghold he was a part of in Lauren. They were all gathered in a corner of the large living room, where most of the Hansen family were milling around talking, sipping their drinks, and snacking on hor d'oeuvres.

Repugnant could barely contain his laughter. He gripped Hideous's large bicep and whispered in his gravelly voice, while not taking his eyes off the demon that commanded his attention. His chest bounced with silent laughter. "Hideous, that's him. That's the one." Repugnant told his little audience again in a whisper, "Remember. Try not to look at him when you laugh. He doesn't like to be laughed at. I don't want to have to pluck those feathers again. That's how I got all of these scratches on my face."

Hideous looked at the pride spirit and grinned with a chuckle. "He's *orange*."

"And?" said Repugnant, feeding the funny moment.

"And he looks like a rooster."

"Exactly! Exactly!" said Repugnant. "A rooster. Look at that puny little head and that crazy crop of red hair."

Another demon added, "And those big eyes."

"And all those feathers and that fat butt," said another demon that was straining to keep his laughter muffled.

Hideous's shoulders bounced with light laughter, but he didn't understand why these demons were on the verge of bursting out into a laughing fit.

"You'll see. You'll see," Repugnant promised Hideous. "Here comes Lauren now. Watch him. Remember, don't look at him when you laugh. That crazy thing knows how to use that beak and those clawed feet."

Lauren's long hair bounced on her flawless bare shoulders as she glided into the room in slow motion with exaggerated movements. Every step a message. Every expression a story.

A few heads turned to look at the first Hansen daughter who had followed in her mother's footsteps by winning the Miss Michigan beauty pageant. At exactly the right moment, she came to a smooth stop and a perfect pose.

Repugnant gripped his friend's arm so tight that his claws dug into his flesh. "Hideous, this is it. This is it. Oh, sin, get a load of this thing."

Lauren began to speak. "On behalf of the Hansen family..."

The spirit of pride's eyes popped double their size. He started strutting. His head snapped forward and backward with each step.

Hideous joined in the growing laughter of Repugnant and his new friends. "A rooster mixed with pigeon," he said.

Then the moment Repugnant and the demons had been waiting on.

The pride spirit stood beside Lauren and bobbed his head around in every direction, getting intense eye contact with as many people as possible.

"Cock-a-doodle-doooo. Look at me. Look at me. Cock-a-doodle-doooo. Look at me. Look at me."

Hideous and his friends howled in uncontrollable laughter. Hideous knew his laughter may get Repugnant shredded again, but he couldn't stop laughing. And each time he felt as though he might get control of himself, that thing would look around with those big bug eyes. "Cock-a-doodle-doooo. Look at me. Look at me."

Then the big, furry spirit began strutting around the whole house. And with each few steps, there was a large popping sound that ruffled the feathers on his butt.

"Tell me that thing didn't just let it go like that?" howled Repugnant. "Ohhh, I can't stand it. Somebody, please, cast me into the lake of fire."

Hideous fought his laughter to get the words. "Now I see why," his head slung back with closed eyes, "...the tyrant of heaven hates pride so much. It stinks!"

The more Lauren spoke, the more her demon of pride strutted, crowed, and passed gas.

Chapter 8

Myra sat her niece on her lap. "Lizzy, your hair is beautiful. I love these curls. Lauren must've spent half the day working on them."

Lizzy's eyes brightened with joy. "Thank you, Auntie Myra. Mother says I should always look as though I'm competing in a beauty contest because all the world is a contest. You don't just win. You have to prepare to win. She says that's how she and Auntie Tina and Grandmother won the Miss Michigan beauty pageant, and how grandmother won Miss America."

Whoa, Myra thought, *four years old and..."* She stopped the thought. This was Lauren's daughter, not hers. *Mind your own business, Myra.* "Oh, Lizzy, you are getting soooo heavy. Are you putting on weight?"

Lizzy's eyes widened in alarm and her little face went into a big frown. She jumped off her auntie's lap and looked down. She started crying. "I knew it, Auntie Myra. Daddy gave me a cookie yesterday. He told me to not tell Mommy or we would both be in big trouble. Now I'm fat and Mommy's going to know. I don't want to get Daddy into trouble."

Myra stared dumbfounded and guiltily at Lizzy. One moment she was criticizing her sister, and the next moment she was her sister. "Oh, baby, Auntie didn't mean it literally."

"What's literally?"

"It means Auntie was just trying to come up with something to say. I just wanted to have a conversation with you." That should do it. Myra smiled.

Lizzie asked innocently, "And that's the first thing that came to your mind? That I'm fat?"

Myra's smile vanished.

"Alright everybody," George said in a loud voice, "you know the drill. Time to huddle up and thank the man upstairs."

"Or the *woman* upstairs," said Elizabeth.

George cleared his throat. "Like I said—the *man* upstairs."

Thank God, thought Myra. "Come on, Lizzie. It's time to pray over the food. Here, let me wipe your pretty eyes." Myra wiped them. "Auntie Myra apologizes for saying something dumb, okay? I wasn't calling you fat. The problem is I haven't been doing my exercises like I should. So I'm not as strong as I used to be. That's why you felt heavier than usual."

The lie had the desired effect. Lizzie's face brightened. "Oh, that's a relief. Now Mommy won't yell at Daddy. I don't like it when Mommy yells at Daddy."

Myra stretched her lips. *TMI.* "Well, now Mommy won't yell at Daddy. I hope Mommy doesn't yell at Auntie Myra."

"I'm not going to tell Mommy you called me fat."

Myra looked at Lizzie. Lizzie looked at her. After a couple of seconds, Lizzie smiled mischievously. "Uh huh," said Myra, and picked her up. She bit Lizzie on the cheek. "I think you're a lot older than four years old."

"Are you calling me old?" Lizzie whispered as Myra carried her to the large dining room, "Mommy, Auntie Myra called me old—and fat."

***

Everyone stood around the perimeter of the two long tables with their heads bowed. George began the prayer. "Dear Lord—"

"Hold up. Hold up. Hold up," said a man's voice from the hallway near the front door. "Cornelius is in the *houussse.*"

Elizabeth gave her husband a look of scorn that may have been a bit more serious than playful. "George, you've had twenty-seven years to teach your son proper manners."

George laughed. "So now he's my son."

"Well, he certainly didn't get his caveman propensities from me."

In walked Cornelius. He was tall. Only a few inches shorter than his father. His complexion was light, like the rest of the family. And like the rest of the family, he was beautiful. "I got my caveman digs from Pops. And got my good looks from both of you."

"Your mother had a little something to do with the good looks, but that's mostly me," said George.

Elizabeth looked at her son with her mouth open. "Cornelius, what is that on your head?"

He smiled, biting his bottom lip and lowering his head. He looked sideways at the man and woman he had brought with him.

"Don't look at me," said the guy, with a thick accent. "You must walk on the road you pave."

Still smiling and looking sideways, he said to him, "So it's like that? Old African proverb, huh? I'll remember that, bro."

"Well, young man?" said Elizabeth.

Cornelius shook his hair, then cupped the sides of his head and rubbed back. He stopped halfway. "These pretty devils would be locks."

"I know they are dreadlocks, Cornelius. What I want to know is what are they doing on your head?"

"I tried to fight the funk, Mama, but..." his eyes twinkled with an idea, "Josiah here just wouldn't let it go."

Elizabeth looked at Josiah. "Then why does he have a respectable haircut and you look like you belong in Jamaica?"

Josiah laughed lightly to himself and said softly, "I think your mother has your number."

"Oh, I've had his number for a long time." She looked at Cornelius, waiting for an answer. "Do you now have a Jamaican girlfriend?" Elizabeth looked at the woman who had come with him. That may have been a loaded question.

"Moms, I've got all kinds of girlfriends. Women won't leave me along. They *love* this hairstyle. And...yeah, I've got a Jamaican girlfriend."

Lauren spoke up. "What?" She looked disbelievingly at the female. "Tell me you're not one of them."

"I am most certainly one of his girlfriends," she answered, with a hint of defiance, and an accent that piqued everyone's curiosity.

George let out a loud, "Hmp."

Elizabeth gave him a look. "Don't even think about it."

"What's your name?" asked Lauren.

"You must be Lauren," said the woman. "My name is Aya."

Lauren didn't like how she said that. "I *must* be Lauren?"

"Yep, Miss Michigan number two," Cornelius interrupted before his sister could find her mean groove, "told her all about you and that beautiful long nose and wicked tongue of yours."

"Long nose?" said Lauren.

Tina moved quickly to Aya and took her by the hand. "I'm Tina," she said, pulling her into the prayer circle. "You're very pretty. Where are you from? I love your accent."

"Thank you. I live in England, but I am originally from Morocco."

"That's my twin," said Cornelius. "The one who's rescuing you. One of my two nice sisters. That one over there is the other nice sister," he said, pointing to Myra." He laughed. "Don't let the mean one talk you out of your blessing."

"I am my own woman. You know this."

"My, my, my," said George. "Morocco."

"George," said Elizabeth, "you better pray over that dead turkey before we have to pray over your dead body."

Myra didn't hear a word of her father's prayer. She was fascinated by what she had just witnessed. She had always admired her brother's independent streak. But for the past couple of years, despite his laid back, jokester personality, he seemed to be in a state of undeclared war against the family's expectations.

She thought of Lauren, Tina, and herself. In each of their own way, they were little moons orbiting and enslaved by the dominant mass of the family. How did he break free? She'd definitely have a private talk with him before she left.

Chapter 9

The family and guests would eventually leave the formal dining room and spread to other rooms to talk. But everyone knew the unspoken rule. This was not done until Elizabeth gave a clear signal that enough time had been spent in the dining room. Until then all posturing, bragging, and veiled and unveiled insults would be done in that one room.

Ironically, the usual family Thanksgiving antics weren't getting the same laughs as they normally did. Even Lauren and her rooster pride spirit weren't getting the laughs they had been getting just a little while ago. Only the empty headed, purely instinct driven demons still found the dinner funny. The more thoughtful demons were troubled.

Elizabeth sipped her red wine and placed her glass on the table. She dabbed her mouth with her napkin. "So, Josiah."

"Yes, ma'am."

"I don't like him. I don't like him one bit," said Repugnant. "Something's wrong with him."

Hideous peered at Josiah's eyes. "Something is wrong with him. I wonder if..."

Another demon said, "Where's that wind coming from?"

Elizabeth continued her inquiry. "Aya is from Morocco. She's a cyber security analyst like Cornelius. She's atheist. She speaks Arabic, French, Spanish, and English. What about you?"

"Hmm, well...my native home is Ghana. I am an application security engineer."

"There's basketball and money," said George. "Nothing else in the world means squat. They make pretty good money, don't they?"

"More than me and Aya," said Cornelius.

Josiah laughed. "That is not necessarily so."

"Oh, it is necessarily so," said Cornelius, mimicking his friend's accent.

"Go on," Elizabeth prompted.

"Unfortunately, I am not in Aya's league. I speak only three languages. English, Akan, and French."

"French?" said Elizabeth.

"Yes, French is very popular in my country." He stole a glance at Cornelius, who was smiling at what he thought was coming next. "And unlike my friend, Aya, I am not an atheist. I am a son of the Most High God, and servant of the Lord Jesus Christ."

Cornelius thought, *Bam!*

***

A brilliant light flashed that temporarily blinded every demon that was walking around the physical home of the Hansens. At the same time, a strong gust of wind hit the blinded demons, toppling and sending some flying, and others rolling on the floor in confusion. Several landed outside the home. These decided on the spot to call it an evening, and to go find something else to do until it was safe to return. There were times when walking through dry places made good sense.

Hideous and Repugnant were not among those demons.

"What was that?" asked Repugnant, asking what he already knew. It had to have been that tyrant, God. He was always doing something unexpected. He rubbed his eyes, blinking furiously in growing alarm that his eyesight was permanently damaged.

Hideous scowled and looked at the detestable African visitor. He got up off the floor. "That, my friend, is a believer who knows who he is in Christ. I hate those kind. I have no success with them. They won't believe my lies."

"Why would Cornelius bring one of those to the dinner? It doesn't make sense." Repugnant let out a breath of relief as his eyesight returned. "Oh, darkness, I thought I was blind."

A heavy, dreadful voice rolled in from every direction. Its sound entered more than the demons' ears. It entered every pore and filled every space of their being. "The angel of the Lord encamps all around those who fear Him, and delivers them."

Hideous and Repugnant looked in every direction for the threatening voice that had invaded them. "Oooooh," Hideous heard Repugnant's wavering voice.

"What? What?" he answered, in an irritated hiss. Irksome Africans. Blinding lights. Thunderous voices. Things were suddenly going bad. Then he turned from searching for the all-consuming voice to see what Repugnant was *Oooohing* about.

Six heavily armed angels surrounded the African. They faced all directions. There was even one at his head looking up, and one at his feet looking down. No way to reach this wretched man without going through those angels and their long swords and short blades. As if anyone wanted to tangle with this man of God. *Well, at least they're not mercy angels.*

"I don't have a lot of experience dealing with angels," whispered Repugnant.

"Neither do I," whispered Hideous. "What do we do?"

"Exercise your rights. Nothing more."

Hideous and Repugnant looked at each other in nervous astonishment at the words of the angel. Repugnant whispered, "He *heard* us? How could he hear us?"

"How do I know?" Hideous answered, taking out his anger on his friend. He looked around. Most of the demons of his stronghold were still there. He could see them positioned on the thick walls of lies in Myra's mind. He had to do something assertive or these blabbermouths would put the word out that he was a coward. "This family has given us rights."

"Exercise your rights, or leave," said the angel. "We will not speak to you again without a sword."

Repugnant whispered, "You think he's telling us we can get back inside of our property?"

"Oh, Repugnant, why are you whispering? This traitor's got ears like an elephant."

"Yeah, but our demons don't."

"Guess you got a point." Hideous thought he saw a slight movement in the angel who was doing the talking. He quickly spoke. "We'll not bother the man of God. All we demand is what's rightfully ours." Hideous whispered to Repugnant, "Order your demons."

They both ordered their demons back into their hosts. The other demon commanders did the same.

"Whew," said Exhaustion, leaning heavily against a lie, "they messed up...the party. But at least...we don't...have to see...that man of God...again.'"

Hideous peered at the man of God from the safety of his stronghold. He didn't share the worn-out spirit's optimism.

Chapter 10

Myra tried not to squirm or show on her face what she was thinking as the inevitable annual conversation arose about how Mother had won Miss Michigan and Miss America back in the day, and how unprecedented it was for two of her three daughters to also win the Miss Michigan beauty pageant. She excused herself to go to the restroom and made eye contact with Cornelius as she left the room. They met in their father's study.

"What a wimp," he said. "They're only going to talk about how beautiful they are for maybe half an hour and you skate."

"I know," she confessed. "I'm just tired of hearing it. Tired of hearing how beautiful they are, and..." She dared not say it. Myra noted an uncharacteristic thoughtfulness in her brother's eyes as he looked at her. She shook her head. "No, no, it's not that. I mean...it's just..."

"Yeah, it is that. *And how beautiful you're not.* It's those three—and you." He said it as though she was an afterthought. "You're not in *Club Glamour*. Good. The club's bankrupt. Shallow. Don't worry about being in their little rinky-dink club. They're not in your league anyway.

"What you have will last forever. What they have will last only until it fades away." Cornelius laughed at Myra's open mouth. "Nice tonsils."

"Oh," she closed her mouth and shook her head with questions. "Thank you." She paused. "I don't know what to say. I had only planned to ask you how you found the courage to...not defy Mom and the others...well, I guess it is defiance. Their words have such power over me. I can't even imagine not trying to live up to their expectations. How do you do it?"

She threw in, "For instance, you know how Mother feels about short men and dark men. What possessed you to try to fix up Tina with an African? And a west African at that! How many times has Mom gotten on her soapbox about west Africans being weak for allowing themselves to go into slavery? Or for being complicit in the slave trade? And you bring one home!"

"Correction," said Cornelius, "our mother doesn't like short men or dark *people.* First of all, Josiah is six-foot-one. Only our mother would consider that short. Second, this whole skin color thing is stupid. Third, Moms is as smart as she is beautiful. And I love her as much as anyone. I mean, she's Moms. But, Myra, I'm just going to be real. I can't believe someone as intelligent as she is can say things only an idiot would say."

Myra's mouth popped open and her neck jutted forward. "You're calling Mom an idiot?"

Cornelius gave a half smile. "Oh, don't get me wrong. I may be doing my own thing, but I ain't crazy. I'll never be that plain talking to Moms. I can be sophisticated when I need to be." He winked at her. "Plus, I like living. And who told you I'm trying to fix up Tina with an African?"

"Mom did."

"Moms? I'm not trying to fix up Tina with an African. I'm trying to fix up *you* with an African."

Myra was shocked. "Me?"

"You think I'd try to fix up anyone with Tina?"

"Tina's a doll. She's nice. Why wouldn't you?"

He stabbed his index finger at Myra. "Right. She's a doll. And she's nice. Too nice. She's Moms' doll. Moms winds her up and she says and does whatever Moms wants. She can't think for herself. You think I'd set some brother up to live with that? And have that dude looking at me funny until he bails? Uh-uh. Not going to happen."

Myra was having a hard time grasping that this was her brother. *Cornelius.* A guy who was charismatic, intelligent, and as beautiful as a man could be, and who, until tonight seemed content with simply letting those qualities bring him lots of money and lots of women, now sounded like a fountain of wisdom.

She didn't see the angel of truth that rested his hand on her brother's shoulder.

"Okay, just for the sake of moving this conversation along," said Myra, "let's assume you are actually Cornelius and not some alien pretending to be my brother. These things you're saying about Mom and Lauren and Tina—"

Cornelius interrupted. "These things I'm saying about *you*, Myra. You can say it. I'm not talking about them. I'm talking about you. I only mention them because I'm trying to get you to see something."

Myra didn't know why her eyes were beginning to moisten. "What's that?"

"That you're beautiful. Just as beautiful as Lauren and Tina."

"Cornelius, I don't know why you're saying this—and I appreciate it. I do. I really do." She spoke as though she was correcting a good-hearted child who had said something really dumb and she was trying not to hurt his feelings. "But you're now being ridiculous."

"Okay," he conceded with a laugh, "Lauren and Tina, they're unreal, right? They've got that beauty it factor thing locked up. It's not even fair what God did with them."

"Nooow we're being honest again."

Cornelius pointed. "But that's if we're just talking physical. If we look at the whole person, you're number one."

She rolled her eyes and turned her head. "Cornelius—"

"Hear me out, Myra. Lauren and Tina, they're a ten plus and a ten plus plus. I'm going to be honest with you. You're a ten. But if we look at the whole person, you're a ten triple plus. Look, they're beautiful and they know they're beautiful. You're beautiful and you don't know you're beautiful. That's why I wanted Josiah to meet you. The man who gets you...now that brother's got something special."

Myra wiped her eyes. "You're full of surprises. You're full of something else, too. But I'm not going to say what it is."

"Won't be the first time I heard that." Cornelius said nothing for a few moments. "Is this where you make your annual getaway?"

"Yeah, I think this is a good time for me leave. Look, your friend tried to talk to me a few times and I wasn't very friendly. I mean, I thought he was here for Tina."

"I'm sure he won't slit his wrists. It's not like he doesn't have women coming after him."

Myra felt her posture involuntarily stiffen at this news.

"To be honest, it was a longshot anyway," said Cornelius. "Josiah's really spiritual. He doesn't date."

"He doesn't?" Myra wished she could take the words back as soon as she spoke them.

"Ahh, so there is some life in the corpse?"

"No, it's not that," she lied. "It's just unusual that a guy..."

"That good-looking doesn't date?" Cornelius smiled. "I mean, even though he is dark, muscled up, got fat bank, and is only six-foot-one?"

Myra's embarrassment temperature went up to a hundred and ten degrees. "No, what I'm saying is it's unusual, knowing how much you like women, that you would hang out with a male friend who doesn't date."

"He has high standards."

Myra was not falling for the bait.

"I know you want to ask about his standards," said Cornelius, having the time of his life at his sister's expense. "He only dates Christian women who love the Lord and are pure."

"When did you start talking like that?"

"Oh, don't get any ideas sister. I don't. And just for the record, I have absolutely no problem with impure women. *He* does. I'm just telling you what he told me."

"I didn't know there was a shortage of Christian women."

"According to him, there's not a shortage of Christian women. There's a shortage of Christian women who don't try to go to bed with him."

Myra shook her head and smiled. Then she laughed. "I have heard it all."

"Like I said, he only dates Christian women. So, it wasn't going to happen anyway."

"And yet you invited him. Why?"

Cornelius looked down and pondered. He looked up with a smile. "Because you're a beautiful person, and I really like this guy. We talk a lot." He chuckled. "He's trying to convert me. Now that's not going to happen. But I figured with you and him...you're a beautiful person, he's a beautiful person. Hey, you never know."

Myra was overwhelmed by her brother's sentiments. She knew he liked her, but she had no idea that he thought so highly of her. Some of the things he said were so sweet and insightful that she couldn't bear the idea of going back and joining the others so they could rip her good feelings from her heart.

"Cornelius," she said, "I need to go."

"I know you do."

"Tell your friend I..." She didn't know what to say.

"That you apologize for being rude. That you were under the impression he was there to meet your sister. And that you would be delighted to talk with him. I'll give him your number."

Oh, no. Now he's going to think I want to go out with his friend. She began a slow shake of the head. "Wait...that's not...he doesn't..."

"I know the Hansen females aren't into dark-skinned brothers, but I'm giving Josiah your telephone number. Maybe he can get an affirmative action exemption."

She looked at him as though she had no choice but to agree. "Okay, Cornelius, give him my number."

"I love it," he said. "A sister who doesn't know she's a fox is willing to sacrifice to go out with a good Christian man who makes two hundred K and doesn't sleep around. This is some serious theater."

***

Hideous waited until she left the house. "I know you don't believe that crap he said about you being beautiful. He said you're a ten just to make you feel good about yourself. I wouldn't give you a two on your best day. I dare you to look in the mirror."

Chapter 11

"Why hasn't he called you?" Hideous taunted. "It's been a week. If he were going to call you, it would have happened by now."

Myra looked at her huge computer monitor and tried to ignore the thought by focusing more intently on the ad's verbiage. No matter how hard she squinted her eyes, she couldn't squeeze away the negativity that was pouring over her like a dark, heavy liquid. She tried to mentally shake it off, but the feeling clung to her.

"Ugh!" she grunted under her breath. *I didn't want to talk to him anyway,* she told herself. But this was only partly true. For even though she had tried hard not to think about Josiah, she couldn't help herself.

As far as she knew, there was nothing about him not to like—certainly not physically. And he was charming...and he smelled good...and his smile was hypnotic. Before she could stop herself, she defiantly thought to her mother and sisters, *Tall, dark, and handsome may be ugly to you, but it's fine to me.*

"Ugh!" she grunted again for thinking like this. It wasn't going to happen. This guy was super religious. She wasn't irreligious, but she wasn't religious either. Although she did believe in God.

There has to be somebody or something out there, she thought. But she didn't know who or what it was, or whether it made any difference. She realistically concluded, If this man is kicking Christian women to the curb, I don't stand a chance.

"Myra, just stop it," she scolded herself in a whisper. "You're practically having this man's children."

Hideous gave his two cents. "You don't stand a chance because you're ugly as sin. There's nothing about you that would attract a man like that. You're not Tina. You're not Lauren. You're *My—ra*. Ugly *My—ra*."

And that was the real reason she couldn't talk to Josiah. It was the same reason all of her relationships miscarried, died stillborn, or were slowly strangled or abruptly killed—by her, directly or indirectly. No man wanted her. Not for long. They said otherwise, but she knew differently. So why begin what could never be, or allow to linger what was doomed anyway?

She looked at Allison's marketing ad, but thought of her therapy and wonder-working therapist. Irrational, hopeful thoughts about the remote possibility of one day living a normal life bobbed up and down like a small boat in dangerously rough waters.

The thought of Dr. Brown securely anchored her uncharacteristic hope. She wouldn't sink. Dr. Brown won't let me sink, she told herself. Who knows? Maybe one day I'll be able to have a normal relationship and not sabotage it.

Her heart warmed at the thought of Josiah, although under any circumstances, that was more impossible than improbable. But if not him, maybe somebody—someday.

Myra exhaled deeply...and enjoyed the new horizon of *maybe*. Half a day later her boat of hope struck a rock and sank.

***

Myra held her private cell phone in her hand, frowning at the abrupt dial tone, and now staring at the iPhone's face. Allison was beside herself. She was crying hysterically. Her words were incoherent. What was that all about?

Myra thought about Allison the whole way home. Her co-worker had never come right out and told her why she was seeing Dr. Brown. But bits and pieces and hints led her to believe she had been sexually abused as a child. Plus, she had lost her mother at a young age. Yet, she seemed to be making good progress. That was one of the reasons Myra had trusted her recommendation to see Dr. Brown for her own problems.

Myra tried calling again. No answer. What could have possibly come out in her therapy session that would cause Allison to lose it like this and not return to work? The answer was devastating.

***

Allison was on the floor between a sofa and the glass coffee table, stretched halfway across it and crying with moans. Myra's face was pained and her eyes big from the news. "Allison, what are you saying?"

Allison screamed, "I'm saying she's freaking dead! The therapist who was telling me how to get my life together killed herself. That's what I'm saying!"

Myra's purse dropped to the floor. Her mouth went dry and she got dizzy. She turned her head left and right in a stupor. The room was moving. *I have to sit down,* she thought. She sat and felt as though she'd been swallowed by a monster of nausea.

"My mother and my therapist commit suicide?" Allison wailed. "How do you swallow a bottle of pills and leave your little girl in the hands of a pervert? How can you be so selfish to kill yourself and abandon your patients? Who does something like this? Myra, what am I going to do? I'm lost."

Myra stared straight before her with the expression of a shell-shocked soldier. Only she didn't hear ringing. Through the numbness, she heard only *What am I going to do? I'm lost.* She had reached the boundary of her new horizon of hope only to find the world was indeed flat, and she was at its edge and going over into the abyss.

"I don't know," Myra whimpered, almost inaudibly. "I thought she would help me." Her eyes wide and lips trembling, she muttered, "I've got to find a way." Without thinking, she absently responded to the prompting of the Holy Spirit and said, "God help me. Show me what me to do."

Chapter 12

A physical hit to the head with enough violence to shake the brain is a concussion. Some of its symptoms are amnesia, confusion, lack of physical coordination, dizziness, nausea, vomiting, and fatigue, among other things—even death.

Allison's words had furiously hit Myra like a baseball bat to the head. Her physical senses were compromised, especially her sense of perception. She'd only been drunk once in her life and hated it—in college. Blurred vision. Stumbling around like an idiot. Throwing up. Waking up not knowing who had done what to her. There was simply nothing about it that was remotely appealing.

Unfortunately, that's exactly how she felt as she sat on the sofa and catatonically stared at Allison. She heard the muffled sounds of her roommate's anguish. She heard her bitterly cry out over and over, "How could you do this to me?" She saw her now rolling around on the floor and beating her fist on the carpet.

Myra felt two odd things happening inside of her. The first was she was becoming more disoriented by the moment. The other was her shock was acting as an anesthetic, and now she felt the numbness wearing off. Something told her that she had to escape this room before she began to feel the pain as acutely as Allison was feeling it.

She consciously steadied herself as she rose to her feet. She knew the sympathetic thing to do was to comfort Allison. But it was all she could do to not—what? Scream? Throw up? Pass out? Her voice was soft and unsure as she headed for the front door. "I've got to get out of here."

Allison didn't see her leave.

***

Three Days Prior

Josiah finished his last pushup and rolled over onto his back to begin his abs routine. He'd barely begun when an angel gripping a dagger kneeled next to him and gravely said, "The burden of the Lord, man of God. The burden of the Lord."

The angel slammed the dagger into Josiah's chest and vanished.

Flashing mental impressions. An angel with a sword in his hand. The great white throne judgment. Tears. Screams. Terror. Dread. The lake of fire. Eternal damnation.

Josiah's eyes widened and immediately moistened with tears. He hadn't thought of Myra since Thanksgiving. Now she had suddenly filled his thoughts, but not romantically. That was out of the question.

Rather, he was filled with concern for her soul. But concern wasn't a strong enough word. What he felt was an all-consuming danger for her and a desperation to see her saved. And he felt something else.

Pain.

Josiah put his hand over his bare chest. The pain wasn't physical. It was much deeper than that. It was spiritual. He knew from experience this was God. The Lord was letting him feel a little of His own heart for Myra so that he'd pray for her.

Ezekiel 22:30-31 and 1 Samuel 12:23, Scriptures Josiah had hidden in his heart, came to mind:

> *So I sought for a man among them who would make a wall, and stand in the gap before Me on behalf of the land, that I should not destroy it; but I found no one. Therefore, I have poured out My indignation on them; I have consumed them with the fire of My wrath; and I have recompensed their deeds on their own heads, says the Lord.*

Moreover, as for me, far be it from me that I should sin against the Lord in ceasing to pray for you; but I will teach you the good and right way.

The man of God began his agonizing prayer. "Oh, good Father, save this woman from her sins. Have mercy on her soul. Don't let her die a rebel. Open her eyes."

Chapter 13

Myra started driving with no destination in mind other than to get as far away from Allison's gut-wrenching wails as possible. She found herself sitting in traffic on tenth street going east toward the 75-85 interstate connector that ran north and south through the heart of downtown Atlanta.

How'd I get here? she wondered.

Maybe she'd go to Piedmont Park. She wasn't far from it. She thought of street parking versus the parking deck. *If there's no street parking, forget it.* Not that she was going to get out of her car. She wasn't. But sitting in a dark parking deck mulling over her therapist who had just committed suicide was creepy. That was too much like she was planning to follow her lead. As hard as life was, she still had many decades to go before checking out of here.

She exhaled as she glanced at the red traffic light before her and wondered where the siren was coming from. A pretty, long-haired, backpack-carrying Georgia Tech student stepped off the curb to cross the street. She smiled widely as she talked on the phone. Her steps had a youthful bounce in them.

Myra watched the joyful girl and drifted away from thinking of her dead therapist to how full of life and promise this young woman looked. She wondered if the girl was talking to her boyfriend. Oddly, she found herself envying this stranger. The girl's relationship with her boyfriend. Her supportive parents. Her healthy self-image. Her bright fu—

A red car with black stripes on it sped from the girl's right side and hit her with such force that it was impossible for Myra's eyes and brain to process how many times the girl's body flipped in the air before it crashed sickeningly to the asphalt in a distorted heap.

The gulp in Myra's throat froze in place and constricted her scream. *Help her! Help her!* The thought came from her as though from someone else. Myra's humanity urged her out of the car to answer her own call. But it was her humanity that also made this impossible. Her limbs wouldn't move.

She watched several people get out of their cars and run to the still body. The car that hit the girl continued driving until it was trapped by traffic ahead. The car skidded until it ran into the back of a car. A guy jumped out of the offending car and ran away. He was chased down by two men who took serious liberties with vigilante justice.

Now she saw the source of the siren. A police car sped from the same direction that the other car had come from and screeched his car to a diagonal halt, blocking the body from other oncoming traffic.

"Ughh," Myra moaned. She felt herself becoming sick. She snatched at her door's handle and pushed the door open just in time.

The angel who had been tasked with getting her to this spot at this exact time had not been told why he was to have the woman here. It was not the first time he had seen a human die. Still, he was mortified. It was never easy.

He watched the young woman's eternal spirit exit her body and hover over it in confusion. The girl looked at him with wide, terrified eyes that searched for an answer to her predicament. There was a loud clank. She looked down at the shackles and chains around her ankles.

Hell's irresistible gravity snatched for sin and found its ripened harvest. It yanked her downward to meet the hungry flames of divine punishment. He watched until she disappeared into the thick darkness and her screams were no longer audible.

The death of the wicked is tragic, he thought, before focusing again on the woman he was directing. She was shaking inside and out.

The angel thought of the dead girl and words from the blessed book. *You fool! This night your soul will be required of you.* "It is good for you to see this," he said of Myra.

The angel looked up and saw two fiery angels descending in the far horizon. He knew they were coming for Myra. He felt his release from this prayer support task. He looked to the left and saw another angel. This one cloaked in ominous darkness and carrying a sword in his hand.

Truth from one direction and judgment from another, noted the angel. They always worked together. He looked in righteousness at Myra. "I hope you are not the fool in the parable," he said, before leaving to help answer another prayer in another place.

Chapter 14

At the last minute, Myra turned right on Peachtree Street. She drank their coffee, but she wasn't one to hang out at Starbucks. If she were going to do a coffee shop, she'd much rather it be an indie. More character and she liked to support small businesses.

But today wasn't about character and supporting the little guy. It was about getting out of her car as quickly as possible—getting away from cars *period*.

That poor girl, she thought.

Myra's hands trembled as she gripped her coffee cup and stared at it. She hadn't put the cup to her lips since she sat down. The noise of the early evening coffee crowd around her helped a little. But only a little.

How fast was that car going? she thought. How she spun in the air and hit the ground... There's no way that girl lived.

Myra had never seen anyone die. She had never even known anyone who had died. Death had been only a distant reality. Something she had seen on television. Something she had heard about on the news or had read about on the internet. But not something that happened before her very eyes.

And so violently.

And suddenly.

The suddenness of the tragedy was in a way more horrifying than the death itself. For whether one thought about one's own death or not, one knew it would happen—one day. One day a long while away. Many years in the future. Decades even.

It would happen only with proper notification and at the appropriate time, so as not to be sudden or inconvenient or premature. When every laugh had been laughed, every joy enjoyed, every dream realized, and every love loved…

And when everything desired had been attained to its fullest, and when the many wrinkles on the face testified that it was only natural that the person should now leave this life, then and only then would the end come.

The death of the young girl swept the dishes of this immaculately set table of illusion onto the floor with a jarring crash. Cruelly, a young and beautiful university girl had done nothing more offensive than to assume her safety as she crossed within the pedestrian crosswalk at a green light. And for this reasonable assumption, she was now dead.

Myra sipped her coffee. It was lukewarm, tasteless, and definitely not her usual drink. What had they given her? She knew the real question was what had she ordered? Her mind wasn't all there. *Forget it,* she thought. *I don't need it anyhow.*

"You need to talk to Josiah," said one of the angels of truth who had descended from the sky. "He can help you with your fears."

Myra's phone rang. She looked at the unfamiliar number and ignored it. This wasn't the moment for wrong numbers or a once in a lifetime timesharing deal. She put the phone on the table and rested her hand over it.

The other truth angel said, "Check your phone message." He studied her non-response. "James, do you think she can hear anything we say?"

"Some." He studied her, too. "But she does hear the Holy Spirit speaking through the girl's death."

The truth angel pondered his friend's words. "Yes, but for how long? And to what extent?"

It was a baffling fact that humans could be exposed to the greatest manifestations of the Creator's creation and yet not see Him. Or even worse, they could actually see Him and yet not believe Him.

But sometimes shocking or traumatic events penetrated the sinner's thick darkness and compelled him to think of the great questions of origin, purpose, and destiny. Questions that inevitably led to God—if the sinner responded to them in honesty and humility.

"Hopefully, long enough," answered James.

One of the great mysteries of darkness was how unpredictable and fleeting were the moments that sinners contemplated eternity. The greatest events could produce the least moments of opportunity; the least events could provide the greatest moments of opportunity. There was a troubling randomness to it all that frustrated the most sophisticated and well-executed strategies.

James saw his friend looking in the distance toward the angel of judgment in the dark cloud. They both knew why he was there. "Micah," said James, "I think of the words from the blessed book in the letter to Timothy, 'Some men's sins are clearly evident, preceding them to judgment, but those of some men follow later.'"

"That is what I fear of this sinner," said Micah. "I do not sense that her sins are clearly evident. She sees herself as good."

James nodded grimly. "And yet she is a child of wrath, a daughter of disobedience, who is by nature an enemy of all that is truly good."

Micah added, "All have sinned and fall short of the glory of God. There is none that do good. They are all together gone out of the way of righteousness."

"The challenge," said James, "is to convince her that she is not good, that her goodness is an abomination to the Most High."

"Isn't that always the challenge when dealing with *good* sinners?" said Micah. "Perhaps the man of God will be able to open her eyes."

James looked at the angel of death and said, "He who believes in the Son of God has everlasting life; and he who does not believe the Son shall not see life, but the wrath of God abides on him."

The upper part of the cloud of darkness around the angel's face cleared for a brief moment, revealing a face of bronze that glowed with the heat of God's anger, and deep eyes of fire that acted as windows into hell. Both angels of truth looked into the fiery abyss of the death angel's eyes and said, "Blessed be the name of the Lord. His judgments are true and righteous."

Myra's phone rang again.

Chapter 15

First, two fire angels of truth. A menace for sure. But at least they had a fighting chance against them. There were rules of engagement. It was lies versus truth. Not this unfair and humiliating mercy trumps all business. Over one hundred demons neutralized without a fight.

Hideous seethed in silence. Every demon in his stronghold—including him, but that was beside the point—was frozen in place through terror of the two mercy monsters who were walking around the place as though they owned it. And those demons who normally hung out around Myra seeking entrance into the stronghold? What a surprise? They were conveniently absent.

All because the tyrant of heaven played fast and loose with the rules in the name of mercy. But these mercy monsters wouldn't be around forever. Sooner or later they'd leave, and things would be back to normal. They'd be able to get back to the business of tormenting Myra and strengthening the stronghold.

***

Myra looked at the number on her phone. It was the same number as before. A flash of irritation hit her. She slid her finger across the screen and picked up the phone. "Yes," she answered, with a tone that said, *Why are you bothering me?*

"Hello. Myra, this is Josiah."

Myra pulled her neck back. "Josiah?"

"Bad timing? I can call back later." He went to the counter and picked up his drink and looked for a table.

"Ooh...no. I thought you were trying to sell me something."

"Good, good." He wrestled with his approach. He didn't want to give her the wrong impression.

She waited through his pause.

"I was wondering...well, hoping that I could see you." Then his words abandoned him. Nothing else came out of his mouth. He hurriedly put his coffee cup on the table and smacked his head as though this would help. It didn't.

He gritted his teeth and grimaced, then shook his head in exasperation. This sounded exactly the way he did not want it to sound. He was not trying to date her. He was trying to save her soul.

Missionary dating?

Josiah bristled at the thought. Missionary dating was for fools and backsliders. This was about her soul. Nothing more.

"See me? Josiah, I don't understand. Cornelius gave me a little back story."

Back story? he thought. He smiled widely. "Ahh, yes, exactly! I am not asking for a date. I would ne—" He abruptly stopped. *Josiah, this girl is turning you into an idiot,* he scolded himself. Now what was he supposed to say? She had to have caught that slip of the tongue.

Pause.

"Yes, exactly," said Myra. "Why would such a holy man as yourself want to see a Jezebel like me? Or would it be more appropriate to say a Delilah like me?"

That answered his question. She definitely heard him, and though her tone was polite, she definitely didn't appreciate his words. He tried to deescalate the situation with humor. She obviously knew the Bible story of Delilah seducing the prophet Samson. "I don't have long enough hair to qualify to be Samson."

Idiot. Josiah closed his eyes and dropped his head. He couldn't be Samson because he didn't have long hair, but what about her? She could still be Delilah. He had done it again.

"That did not come out the way—"

"Josiah," she cut him off, her voice tired, "I'm sure it didn't. Perhaps comedy is not your calling. Don't worry about it. Stay the course. Leave girls like me alone." She wasn't trying to be mean. She just didn't need this right now.

"Myra, my words...they are coming out wrong. I didn't mean to insult you."

Pause.

Against her better judgment, Myra's curiosity got the better of her. "What *did* you want to see me about?"

"Your soul."

"My soul."

"Life is short, Myra. The next moment is not promised to us. God put it on my heart to talk to you about eternity. Heaven and hell. You are going to spend eternity in one of these places."

Her therapist killing herself.

Her roommate wailing on the floor.

Her waiting at the traffic light.

The girl's body flipping and spinning in the air.

The body hitting the ground.

Her throwing up out her car door.

She still feeling sick from it all.

"Josiah, don't take this personally, but I prefer that you not contact me again." She stood up and began walking toward the rear of Starbucks, waiting for an affirmative response from Josiah.

Josiah didn't know what to say. He was sure that God had told him to pray for her. And up until now he had been sure that God wanted him to speak to this woman about her soul. Now he wasn't sure. *Had he fallen for the fleshly trap of calling himself to the spiritual rescue of a beautiful woman?*

He was about to resign to defeat and say, "Of course," when he saw her, and she saw him. They both froze. Only a couple of yards separated them. Their eyes locked in surreal disbelief.

"Mercy me," said Josiah, "I think the good Lord has other plans."

"Wow," muttered Myra. "Just...wow." *You have got to be kidding me,* she thought.

Chapter 16

Sitting across from Josiah, and smelling his cologne, Myra found it considerably more difficult to be angry at him. Difficult, but not impossible. Not if she worked at it. "Well, here we are," she said.

He smiled, showing sparkling white and even teeth. His jawline was sharp and his face smooth and flawless. He had a light mustache that went down to the chin to meet a short, perfectly groomed beard. His lips—

Stop it, Myra! she ordered herself. Leave this man's lips alone. They are his lips, not yours.

"Yes, here we are. I must thank you again for agreeing to speak with me. And I must apologize again for insulting you. I am not normally clumsy with my words."

"Just something about me, I suppose." Her quip was with an expression that might've been a faint smile or a cynic's smirk. His expression was apologetic. She was pleased at her response and his.

"I deserve that. And more," he said. "Inexcusable."

She said nothing.

"Insensitive," he added.

She slowly nodded. "Self-awareness and personal responsibility are good. You're getting there."

"Unforgivable," he said, "although I do hope you will forgive me."

It wasn't a smile he saw, but her expression was soft. "You're in luck," she said. "For all of my ungodly, heathen ways, unforgiveness is not one of them."

"So I'm forgiven?"

"Are you asking for forgiveness?"

"With all my heart."

His smile was lovely. She reminded herself that she was angry. "Yes, you're forgiven."

"Okay then."

"Okay then," said Myra, in a business tone.

"Your brother has told you that I am a Christian?"

"Uh, I remember you telling all of us that you're a Christian."

"Oh, yeah. Right. Thanksgiving."

Myra looked him in his eyes. "Josiah, what do you want to say to me?"

He briefly grinned. The grin faded. "I am an intercessor."

"What's that?"

"It's someone who prays for people a lot. Sometimes God moves on my heart with great urgency to pray for people."

"And He moved on your heart to pray for me? That's why we're here?"

"Yes. I mean no. Not to pray for you now. I have been praying for you."

"Okay, God told you to pray for me. You've prayed for me." She turned at an angle and looked inquisitively at him. "There's obviously something else."

He decided that he'd tell her everything God showed him only if he had to do so. The last thing he wanted was to create a false convert. If she came to Christ, it had to be because she wanted Him, not because of a temporary scare that would inevitably fade away.

"There is something else, Myra. I will speak plainly, and we can work from there. You are a sinner. You have sinned against God and others. You, me, everyone. We're all guilty. The whole world stands guilty and condemned before a holy God."

Myra shifted in her seat. "My, my. And this is your tactful version of yourself." She chuckled in disbelief that such brashness could come from someone so good-looking. Then she thought of her sister, Lauren. "So, is this where you tell me that Jesus died to pay the price for my sins?"

Josiah's face brightened. "Yes. Jesus died to pay the price for your sins."

"So what's the problem?"

Josiah looked at Myra, wondering whether she was serious. She was serious. "The problem is the gift of God has to be received for it to do you any good."

"I asked Jesus to come into my heart when I was a little girl."

"You did?"

"You look surprised."

"Do I? I'm sorry. I'm not insinuating anything, but may I ask you about this experience?"

"Sure." You've already called me a sinner and strongly implied that I'm going to hell, she thought. Why not ask a question?

"How did this come about?"

"We were at vacation Bible school. Sister Colleen asked if anyone wanted to receive Jesus in their heart so they could go to heaven when they died."

"And you said yes."

"Of course, I did," said Myra. "Who doesn't want to go to heaven? All three of us did."

"All three of who?"

"Me and my two sisters, Lauren and Tina."

Josiah nodded a couple of times. "I see."

"Said the sinner's prayer and got baptized. All three of us."

He nodded again. "I see."

"What do you see, Josiah?"

"I am not your judge, Myra. I am not Lauren's judge, or Tina's judge."

"But..." said Myra.

"But the word of God judges us. Did you notice a dramatic change in your life once you said this prayer and was baptized?"

"Hmm, not really. I was always a nice person. So, no."

"What about your sisters?"

"No."

"What about as you grew older? When you were a teenager?"

"I went to church a few times, but that's about it."

"What about your life? Would you say you lived for Jesus as a teenager or for yourself?"

"I wasn't perfect, of course, but I wasn't what I would consider bad. I've never been into hurting people or taking something that wasn't mine. I can't say honestly that I was into Jesus as a teenager. But I've always believed in God."

"I see," Josiah said, again. "What exactly do you believe about God?"

Myra pondered. "That someone or something created everything. That God is out there somewhere."

"That's it?" Josiah was surprised.

"Yeah, that's it. At least for me."

"What about what you learned about Jesus? What about the Bible?"

"I used to believe in Jesus, but the older I got, the less I believed in Christianity. I mean there's so much about it that doesn't add up."

"Such as?"

"Such as you have a god of love sending people to hell just for being human. It's ridiculous. None of us asked to be born. You're born and the first thing God does is put you on His hit list? And what about all the people who never hear about Jesus? Those innocent people go to hell just because they're born in some remote village in India? Or because they happen to be born in an Islamic culture?"

"Those are good questions," said Josiah.

"And the reason you want to talk to me," said Myra. "That's another reason I don't believe. You believe God told you to pray for me because I'm in danger of going to hell, right?"

"Yes."

"So me asking for forgiveness when I was little and being baptized mean nothing. And all of my good counts for nothing. He has never said one word to me, but he's going to send me to hell when I die. Right? Isn't that why we're sitting here in Starbucks? Because God's got a bull's eye on me right now?"

Josiah was surprised at Myra. The more she talked, the more her anger at God and defiance of Him was revealed. One of the angels of truth placed a hand on his shoulder and spoke closely into his ear. He felt his chest warm as the Scriptures filled his mind.

And you He made alive, who were dead in trespasses and sins, in which you once walked according to the course of this world, according to the prince of the power of the air, the spirit who now works in the sons of disobedience, among whom also we all once conducted ourselves in the lusts of our flesh, fulfilling the desires of the flesh and of the mind, and were by nature children of wrath, just as the others.

"Why are you looking at me like that?" asked Myra.

Josiah blinked hard. "Like what?"

"I don't know." She shook her head. "Like you're here and somewhere else."

Thank you, Holy Spirit, he prayed. He had dropped his guard, but he was back on track. He wouldn't let this woman's beauty and sweetness cloud his vision. She was a sinner, a natural enemy of God who needed to be saved. That was the only reason he was here. To save her soul.

He changed his mind about not telling her everything God had shown him. She needed the fear of the Lord. Josiah scooted his chair closer in even as he moved his heart farther back. "Myra, I have something I need to tell you."

Chapter 17

Myra had had enough of this talk about hell even if she hadn't had enough of talking to Josiah. But he didn't seem to be the kind of person who could keep his religion separate from the rest of his life. So she decided that he was down to his last few moments of preaching to her.

"And what's that?" asked Myra. Let's shelve this conversation and enjoy the rest of the evening? she toyed. Myra, would you like to go out to dinner? We can spend time getting to know one another. We'll talk about everything except religion. How does that sound? Sounds great, Josiah. I know a really cool place we can go.

"I saw a tiger eat you," said Josiah.

Myra was dumbfounded. She looked at him with an open mouth for a few seconds. "You—

what?"

"You recall that I told you I am an intercessor."

Myra held the same *I am talking to a certified nut* expression for a few seconds and put her hand on her purse.

"Sometimes I see things when I pray."

"You see things?" Myra pulled her purse. "Well, Josiah, you told me that God told you to pray for me. You did not tell me that you see things and that you saw me get eaten by a tiger. Perhaps that's a common occurrence in Africa." She stood up. "But it's really rare here in Atlanta."

"We do not have tigers in the wild in Africa. That is a misunderstanding many people have."

Myra's expression was unchanged.

"That Africa is a land of tigers," he added. "We have many lions, but very few tigers."

She shook her head at him. "Josiah, I really don't care about your lions or your tigers." She started on her way.

"You are leaving?" said Josiah.

"Josiah, what else is there to talk about once you've been eaten by a tiger? Yes, I'm leaving."

"Don't leave, please. It happened suddenly. You were standing at a light, waiting to cross the street. The light turned green and you stepped off the curb. That's when a red tiger pounced on you."

Her face appeared to have been drained of all fluid.

"Myra, are you alright? I do not mean to frighten you, only to be faithful with what the Most High God has shown me."

"I—please, I need to sit down." She clasped his forearm. "Please, help me to sit down."

He did.

"I saw a girl get killed today. Hit by a car. She was waiting at a traffic light. A red car with black stripes on it ran her over."

"God have mercy," said Josiah.

"Mercy?" she asked, incredulously. "She's dead. What good is mercy now? When did you have this dream or vision or whatever it is you had?"

"Three days ago."

"Josiah, I don't know what this is. A vision from God. Your subconscious mind. ESP. A coincidence. I don't know. But I know that if I could've prevented that girl from being killed, I would've done so." Myra was puzzled at Josiah's expression. He didn't agree with her. "You would not have saved her?"

"Of course, I would save her—as a human, yes."

She looked at him, interpreting the way his voice trailed off that he held reservations. "But?"

"But I am not God. As a man, yes, I see someone in danger, I help them."

"Because that's what good people do," said Myra. "They help people in need."

"But we can not judge God actions. He is altogether good."

"That's not how it sounds to me, Josiah. It sounds to me like you are good and your God is not."

"Myra, I am simply saying that I am a man. If I see a person in danger, I help them. That is my responsibility. I am a limited, imperfect human being. Everything I do, I do in that context. God is not me. He is not only all-powerful, He is all-wise. It is not always a question of whether He is able to do a thing, but whether He should do a thing."

Myra's voice raised. "She was a college student, Josiah. She couldn't have been more than twenty years old. Are you really telling me that you think there is any scenario where God should not have saved her?"

They looked one another in the eyes. Each knew this would be the last time they did so. She walked away. Josiah spoke up after her. "I don't know why God didn't save the girl, but He's trying to save you."

She whipped around. Her mouth opened, but she was more frustrated than angry and more confused than resolved. Her words were garbled in her heart.

Josiah showed the palms of his hands as he spoke. "That's why the good Lord let you see that girl lose her life. It was His mercy. He always offers mercy before He is forced to judge sinners. He wanted you to see that old age is no guarantee, and that your life can be required of you in an instant." He read her eyes. "No one is exempt."

This man had just put *good* and *Lord* in the same breath with a lame excuse to justify an almighty god letting a young college girl get hit by a car. Myra looked at Cornelius's friend—and that's all he would ever be—as though he was insane. "I must be a hell of a sinner to get this kind of attention." She shook her head. "I can't get with this Viking god of yours, Josiah."

Josiah watched her walk away and wondered what would become of her. He had the awful feeling that she was running out of time.

***

The mercy angels walked away from the stronghold as Myra walked away from Josiah. Hideous and his crew watched in happy relief from the ground floor. "Good riddance," he muttered. He looked beyond the walls of his stronghold at the angels of truth. *She'll never choose you over us?* he thought.

Chapter 18

Hideous looked around, his eyes darting here and there, fixing on prominent points of the stronghold. Everything looked the same, but he could feel it. Something had changed. He raced back up the stairs to the top of one of the walls of lies and slapped both palms heavily on a ledge of Myra's insecurities. It felt as sturdy as ever.

Still, he tried pushing it. The huge stones didn't budge. He glanced around, feeling foolish and now a bit paranoid as demons watched him do his own security check. He knew his worthless demons would crack jokes about him behind his back.

So what, he thought defiantly. Better to have these idiots crack their jokes than to sit on my hands and do nothing when I know something's not right.

Hideous ended his security check in one of the guard towers that rose from the very top of the large structure. The demon on duty said nothing as he watched his lord stare out beyond the stronghold.

A gurgling sound bubbled in the throat of Hideous. The two truth angels were still present. They weren't doing anything. Just standing there. Hideous didn't care that they appeared to be doing nothing. *What sneaky trick are you angels up to now?* he wondered. "What is it?" he yelled at them.

They ignored him totally.

"I know you hear me," he yelled again. "What are you up to? Myra is ours. Your words mean nothing. She's ugly, and she will always believe she's ugly."

Hideous was incensed. He knew the angels heard him. Yet they treated him as though he were a fly on an elephant's back. Of course, angels regularly ignored the taunts of demons. And truth angels rarely spoke to demons, and when they did, they just repeated the words of the tyrant, like a bunch of parrots. So maybe it was good that they didn't flap their gums at him.

Nonetheless, Hideous couldn't stop himself. He was the master of this stronghold, and no angels of truth would remove him. Not these two glorified lightning bugs, and not even an army of them.

"Stand there all you want you impotent bonfires. The woman belongs to me. Where's your mercy angels? It's just your words versus ours. Who do you think Myra will—?"

Hideous stopped in mid taunt. His mouth popped open. The mercy angels. He looked at them in the far distance and lifted his hands with his palms facing them. He closed his eyes and *felt* what was troubling him.

After a couple of seconds, he opened his eyes and smiled. His eyes hungrily found the dimming glow of the mercy angels as they got farther away. "That's what I felt," he said, gleefully. "That's what I felt. I thought it was something bad."

The tower guard demon said nothing about his lord's odd behavior.

Hideous looked down at the angels of truth. "That's what I felt," he yelled. "It's your precious mercy angels. They're gone and they're not coming back. The woman has been abandoned, hasn't she? You may be mute, but you're not deaf, angels. No. More. Mercy. It's just lies and truth!"

Both truth angels looked at Hideous.

"You see. You can hear," he roared. He watched in surprise as they walked closer to the wall. They were actually going to answer him. "Speak up. I'm not a mind reader."

The angels spoke in unison. "It is written, 'Let Your mercies come also to me, O Lord—Your salvation according to Your word."

Hideous gasped. *Is that really in that horrible book?* He gasped again when the angels disappeared.

The tower guard demon watched in silent satisfaction as his smug lord clutched his chest. He said as innocently as he could,

"That sounds like they're saying mercy doesn't only come through mercy angels. Sounds like they're saying mercy is in the word of the Lord. And, my lord, since truth angels only speak the word of the Lord, it sounds like they're saying any time they speak, mercy may come—with or without mercy angels."

Hideous's eyes flashed anger at the petulant demon. "And it sounds to me like you're trying to build a church," he snapped. "Did anyone ask you for a sermon?"

The demon smiled inside. "No, my lord."

"Then shut your ugly face."

"Yes, my lord."

Hideous descended the winding stairs of the guard tower in a daze. How had things turned so badly so quickly? He steeled his resolve. *I'll work faster and harder than ever. This ugly bat is mine. I'll never let her go.*

Chapter 19

Hideous couldn't get the words of those horrible angels out of his mind. He looked at his large, rickety wooden *chair* in contempt. It was anything but a real throne. A humiliating physical reminder from his region's leadership that his stronghold had not yet arrived. He'd spit on it if he weren't going to sit on it. He spat on the floor instead and sat down heavily. His large crusty hands covered his forlorn face. A low guttural sound passed through the palms of his hands. "What am I going to do," he said.

Someone cleared his throat in front of him.

Hideous dropped his hands from his face and planted them firmly on his chair. It was that tired spirit of perfection, Exhaustion. Just looking at this listless demon prompted a yawn from Hideous. "Don't say it. I warn you, Exhaustion, I am not in the mood to be told to try harder."

"I wasn't...going to say that," he lied.

"Then what were you going to say?" Hideous knew the demon was lying.

"I have an idea."

"Now that's original," Hideous said, condescendingly. "Every worthless demon in my worthless army has an idea. Cutting says this. Bulimia says that. Anger says, 'No, we need to do this.' Even fat boy's got ideas."

"Gluttony?"

"Yeah, Gluttony," he spat. "That dwarf rhino. What a waste of space." The ugly spirit's face was tight with anger. Exhaustion represented his frustration. He jabbed an accusatory finger at him. "What you demons don't understand is there's something missing.

We can't take this woman to the next level of bondage simply by snapping our fingers."

Hideous looked past Exhaustion into an imagined, decisive victory. "I can see it," he said, dreamily. "I just need a bridge to cross over into the promised land." A thought snatched him out of his dreamy state. "And I need it before that African messes up everything. He's trouble."

"That's what I want," Exhaustion took a deep breath, "to talk to you about, my lord." Exhaustion's eyebrow lifted. "I can give you...that bridge. I've done it before." He paused for rest. "I can do it again."

Hideous looked at Exhaustion with a hard expression that hinted at his hopeful thought. *What if this half-sleep demon is on to something?*

Exhaustion knew what his lord was thinking. "The tyrant took my energy," a few pants, "but I'm good at strategy." He blew air out of puffy jaws. "I know you...want a real throne."

Hideous waited with growing interest for the spirit to catch his breath.

"Let me get it for you. It's amazing...how pliable a woman can be...when she's physically...and emotionally exhausted...When I finish with her...Cutting and Bulimia, even fat boy...will be able to touch her...I'm tired, yes...but I have a rich resume."

Hideous perked up. Surprisingly, the yawn sounded convincing. Something about this demon's confidence was different from the other mouthy demons. "Resume?"

"A *rich* resume."

An evil smile grew on Hideous's face. "Why didn't you mention your resume earlier?"

I did mention it earlier, you half-wit, no-strategy bag of hot air, thought Exhaustion. His body was tired, but his mind was sharp as it had ever been.

Hideous pointed to a stool. "You look tired. Have a seat and refresh yourself. Tell me what you need."

"Four demons."

"Only four. Specialists?"

No, general contractors, you non-thinking idiot, thought Exhaustion. "They're already here. I just need total authority over them."

"Who are they?"

Exhaustion gave their names.

Hideous was unimpressed with the list, but if this tired demon had succeeded with other women, maybe he would succeed with this one. And if he didn't, he'd rip his sleepy head off. Besides, he had to do something fast. That African was gone now, but he'd probably pop up again. "Done," he answered.

Chapter 20

Josiah's eyes popped open. His breathing heavy. His forehead wet. His alarm high. He raised up from his bed. *Oh, man,* he thought, as he looked at the time on his phone, anticipating a day of sluggishness and heavy eyelids at work.

The plan had been to get to bed early Tuesday night to make up for Monday night's late intercession. That Tuesday he had prayed for a couple of hours and had gone to bed at eleven, only to be awakened by another dream about Myra being in trouble. He had prayed nearly another hour before feeling it was okay to stop.

Now it was 3:33 a.m. on Wednesday. He let his breathing and heart rate slow to normal. It was only a dream. A very lifelike dream. The tiger was not real, thank God. But his sense of alarm remained high, nonetheless.

This woman is in terrible danger, he thought. But he'd been thinking this very thought ever since he had watched her walk away at Starbucks. He'd also come very close to contacting her even though she had made it clear that she didn't want to hear from him again. But he was willing to suffer her anger if it meant saving her soul.

Yet it wasn't only her desire to be left alone that was keeping him from contacting her. Apparently, it was the good Father's desire that he leave her alone. This was beyond troubling.

If Myra was in immediate danger, why did he get such a strong feeling of nausea each time he had come close to contacting her? Why did he feel like God was telling him to pray and do nothing more?

He could hear his mother giving her usual concise admonition to wives whom she felt were getting in the way of their own prayers. *Your part is to pray. God's part is to save. Pray and be quiet. Don't get in God's way.*

That's exactly what he felt like he'd be doing by contacting Myra again. His heart embraced his mother's advice. He got out of bed and thought of showering first. *Why not? I'm not going back to sleep.*

Making sure he was fully awake before starting to pray had proven to be the way not to fall asleep while praying. After he showered and dressed, he fell to his hands and knees in the living room.

"*Faaaather*, oh, good Father, I stand in the gap for this woman and plead Your mercy," his anguished cry began.

***

Josiah erupted into a blue flame that emitted thousands of fragrant embers that were carried intelligently on an active wind that moved delicately in every direction. The uniform floating of the sweet-smelling embers resembled a flock of blue birds in poetic dance, going this way, then another, before forming replicas of sacred items. Each lasted seconds before it was replaced with the next.

An ark.

A staff.

A cross.

A throne.

The longer Josiah prayed, the more the room filled with embers. The more intense his agony, the more active the wind became. Finally, Josiah screamed, "Father," and released his spiritual pain in a yell that left him in a crying heap on the floor.

The embers began to come together and slowly swirl into a large whirlwind. For several seconds, the whirlwind moved in slow motion. Then Josiah got to his hands and knees. His tears landed on the floor. Each dropping tear caused corresponding small explosions in the whirlwind.

Then Josiah said something that left his trembling lips as a humble whisper and arrived in the throne room of God as a bold roar.

> "It is written, my God and my King, I cried
> to the Lord with my voice, and He heard me
> from His holy hill...the eyes of the Lord are
> upon the righteous, and His ears are open to
> their cry...put my tears in Your bottle."

"Who is this man who puts Me in remembrance of My word?" asked the Lord, for the benefit of the attending angels, and for the official record.

An angel answered, "He is Josiah, the man of God who bears the burdens of the Lord in prayer."

"He is My friend. I will hear Him."

***

Josiah knew he had entered the burden of the Lord because his own heart was broken for a woman he didn't even know. He tried to put his brokenness into words, but the pain and need was too deep to articulate. All he could do was feel the Holy Spirit's spiritual pain and desire and groan with utterings too deep for words.

An armored angel, a ministering spirit, assigned by God to minister to those who are heirs of salvation appeared in the room. In one hand he held a long sword. In the other, an ornate bottle with a wide opening, a long neck, and a wide jeweled base. The man of God was oblivious to the angelic courier.

The angel stepped inside of the whirlwind. Josiah's prayers swooshed inside of the bottle with such force that the angel braced his legs to keep from being knocked over. He secured the bottle's top and ascended through the ceiling.

Josiah spent the rest of his work day encouraging himself in the Lord and knowing in his heart that God heard his prayers. But Satan continued to harass him with spirits of doubt that tried to get him to focus on Myra's rejection of God instead of God's ability to save her.

***

An angel from the altar in heaven watched the courier angel arrive at the glorious entrance of the altar with his bottle of prayers mixed with tears. He knew exactly how beautifully overwhelming it was for him, even though the angel had performed this blessed duty many times before.

The courier angel placed both hands on the neck of the bottle and walked forward until he stopped in front of the designated altar angel. The altar angel stretched forth a golden bowl. The courier angel poured the prayers and tears into the bowl and gave a slight grin of camaraderie to the altar angel. The grin was returned to him.

He walked away knowing that he had performed a most important and honored task. Just before he exited the altar area, he stopped and turned to do what he did each time he performed this most solemn duty. He watched the mixture of the blood of the eternal Creator with the prayers and tears of an offspring of Adam.

A created being.

A sinner made righteous.

A sinner made a child of God.

A sinner who would one day sit with God on His throne.

The angel repeated the Scripture in his mind as though it would help him understand. To him who overcomes I will grant to sit with Me on My throne, as I also overcame and sat down with My Father on His throne.

This only served to remind the angel of the grandness of the mystery. It was all too deep and incomprehensible to understand. All he could do as he watched this mixture of the divine and the degraded was to do what every angel did when contemplating such ability, wisdom, and love. He praised God for being infinitely powerful and good.

"All praises be unto the Lord my God," said the angel, as the sweet smell of Josiah's prayers filled the altar.

He was not there at the conclusion of the presentation of prayers to hear God say, "Josiah pleads for the woman's safety and salvation. Send angels to help her as she decides her eternal fate. Get the woman, Myra, to the funeral of her therapist for my purposes."

Chapter 21

Hideous was not unaware that even a tired-butt demon like Exhaustion could get full of himself if given the chance. Yeah, he had given the snoozer authority over a few demons because of his self-proclaimed proficiency at strategy, but he was still master of this stronghold.

As master of his stronghold, Hideous called a special meeting to share his own strategy with his inferiors. Every demon in the stronghold, except the tower guards, stood in block formation in the meeting area.

Hideous paced back and forth several paces with his hands clasped behind his back. He wanted to milk the moment. Keep them waiting. Waiting on him. The master of this house. He looked at that sleeper of a demon, Exhaustion. "I have a plan," he said, in a loud voice, "a strategy," he said, looking at Exhaustion.

Give me a break, thought Exhaustion.

Hideous twitched at Exhaustion, as though he knew the snore was laughing inside. "The woman is traumatized by the death of her skinny little know-it-all therapist." He looked at one demon then another. "We are going to cram this failure in her face. I want her to know that her hope is dead!"

Hideous sensed with delight the curiosity of his demons. They were waiting on the master of the house. Not some two-bit sleepy demon who could barely stand up without a prop. "I want her to attend that funeral. I want her to see her high and mighty therapist lying dead in a casket. Is that understood?" he barked.

"Yes, my lord," answered the demons.

Chapter 22

"Allison, I don't think it's a good idea," said Myra. "I mean, this thing has really affected you. Why do you want to attend her funeral?" Myra had successfully hidden that she was as devastated as her roommate that the woman with the answers had committed suicide.

Allison had wiped her face dry a couple of times. The intermittent tears didn't stop. "I never said it was a good idea," she sniffled.

"Then why go?"

"Because I have to, Myra. I don't know. Maybe it's because I can't believe it's over. Maybe it's," she paused, "because my mom left me high and dry like this." She looked at Myra with a pained face. "Maybe I see my mom in that casket. I don't know, Myra. I just know I need to see her one last time."

Myra didn't protest. It was obvious that as badly as Allison was taking Dr. Brown's death, she needed to go. Maybe she would get closure with her mom by going to the funeral. But as for her, she wasn't going near that funeral. *How could the lady kill herself?*

Allison grabbed both of Myra's wrists and said with tears, "This thing is eating at me. I'm scared to go, but I have to go. You're my friend, Myra. Please go with me."

Oh, my goodness, thought Myra, in stunned silence, I'm going to this lady's funeral.

***

Myra had not intended *not* to go to the funeral because that would have required her to actually think about attending. Something she hadn't done until Allison had surprised her with the news that she was planning to attend. Nor had she thought about not actually viewing the body because the thought was too ridiculous to contemplate. She didn't need to look at a dashed hope up close and personal and *dead*. It wasn't going to happen.

Nonetheless, she found herself in the unlikely position of walking Allison down the aisle toward the casket. Her arm under hers, providing her moral and physical support. Physical support that, from the way Allison leaned heavily into her, she could not do without.

"You can do it," Myra whispered supportively. "We're almost there." Myra wasn't trying to be judgmental or uncompassionate. But she found herself involuntarily wondering at the depth of Allison's grief. After all, this was not really her mother. It was her therapist.

"I'm sorry," Allison whimpered. "I know this doesn't make sense."

Myra's heart broke. First, for her friend. Then for her own lack of sympathy. They arrived at the body. Myra placed her second hand on Allison's arm and bowed her head, but not to look at the body. She was not going to look at this woman.

Myra heard Allison haltingly say, "Dr. Brown, why did you do it? I needed you. Mother, why did you leave me?"

Myra listened through closed eyes as her friend spoke to Dr. Brown and to her mom. She was surprised and relieved that Allison now felt more steady and sounded less fragile. Only a few more words and she'd be able to get away from Dr. Brown and this casket.

One of the two angels of truth who had appeared around her days before touched her eyes. It was James. "See," he said.

Myra's eyes were still closed. But this didn't stop her from *seeing* Dr. Brown. In fact, she saw this woman with more clarity than if she had her eyes open. She seemed to study not only every feature of this woman, but the sum of every thought, hope, disappointment, and achievement she had ever experienced.

Gone forever. A life wasted.

These overwhelming thoughts reverberated through Myra's soul.

As she looked at her dead therapist, she seemed to back away as though she were looking through a camera lens and it was zooming out. The focus was the casket. Again, something was making her study everything about the casket. For a moment, it was like every physical fact about the casket passed through her mind and converged into one powerful thought.

Eternal finality.

"See," James said, again.

Myra opened her physical eyes and looked at Dr. Brown. Her therapist. The person with the answers. Dead by suicide.

Allison jerked to the left with Myra's sudden pull on her arm. She couldn't catch her balance and fell to the floor with Myra.

"Oh, God, what am I going to do now," Myra cried. "I trusted her. I trusted her to help me."

Allision got to her knees and tried to console her. "It's going to be alright, Myra."

"It's not going to be alright," she cried. "She killed herself. How can I believe anything she told me?"

***

Hideous congratulated himself for smearing the doctor's death in Myra's face. A few wise demons went through the motions of congratulating their lord for his brilliant strategy. One, however, had disturbing news. Exhaustion said, "Those truth angels are back."

"Where? I don't—"

The stronghold's siren blared.

Demons scrambled to the safe places in Myra's mind that comprised the stronghold. Hideous looked beyond the stronghold to the two truth angels. He was ticked at their presence. They were probably why Myra had ignored him until she had her little falling out fit.

Then he saw something that took him way beyond being *ticked* to being scared. There were angels coming from three directions. *Armed angels.* Maybe fifty of them.

He didn't have fighters. He only had specialists. What was he supposed to do? Why were fighting angels here? And so many!

***

James and Micah had been expecting the contingent of fighting angels as soon as they heard of Josiah's prayers. The truth angels watched the fighters move in, separate into groups of twos, threes, and fours and move strategically around the stronghold.

The truth angels established eye contact with Jezrael, their leader, and disappeared into another dimension. They were invisible, but not gone. Their primary job was not to fight demons. It was to fight lies and every thought that exalted itself against the knowledge of God.

Jezrael didn't recognize the two truth angels that had disappeared, but he had worked closely with many of them. Truth angels worked behind the scenes. He and his angels, they were front-line, hand to hand combat fighters. But today they weren't here to fight. They were here for reconnaissance, a show of force, and to train two angels who had been newly assigned to observe front-line duty.

They were also here to drop off a squad of fighters for the woman, Myra.

Chapter 23

Myra had welcomed the news when Allison informed her that she was taking off from work to spend some time with her sister in Colorado. Why, with her own growing self-esteem problems, and her therapist committing suicide—*her therapist!*— seeing someone run off over by a car...

She thought of Cornelius's fanatic friend. Josiah. Him and his tiger. Him and his God of judgment. The audacity of using scare tactics to get converts.

Her thought had naively been that with Allison gone, she'd use the quietness and lack of distraction to emotionally rest. To recuperate from what had, surprisingly to her, become a larger than life issue.

She had only seen Dr. Brown a few times. Why should she be consumed with the woman's death? Good question. Better question. Why did she break down at this woman's funeral?

Really, Myra, that was just ridiculous, she mentally scorned herself.

But why had it happened? Nothing came to mind. She answered the non-answer by hopping up off the sofa and going to the refrigerator for something cold to drink. *Coca-Cola.* Orange juice. Peach-Mango iced tea. Allison's beverage kingdom.

Myra rarely drank anything other than water and coffee. Sweet drinks didn't do anything for her but leave her thirsty and needing to drink water to get the sugary taste out of her mouth. But this was one of the rare times.

Exhaustion's team of demons flexed their muscles when her eyes fixed on Allison's iced tea. Myra got a bad feeling when she looked at the bottle. She dismissed the feeling, grasped the bottle, and closed the refrigerator door.

In the short time it took to return to the softness of her seat on the sofa and to open the bottle's top, she felt as though she had done something terribly wrong. Condemnation cascaded over her from head to toe.

You're going to add fat to ugly? How much sugar is in that drink?

Did you notice how in shape Tina and Lauren were when you saw them? It's like they both just won their beauty pageants a week ago. Even your mother's still hot. They didn't get that way by drinking sugar water.

You're the fattest person under thirty on your floor. Allison's much thinner than you.

You need to purchase a scale.

Your weight's out of control.

You eat too much.

You need to go on a diet.

You don't exercise enough.

You need to put your heart into it. Get up earlier. Do more aerobic exercises. Get that heart rate going. Run more. You don't have to be ugly and fat. You can look better. You can do it if you try harder.

Try. Harder.

The demons hurled their wisdom and a hundred other taunts, lies, and accusations at Myra.

***

Jezrael had lost count of how many thousands of assaults like these he had witnessed. It was basic spiritual warfare. Page one of the enemy's playbook: Get the victim to believe a lie. Once this happened, the victim's behavior automatically followed the lie. But he had two angels newly assigned to him who knew little of spiritual warfare.

He saw the astonishment and horror on their faces as they watched the fiery darts, arrows, and spears pierce the woman's soul and spirit. "You've never seen anything like this," he said, with a question's inflection.

Neither angel answered. They were totally absorbed by their first face-to-face exposure to seeing something so spiritually brutal. Jezrael understood their silence. "Mishnak?"

"No, Commander, I have never seen anything like this."

Jezrael sensed that Mishnak was contemplative and deliberate. *You were chosen for your strategy,* he thought.

"And you, Aaron-Hur?"

"No, never." The angel was shaken. "I had heard stories, but..." His gaze was pulled back to the woman. "Look at how they attack her. She has so many wounds. The demons...they've...she looks like a human pin cushion."

And you are here for your tactical gift, the commander thought of Aaron-Hur.

Mishnak looked at the mess of blood that oozed out of her body. "Commander, how does the woman bleed from these wounds? They are not physical."

There were as many mysteries as there were certainties in spiritual warfare. The commander would share what he knew. "The blood comes from her spirit and soul. It is as real as the blood in her physical body."

"The human spirit and soul have blood?" said Aaron-Hur.

"Yes, but not in the same way the human body has blood. The human body cannot live without physical blood. The human spirit and soul are eternal. The blood you see coming from the woman doesn't give her life. It shows what is happening to her life." Jezrael let this sink in for a few moments. "Are you familiar with disease?" he asked him.

Aaron-Hur answered, "I've heard of this condition. It has signs that reveal what is going on inside of people."

"Often, yes," answered Jezrael. "They call them symptoms."

"The woman's spiritual blood is a symptom of what is happening in her soul and spirit," said Mishnak.

"That is correct."

"Can her spirit and soul run out of blood the way her body runs out of blood?"

"I do not know, Mishnak," said Jezrael. He thought of something that brought trouble to his eyes. The angels waited for further explanation. "But if they lose enough blood, it causes great damage. Sometimes permanent damage."

Mishnak and Aaron-Hur focused on Myra's blood-soaked clothes.

"You both have questions," said Jezrael.

"I do, Commander," said Mishnak.

"And I," Aaron-Hur joined.

Jezrael waited.

Mishnak was first. "What are they doing? The demons. Why are they saying those things to the woman?"

Aaron-Hur asked his question with wide eyes. "Their words...they..."

"They turn into fiery darts and spears—and other weapons," Jezrael finished.

"How does this happen? They are only words," said Mishnak.

A long moment of thought followed. Mishnak and Aaron-Hur looked at one another, then at the commander. All three angels said in unison, "God created everything with words."

No matter what you do, you will never be anything but ugly.

The angels saw the fiery dart shoot from the mouth of the demon called Hideous. It hit and lodged in the bleeding woman's head.

Mishnak asked, "I do not understand, Commander. Some of the darts hit her and some didn't. Some hit her and bounced off. This one...this one that says she is ugly..."

Aaron-Hur added, "But she is not ugly. She is a physically beautiful woman. How can an obvious lie find a target?"

"I will explain to you the mystery of the darts, arrows, and spears," said Jezrael.

Chapter 24

"Do not assume that people must be told a lie to believe a lie, or be denied the truth to believe a lie," said Jezrael. "They believe lies for many reasons. Some people actually choose to believe a lie knowing it is a lie."

Both angels appeared puzzled.

Jezrael continued. "If the truth is unacceptable, they will reject it. They have to replace what they reject with something that will protect them from the truth. So they believe a lie. It is the human condition. The heart is deceitful above all things and desperately wicked."

"People actually live this way?" asked Mishnak.

"Yes," answered Jezrael. "There are people known as atheists. The truth of God's existence is unacceptable to them. In place of this obvious truth, they believe the lies that the universe popped out of nothingness on its own without God and that people evolved from apes."

This shocked both angels. "How can a universe create itself?" Mishnak asked cynically.

"Apes?" said Aaron-Hur.

"Many believe these lies," said Jezrael. "Then there are others who murder babies in the womb for convenience and money. They do not call it murder. They call it abortion. Or they call it a medical procedure."

"But a medical procedure is to help people, is it not?" asked Mishnak.

"It is," said Jezrael. "They justify the extermination of babies in the name of helping pregnant women."

"How does killing a child help pregnant women?" Mishnak asked.

"It relieves the woman of the responsibility of taking care of the child. Some women are hardened and will admit this truth. Others convince themselves to believe the lie that the baby in their womb is not a baby."

"What is it if it is not a baby?" demanded Aaron-Hur.

"They tell themselves it is a blob of tissue."

"They take away its humanity," Mishnak thought aloud. "Like the Nazis did to the Jews."

Aaron-Hur was incensed at this offense against the Creator. "But how can a mother and a doctor not know that a baby is a baby? Their own science tells them it is a baby."

"This is the depth of their depravity and deception, Aaron-Hur," said the commander. "If the woman desires the baby, she calls it a baby. If she does not desire it, she calls it a blob of tissue and pays a doctor to kill the baby."

Aaron-Hur's eyes were as wide as they could get. "It does not matter what they call it, Commander. The Creator calls it murder. This will not go unpunished!"

"Yes, but you see now how even the most obvious truths are disregarded for the sake of convenience. Truth has very little to do with what they believe. They have the ability to believe whatever they desire to believe, with or without evidence. This is the human condition."

Both angels were shaken by this conversation. They had both desired this assignment and knew they would see and learn troubling things, but this was shocking. Yet this path of shock was the necessary journey to qualify to provide more direct support to the sons and daughters of Adam. *They had to understand more if they were going to help more.*

Mishnak was the first to recover enough to ask about Myra. "This woman wants to believe these lies?"

"It is complicated," said Jezrael. "She does not want to believe these particular lies because they cause her discomfort. But there are other lies she desires. If you submit to one lie, you open yourself to other lies."

"What are those lies?" asked Mishnak.

"She rejects God," said Jezrael. "She finds him offensive."

Aaron-Hur shook his head. He wasn't even going to ask how a created being could find her creator offensive.

Jezrael continued. "She has rejected that which is above. All that is left is that which is below. She must get her life from this world."

"But it is written in the blessed book that this whole world lies in the grip of the evil one," said Mishnak. "One cannot eat from a filthy garbage can and remain healthy. Whatever life she gets will be rotten."

Jezrael lifted an eyebrow in surprise at the angel's use of human jargon. He was not as sheltered as the commander had assumed. "That is true, Mishnak, but if it is all she has, she must fight for it, nonetheless. Otherwise, she is left with nothing. People cannot live with nothing. They must believe something."

Aaron-Hur and Mishnak studied the woman's wounds and bleeding condition as they contemplated this information.

"This world is all she has," said Mishnak.

"Yes," said Jezrael.

"The lust of the flesh. The lust of the eyes. The pride of life," said Mishnak. "If this is all she has...and if people without the Creator must have this to live... She is a fish out of water without these things."

Another human jargon.

"Then Satan can harm her by attacking that which she values, even if what she values is eternally worthless," said Aaron-Hur. "The demons can deprive her of what she needs."

The commander smiled ever so slightly at the light entering the apprentice angels. "Yes, exactly. All of these wounds are possible because she gets her life from this world. These demons have access to her only because they can threaten that which gives her life."

Aaron-Hur's eyes were lively with revelation. As shocking as close exposure to the front lines was, this is exactly what he had hoped to experience. "Commander, all of these darts and arrows and spears, even the axe, are from attacks on her appearance."

"And how she feels about herself," said Mishnak.

"And how others feel about her," said Aaron-Hur.

"Now you see," said Jezrael. "The weapons find their target because there is something to hit. Because she gets her life from this world."

"Now I do see, Commander," said Mishnak, with the excitement of a student accurately figuring out a hard problem in front of his teacher. "If she repented and submitted to God, she would get her value from her Creator. The demons would have nothing to work with."

Aaron-Hur nearly clapped his hands in joy, sharing in Mishnak's excitement. "That is so, is it not, Commander? The Almighty has given His Son as a ransom to make the woman His own daughter. If she were a daughter of the Most High God..." he searched through his excitement for the right words, "no lie could touch her. The demons' attacks would be impotent."

The commander's expression told the enthusiastic angel this was not the case.

"Is this not true?" Mishnak asked slowly, not seeing how it could possibly be untrue.

"It should be true," said Jezrael, "but more often than not, it is not true."

"Why?" asked Aaron-Hur. "If she were a daughter of God, she would be a child of God and a citizen of heaven. None of the demons' lies would mean anything. They could all fall harmlessly to the floor, as these other weapons have fallen to the floor."

The commander looked somberly at both angels. "She does not believe every lie. Therefore, some fall to the floor. You will both eventually see for yourselves that God's own children believe many of Satan's lies, and therefore are stricken with his weapons of war."

Mishnak and Aaron-Hur were silenced, stunned, and saddened.

"Take heart. All is not lost," said Jezrael. "Those who do believe God instead of the devil are strong and do many exploits. You will see that truth, also. But for now, observe this attack on the woman and see how demons go about their evil work in those who believe their lies."

Chapter 25

Myra could drink only a little of the iced tea before guilt made her put it down. Yes, the sugar content was high. But she rarely drank high-sugar beverages. So why did she feel like she was spitting on the Pope just because she wanted to treat herself to a rare sweet tea? It didn't make sense.

She hopped up from the sofa instantly at the thought of her suddenly being well on her way to becoming overweight and went to her bedroom. She looked into the full-length mirror. Her eyes told her she was being ridiculous. But her mind accused her of being a fat liar.

She turned away from the mirror in defiance and strode toward the bathroom. "This is just plain silly," she said to the persistent accusation of sudden fatness. Myra kicked off her shoes and stepped on a scale. It was two-tenths of a pound more than she expected.

There it was. Irrefutable digital proof that she was on her way to obesity.

The feeling of being fat pressed its case with a vigor that left Myra searching for answers. Just a few minutes ago she had had problems. Lots of problems. The main one being that she was obsessed with her unattractiveness. But now she was suddenly ugly *and* fat.

"I'm five-seven," she said to a dismissive audience of no one. "A hundred and thirty pounds is not fat for someone five-seven."

But Myra's mind wasn't in the mood for reality. The facts were in her mind—and on the face of the scale. Two-tenths of a pound. *She was getting fat.* She stripped off her clothes and studied the figure in the mirror. She turned to the side. To the other side. Then to the back, looking over her shoulder. Her alarm grew exponentially by the second.

She put her clothes back on. She didn't want to see her naked body. How could she get so fat so quickly? And how could two-tenths of a pound have such a dramatic effect on her body? What was two-tenths of a pound? she wondered. She speed-walked to the living room and looked it up on her phone. It was 3.2 ounces.

Myra shook her head no. It didn't make sense.

Hideous went berserk screaming in her mind. She didn't hear his words as words. She perceived them as powerful thoughts encroaching upon her from every side. A pack of wild dogs encircling a wounded animal. Escape was impossible. There was nothing to do but to wait for the first painful bite.

Instinct kicked in. She tried to escape.

Her fingers punched frantically at the phone's screen. A hundred and thirty pounds multiplied by sixteen ounces is...two thousand and eighty ounces. Two thousand and eighty divided by 3.2 equals...six hundred and fifty.

Myra felt as though she were on the sideline of her mind listening to an argument of reason and irrationality. She concluded the debate with logic. Three point two ounces was only one part of six hundred and fifty parts of her body weight. There was simply no way the addition of a single 3.2-ounce part to a whole of six hundred and fifty parts could have such a dramatic increase in her body's appearance. It was impossible.

And, yet, there it was. Staring back at her from the mirror. Daring her to try again to think away or to rationalize away or to multiply and divide away the fact that she was turning into an oinker.

Her heart sagged and the last grains of sand in her hour glass of hope dropped to the bottom. There was no fight left in her. Somehow a few swallows of iced tea had just added obesity to her problems.

Try the scale this time with your clothes off, came the thought.

Myra gasped as though she had been deprived of air and it was suddenly available to burning lungs. She stripped again and rushed to the scale. She didn't step on it. She hopped on it. The digits horrified her. She stared at them for several baffling seconds. Shouldn't she weigh less with her clothes off? Then why did she weigh the same with and without clothes?

Myra slowly put her clothes back on. She walked like a zombie to the living room sofa and sat.

You're an ugly, fat pig.

How did you let this happen?

Can you imagine what your mother and sisters are going to say when they see how much weight you've gained?

You were already ugly. What guy is going to want you now that you're ugly and fat?

The barrage of demonic thoughts was relentless. Fiery arrows, darts, spears, and axes found their targets in Myra's soul and spirit. Some of the weapons penetrated and hung from her. Others hit her, then slowly sank fully inside like objects being pulled into a mound of soft clay.

Finally, the pain and weight of the weapons of lies, accusations, and demonic wisdom were too much to bear. Myra rolled onto her side on the sofa and cried in despair. She didn't know how much more she could stand.

Then a thought pushed itself to the front of all the others that were assailing her. This one offered her hope. Not a lot, but something.

You have to try harder.

"What can I do?" Myra asked herself.

Exhaustion answered, "Diet and exercise."

Myra thought of something. Maybe she should get on a diet and really start exercising, instead of playing at it. Her dim hopes brightened a little. She felt as though she were in the middle of the ocean in a row boat, exhausted, disoriented, dehydrated, and starving. But, yes, maybe if she tried rowing harder, she'd reach the safety of land.

"I'm going to try harder," she said.

Hideous laughed. "You do that," he mocked.

Chapter 26

"Tell me what you see," said Jezrael, to Mishnak and Aaron-Hur.

"The demons work together to get her to believe a lie. That she is overweight," said Mishnak. "Commander, I have only a little experience with people. She is not overweight, is she?"

"No, Mishnak. By the standards of her culture, most would judge her weight to be perfect."

"Why weight?" asked Aaron-Hur. "Why waste time getting someone to believe they are overweight? They could cause so much more damage by getting her to believe a false religion or to become a drug addict or a million other things. Why weight?"

"Because it is easy, and it opens the door to other lies," said Jezrael. "Physical beauty is part of the woman's calling. To be physically beautiful is deep in the woman's nature."

The two apprentices looked at one another. Aaron-Hur spoke for them. "Is this not vanity?"

"It can be," Jezrael answered. "In their fallen condition, often it is vanity. But the gifts and callings of God are without repentance. Eve was created to help Adam rule and to bring him pleasure. Her softness of heart and beauty of flesh complemented him and brought him pleasure. The great fall did not change her calling. It only perverted the fulfillment and expression of it. It is through this perversion that Satan finds his access."

"What is the perversion?" asked Mishnak.

"The perversion is in the man and the woman. In the blessed book it is written in Genesis, 'Your desire shall be for your husband,

and he shall rule over you.' This is the curse of the Lord for the rebellion of Adam and Eve.

"Part of the woman's curse is that her desire for her husband is perverted. It is now unnatural and imbalanced. Sometimes the perversion manifests as a need for approval from the husband that effectively makes him God. Other times it manifests as a rejection of his authority as husband that makes her God. Ungodly submission. Ungodly defiance.

"Whether the perversion manifests one way or the other, she still finds herself driven by her original design to be beautiful. You will find this in one way or another in every place and culture— except where the men in their hatred for women prohibit it."

Aaron-Hur said, "She will be beautiful for the man or for herself or for no other reason than she was created to be beautiful."

"Yes, that is correct," said Jezrael. "So, you see, it is not about weight. It is about purpose and identity. When a demon attacks a woman's sense of beauty, he attacks much more than an expression of possible vanity—although the woman may or may not be vain. He attacks the reason she was created and her natural design to make the world beautiful by her presence."

"But the woman was created for more than physical beauty," said Mishnak.

"Infinitely more," said Jezrael. "She was created to rule and reign. And we know now after the birth, death, and resurrection of the Lord that her destiny in the Lord's family and eternal kingdom is honor and power and authority and glory unimaginable. But this does not diminish the origin of, or the purpose for, her physical beauty."

"Commander, what about the rest of the curse you quoted?" said Aaron-Hur. "You said that both the man's and woman's ability to fulfill their calling have been perverted. What about the man?"

Jezrael said, "It is written, 'He shall rule over you.' As this relates to Myra and the design of women to be beautiful, there are two things to discuss. First, when Adam and Eve sinned, pride and lust gained the ascendency. The woman became proud of her beauty and began using it as a weapon to get what she desired from the man. The man became lustful of her beauty and began using his strength to satisfy his lust for her beauty.

"This helps to explain the second thing. Man was created to rule. He was given the gift and responsibility of primary ruler of the world. The great fall did not take this gift. It perverted it. When the blessed book says, 'he shall rule over you,' it means a perversion has taken place in the execution of the gift.

"In the beginning, the man was to rule with his wife. But after the fall, he seeks to rule over his wife. This is not speaking of the holy rulership of love and responsibility delegated to husbands. It is speaking of a rulership that is birthed in a corrupt heart that seeks to dominate."

Jezrael pointed to Myra. "This is the world of this woman. This battle is not simply between these demons and this woman. You need to understand the entire conflict if you are going to understand this singular battle. Superior numbers and weapons are not as critical as superior intelligence and wisdom."

The apprentices both looked at their commander with ready eyes. "Teach us, Commander. We want to learn these things," said Aaron-Hur.

"It is why you were chosen for this assignment," he answered. "The demons that are attacking this woman are not the most intelligent you will encounter. Yet they are prevailing against her because of the things I have shared with you.

"Myra is not only being directly attacked by the demons. She is being indirectly attacked by many demonically influenced support systems. Some of these systems are local. Some are international. All feed into the worldwide system of exploitation and domination of women."

"A worldwide conspiracy against women?" asked Mishnak.

"These demons you see attacking this woman are the least significant and powerful," said Jezrael. "They are foot soldiers doing only what they are told to do, or what their nature and instinct compel them to do. They often understand little of the part they play in the larger battles.

"At the higher levels of Satan's hierarchy are powerful angels who devise strategy. These are the ones responsible for creating antichrist philosophies and religions. There is a council of fallen angels that work specifically to hurt women."

Mishnak gasped. "A special council of angels against women?" He looked at Myra. Her hands covered her face as her sobs rocked her body. Weapons of every sort protruded from her bleeding wounds.

"They call themselves the Council of Hatred of All Women," said Jezrael. "They are the dark powers behind abortion, sex trafficking, pornography, female infanticide, female genital mutilation, dowry deaths, and a host of other atrocities against women."

Mishnak and Aaron-Hur had been surprised that there was a council of powerful angels solely committed to hurting women. But they had not been surprised by the methods used to hurt women. These things were well known among angels. Yet, the commander did have information that would shock them both.

Chapter 27

"The Council of Hatred of All Women is also behind the cosmetics and diet industries."

The two angels appeared baffled, as Jezrael anticipated they would be. Neither spoke their questions aloud. Instead, they silently contemplated these words and pondered why a council of high-ranking angels that were in charge of things like female infanticide and bride burning would also be behind industries dedicated to making women look and feel better.

"It doesn't appear to make sense, does it?" asked the commander.

"I can see no connection," said Mishnak. "They appear to contradict."

"Neither can I," said Aaron-Hur."

"And that is one of the reasons the council is so successful." Jezrael looked intently at them both. "Listen closely, and never forget what I am about to tell you. What does the blessed book say about the forbidden tree in the Garden of Eden?"

Mishnak saw it immediately. "That it was good, pleasant, and desirable."

"Exactly. Never forget this. Satan can work through that which is good, or that which is bad and appears to be good, as effectively as he can that which is bad and appears to be bad."

Both angels again contemplated the commander's words in silence.

The commander began to explain. "The cosmetics and diet industries are run by people who understand a woman's need to feel beautiful and desirable. They construct elaborate lies and spend billions of dollars in advertisement to get women to believe these lies. The object is to convince a woman that she is deficient, but that if she purchases their product or goes on their diet, she can overcome the deficiency. Of course, the industries and dark powers never allow her to believe she has arrived. She will never be whole without their products or approval.

"This woman, Myra, must overcome her original calling to be beautiful—which is corrupted because of the fall—the manipulative greed and lies of these industries, and the Council of Hatred of All Women."

Aaron-Hur said, "That is why the demons lie to the woman about her appearance and tell her to go on a diet."

"That other demon," said Mishnak, "the one who appears tired. He tells the woman to try harder. That is the song these demons sing. Try harder. Try harder. Always try harder. The woman is a hamster on a wheel. She runs, runs, runs, but gets nowhere."

"That is the object," said Jezrael. "No matter how much women spend, these industries will never let them feel satisfied. They need women to feel deficient to increase their own riches."

Aaron-Hur said with resolve, "They should stop. Refuse to be manipulated. No more cosmetics. No more diets. Say no to these manipulators."

Jezrael placed a hand on the shoulders of both angels. "If that's all the woman does, Satan wins. She should not refrain from either simply because the enemy seeks to pervert and manipulate. That course would allow the enemy to control her by denying her these things."

"Mishnak asked, "Is that what you meant when you said that men in their hatred for women may prohibit her from showing her beauty?"

"I was speaking of the other extreme of the council's attack against the beauty of the woman. The dark powers will either tell women they are not beautiful enough, or they will tell them they are too beautiful."

"How can a woman be too beautiful?" asked Aaron-Hur. "If you are created to be beautiful, you must be beautiful. It is your calling and duty to express the Lord's beauty through the beauty He gives as a gift."

"The answer has many layers of truth," said Jezrael. "A woman is never too beautiful. But a man or culture or religion that is influenced by the Council of Hatred of All Women will seek to suppress the beauty of the woman. They do this because they hate women. But they do it more because they hate the Creator, and the beauty of the woman reflects the beauty of the Creator."

"Islam," said Mishnak. "Is that why their women must be covered?"

"What kind of covering?" asked Aaron-Hur.

"I have seen this," said Mishnak. "A woman must wear clothing that reveals nothing but her face, hands, and feet. In some places only her eyes may be seen."

"The men make her wear this clothing?" asked Aaron-Hur.

"Yes. If she does not, she will be beaten," said Mishnak.

"Aaron-Hur," said Jezrael, "that is the extreme. But that oppressive spirit manifests in many ways in different cultures and religions. It is not always as easy to identify because it can be subtle. That spirit also works in some Christian churches to make women feel shame for their beauty."

"Commander, it is all so…much," said Mishnak. "This woman, Myra, how does she stand any chance? If, as you say, Christian women who are daughters of the Most High God fall prey to this conspiracy of evil, how can she escape? She is a daughter of the evil one."

"Mishnak, I truly do not know. But these demons and the dark powers of the Council of Hatred of All Women are not her greatest problem."

This caused quizzical, worried expressions on both angels. They had only been on this assignment for a short while, and although they did not love this woman, God was concerned about her. This made her their concern.

"What else is there?" asked Aaron-Hur.

"Can your army help her?" asked Mishnak.

"Look to the east," said the commander.

They did.

"I see nothing," said Mishnak.

"Neither do I," said Aaron-Hur. "What should we look for?"

The commander turned his palms upward and lifted his face. "Lord God, open their eyes so they may see."

"Commander!" they both exclaimed.

A large angel with a sharp sickle in his hand stood in a dark, smoky fire that covered his entire body, except for the arm that held the long sickle. His silhouette was distinguishable inside the fire, as were his eyes, which burned brighter than the fire surrounding him.

The fear of the Lord fell upon Aaron-Hur. "Who is *he*?" he asked.

Even from this distance, Mishnak saw that the angel's eyes looked penetratingly at Myra and nothing else. The angel's voice quivered. "Commander, the angel of the Lord looks at the woman. He is here for her."

"Yes, but not yet."

"Why? What evil could she have possibly done to be marked for judgment?" asked Mishnak, protectively of the woman, but in full submission to the will of God. *God's judgments were always just and good.*

"Mishnak, have you never read in the blessed book, 'he who does not believe the Son shall not see life, but the wrath of God abides on him'? She has done what every person has done. She has sinned against the Almighty God. Therefore, she is marked for destruction, as are the others."

"But why is he here now?" asked Aaron-Hur.

"It is written again in the blessed book. When the natural brothers of Jesus told Him to do something that would cause His death to occur before the Creator's designated time, He answered them, 'My time has not yet come, but your time is always ready.'"

"She can die at any moment?" asked Aaron-Hur.

"Every sinner can die at any moment. Every moment they do not die is a gift of mercy from the God they despise."

"But this woman has so much against her," said Mishnak. "These demons harass her constantly. The Council of Hatred of All Women. She does not know that the death angel is so near. She is distracted by her troubles."

"Mishnak, that is the condition of this world. People choose to serve that which takes away their sight. The blessed book says, 'take heed to yourselves, or your hearts will be weighed down with carousing, drunkenness, and cares of this life, and that Day come on you unexpectedly.'

"We can only hope that the woman's love of sin and the distraction of her problems don't lead her to final ruin. Now come with me. The demons are strengthening the stronghold, and a greater evil is coming."

Chapter 28

Myra was so desperate for relief that she didn't think how odd it was to listen to a thought in her mind that was so loud it may have been an actual voice. She sat up on the sofa. She'd definitely have to reapply her make-up to cover all of the crying she had done.

Two hours later she left her apartment. No more playing at working out. She was on her way to Atlantic Station LA Fitness. She had to lose weight fast.

When she arrived at the entrance to the Atlantic Station parking deck, she got in the line with only two cars ahead of her. The creature that awaited her at the ticket machine moved to her line. He was more monster than demon. He wasn't discernibly tall or large as some demons. But what he lacked in size, me made up for in depth.

If Myra were able to see the monster's dimensions, she would have seen a creature that was only six-foot tall and a few feet wide. His weight would be guessed at maybe two hundred and fifty pounds. She would be totally and immeasurably wrong.

Her assessments would be so completely wrong because the demon's discernible dimensions were like the tip of a demonic iceberg, revealing only a fraction of the monster's true size, which manifested more invisibly inside his form than visibly outside.

This invisible, but true size fluctuated constantly according to the richness of the nutrients in the victim he fed upon, or didn't feed upon. He was always increasing or decreasing in size. Increase brought intense pleasure. Decrease brought intense pain. He was in serious pain.

The creature was ravenously hungry. He was always ravenously hungry. He peered at the woman in anticipation of satisfying his deep hunger pains. If it were up to him, he would have begun his feast on her at the apartment. But when he had moved toward her, he found himself surrounded by four angels and eight sword tips only inches from his body.

One of the angels had put the tip of his sword's blade at the edge of his meaty nose and pressed in, drawing black blood as he said, "The woman must come to you if you are to have her."

The creature didn't know under what authority the angels had interfered with his meal. Nor was he now less angry with the angel's arrogance in telling him that he could wait for the woman at the parking deck. Nonetheless, here he was, still seething at the humiliation, but at least he would get a meal.

The woman was coming to him.

The creature's hunger moved him a step towards her approaching car.

"You will wait."

The creature froze. He saw no one, but recognized that voice. It was the uppity angel who had punctured his nose.

***

"What is taking you so long?" Myra said of the driver in front of her.

Her phone's ring interrupted her irritation. She looked at the number for a moment, shaking her head at Josiah's total lack of respect. *Oh, I see,* she thought, *I'm going to have to block you.* But for now, she chose to ignore him.

Next came a text notification. She read it.

Myra, the Lord has given me a release to talk to you. I know you told me to not contact you again. A vicious tiger—

Myra swiped the tiger text into oblivion without reading the rest. "I told you, Josiah. I'm done with you and your tigers—"

The invisible angel who stood near the ticket machine waited in somber anticipation of the woman's instructions.

"—and your Viking God," said Myra.

Those were the words.

The ticket machine began working again.

"The woman beckons you, demon," said the angel. "She is yours."

Myra felt the strangest sensation as the car in front of her pulled off. She watched it curiously. It was as though safety itself was driving off.

Weird, she thought. She drove forward and pushed the button to get her ticket. She pulled the ticket and felt something odd—and terrifying.

Chapter 29

The creature descended upon his meal and covered every inch of her body.

Myra's eyes and mouth were wide with the sensation that something had just covered her. Whatever it was, it clung to her. Was it wet? It felt clammy. She couldn't tell. But whatever it was, it had a chill and it seemed to have a million tiny points that pressed against her skin just enough to secure a super snug fit that couldn't be adjusted left, right, up, or down without discomfort.

A fit of what?

What is on me? thought Myra. Her bewildered eyes studied her hands.

BEEEEEEEEEEEP!

The car's horn behind her startled her. She flinched and drove forward. The feeling that increased in her as she looked for a parking space added disorientation to her alarm. She felt like a driver who had just looked in her rearview mirror and saw an out of control truck coming at her at high speed. The only way of possible escape was to dart across the path of a speeding train.

Myra parked and got out of her car. She closed the door and didn't move. She took deep breaths that seemed to help—a little. What was wrong with her? She was unravelling. She quickly scanned the family tree. There was no mental illness...as far as she knew.

But what if someone in her family was mentally ill and it wasn't known. She thought of herself. Maybe her problems weren't severe enough to be considered mental illness, but she sure hadn't told anyone about them. So, it wasn't a stretch to assume that she may have inherited a mental illness that was undisclosed in the family line.

Wait a minute! I am not crazy, Myra told herself, fighting the anxiety that was feeding on her. She reached for the obvious non-mental illness explanation only to grab air. She pushed through the panic and moved her feet. She had to get to the gym and exercise.

She had to.

***

"Sign me up," said Myra, to the gym representative.

The woman chose another feature to discuss.

Myra's anxiety grew. "I don't need to hear anything else. Give me the papers and show me where to sign." She heard how horrible she sounded, and she was ashamed to be so short. But this woman didn't understand. Time was running out. She had to lose weight now.

The woman looked at Myra with a plastered smile that hinted at what she was saying about her in her mind. "Give me your credit card and driver's license."

Myra ignored the woman's surly attitude and gave them to her. The woman filled out her portion of the contract. She curled her lips and pushed the contract across the table, with a look of contempt. "Sign," she said.

Myra signed, took the contract, hopped up without saying a word and hurried toward the treadmills to satisfy this new and growing compulsion. *I'm sorry,* she thought to the woman. *I'm not trying to be mean. I just have to lose weight now. Time is running out.*

Myra selected a treadmill. She placed her contract in her purse and placed her purse on the floor beside the treadmill and hopped on. Not thirty seconds later the surly contract lady stood beside her.

"You need to put your purse in a locker." The woman's tone of voice didn't sound like someone who cared a great deal whether she got fired or not.

Myra placed her hands and feet on the sides of the treadmill. She needed to apologize to this woman. "Look, I'm sorry for—"

"Or you can put it in your car," the woman cut her off. She returned Myra's look of surprise with one of her one. Her expression said, *And what part don't you understand?*

"Where are the lockers?"

The woman silently pointed.

Myra didn't have time to deal with this woman. She had to deal with the anxiety that was eating her. "Okay," she said.

She snatched her purse off the floor, not because she was angry, but to save time. She walked as quickly as she could, hoping not to look as odd as she felt. She locked up the purse and quickly returned to the treadmill.

Myra didn't stretch. She didn't have time to stretch. Myra didn't start her routine by walking. She didn't have time to waste walking. She needed results now. She pressed in five and began jogging.

Look at her, came the thought.

Her was a twenty-year-old female who had swam and run competitively since she had been in the seventh grade. She had won a number of high school and college swimming and track and field events, and never finished a race lower than third place.

Myra looked at the woman run at a much higher speed. She was breathing as normally as if she were walking. Under normal circumstances, the woman's beauty would have been what Myra would have focused on. But it was the ease at which the woman was running that commanded her attention.

Look at how toned she is. She's not like you. Not an ounce of jiggle anywhere.

Myra agreed with the thought. The woman's exercise clothing revealed perfect legs, perfect arms, perfect abs. Perfect. Perfect. Perfect. There was nothing about the woman's appearance that would have revealed the cervical cancer that had been growing in her for over a year.

Myra ceased her secret assessment of the woman's perfect body and looked straight before her, feeling jilted for her imperfections. She wondered what it would take to look like that.

You have to try harder, said Exhaustion.

She stole another long look at the perfect young woman to her left and increased the treadmill's speed. Myra's body told her immediately that she was running too fast for someone who was not really in shape and had already run past her safe limit.

But Myra couldn't stop. Not if she wanted to lose that two-tenths of a pound. And not if she wanted to be like Miss Perfect two treadmills to the left.

Try harder.

Myra resisted for a couple of minutes. Not because she disagreed with the thought, but because she was exhausted.

Exhaustion persisted. You don't have to be a fat slob. If you want to look like her, you have to try harder. Look at how much effort she puts into it.

Myra glanced at the woman. *You're right. I have to try harder,* Myra said to Exhaustion, thinking she was speaking to herself. She increased the speed again. She was now at seven. Her body was screaming for her to stop. She couldn't. Not if she was ever going to get back to a normal size.

The perfect woman increased her speed until she was sprinting. Myra looked from the corner of her eye in fascination. She was still not breathing hard. How fast did these machines go?

Do you want to look like that?

Yes.

If you want to look like her, you have to work like her. You have to try harder.

Myra knew it was ridiculous to increase the treadmill's speed. Her body couldn't take it. She already felt nauseous and like she was going to pass out. She didn't know how her legs were still moving. They just were.

Try harder.

Myra steeled her resolve and pressed the speed button until it was at ten. Immediately she lost control. Her weary legs took off into a desperate sprint to keep from face-planting into the spinning surface beneath her feet. She felt like a rodeo cowboy on a bucking bull. This machine was trying to kill her.

"I think you should slow down," said the perfect woman to Myra.

By this time, Myra didn't need this woman's advice to convince her to slow down. The problem was she couldn't slow down. She frantically reached for the sides of the treadmill so she could jump off. The moment she did, the machine sucked her down face-first into the spinning belt. The belt kept spinning against her face and body at the machine's maximum speed until she was thrown off.

A crowd gathered around Myra, who was lying face-down. She was conscious, in pain, and humiliated.

"Are you okay?" several people asked.

Myra felt her face burning from where she hit the belt. It was on fire. What kind of an idiot would go straight from the sofa to trying to run on this thing at full speed? She did not want to turn over and face these people. But she couldn't lie on her belly forever.

"Oh, your face. It's bleeding," said someone.

That was all Myra needed to hear. She thanked the little group of helpers, assured them she was more embarrassed than hurt, which was a lie, and hurried to the restroom. She looked in the mirror and expressed her horror by silently going to the locker to get her purse. She walked toward the gym's front doors.

The woman who had processed her contract caught up with her. The angel of truth called James was with her. "You need to put something on that," she said.

Myra turned around. The woman had a first-aid kit in her hand. By the unhelpful tone of her voice, Myra guessed that offering assistance to someone hurt on the premises must be official gym policy. "That's okay. I'll take care of it at home."

The woman said, "You know, you're not the first one to get hurt in here trying to keep up with someone else."

Myra looked at the woman as though she had no idea what she was talking about.

"Mmm, okay," said the woman. "If you say so. Maybe I didn't see what I know I saw."

"I don't know what you're talking about," said Myra, trying not to let this woman see her grimace.

The woman shook her head with a smile that said, *You're full of it.* "Well, just for the record then, Miss Hanson. The official policy of LA Fitness is that members exercise safely and not try to perform unreasonably beyond their capacity. This could be dangerous."

Myra couldn't believe this woman had a job interacting directly with customers. She could keep her first-aid kit. She walked away.

The truth angel said something to the woman. She called out to Myra, "This time it's a burnt face. Could be worse next time."

Next time.

The thoughts were already pressing her about working harder next time.

Chapter 30

"Exhaustion is doing what?" Hideous snapped loudly to the whispering demon. "Where is he?"

He couldn't believe that some new demon would march his arrogant behind into his stronghold and start barking out orders. And just who was this other demon of compulsion that had dropped out of nowhere.

The two incursions had to be linked. It sounded like a takeover. Well, this wouldn't be the first time Hideous would stick his clawed foot into the butts of opportunistic demons. He walked with quick, angry strides to the general meeting area. The short, informing demon struggled to keep up with his master.

Hideous stopped as suddenly as if he'd hit a wall. His demons were standing silently at attention. They appeared to be frightened. He hadn't called a meeting. What was going on here?

"What are you doing?" he yelled at his servants as he approached. "Who called this meeting? Why do you look so scared?"

A voice deep and heavy with dread answered from far behind Hideous. Hideous had walked right past the demon in his rage to get before the formation. "What are they doing? They are doing what their master ordered them to do. Who called this meeting? Their master called this meeting. Why are they scared? They are scared because their master is worthy of fear."

"Who said that?" yelled Hideous, ready to tear into the intruder. He walked to the right of the formation to see past his demons.

The challenger sat on a jagged boulder. He had the appearance of a thick, tall, and immensely ugly human. He wore a long black coat and black top hat that covered long black hair. His face was bony and disproportionately large. "It is the voice of your master."

"My master?" He had been right. This was a full-blown takeover attempt. He would make an example of this challenger in front of everyone. A slow and brutal reminder to his servants and a message to any marauding pirates looking for easy booty that he was not to be trifled with. Hideous spat a wad of black spit in front of him. "Come to me. We will show my demons who is master of this house."

The challenger slowly released a heavy breath. "You have disrespected your master before his servants." He paused. "I will not destroy you for this transgression. I will instead allow you to show your respect for me by allowing you to carry my hat."

"Enough talk. Come and fight," demanded Hideous.

The challenger stood. He wore a derisive grin as he slowly walked toward Hideous. He pushed back one side of his long coat and pulled out a sword. He kept his eyes on Hideous and tossed it to the side. He kept walking and pushed back the other side of his coat and pulled and tossed his other sword. Hideous watched with glee as the challenger got closer to his own destruction.

They both now stood before the formation. Only five yards separated them. Hideous thought of slicing through the unarmed challenger. But that wouldn't strike fear in the heart of other outside challengers. He pulled out his sword and prepared to toss it.

"You may keep your sword," said the challenger.

Hideous's eyes widened. His nose flared. He threw the sword aside.

"You should have kept the sword, Hideous. I only tossed mine because even I can't make a dead demon carry my hat. I need you just barely alive."

Hideous's smile was dark with confidence. This challenger had no idea. He constricted his throat. His body began to swell, and swell, and swell. Hideous, the master of the stronghold in Myra, looked down at the challenger. He didn't see the surprise he had expected to see in his opponent's eyes. It made no difference. He stepped towards him. "Unfortunately for you, I don't wear a hat. So I have no openings for a hat carrier."

Every demon in the formation would later discuss with fascination and terror how the fight had ended. They would not, however, come to agreement on whether the challenger had taken two steps or three before it started.

Hideous felt the kick that crushed his knee. He did not feel the hammer fist to his forehead that dropped him onto his crushed knee.

The challenger threw a hook to his jaw and Hideous fell like a tree onto his side. It was here that the fight turned as cruel as it was vicious. The challenger kicked Hideous several times in his belly before lying him on his back. He stretched out the leg with the crushed knee and repeatedly stomped the entire leg from top to bottom. He did the same with one of his arms.

Then he sat on his chest and pounded his face until everyone wondered whether their former master was dead. The last thing he did made more than one demon throw up. The challenger pried open the mouth of Hideous and forced his hand down his throat. He yanked once unsuccessfully. He yanked again and pulled out the organ that gave Hideous his ability to swell. He tossed it.

The challenger stood up and turned to his demons. He pushed his coat back on both sides and put his hands on his hips. "Get your eyes off him. He wishes he were dead, but he is not dead. He is my servant, as are you. My name is Vicious Hatred of All Women. You will call me Lord Vicious or Most Vicious. Do you understand?"

A chorus of "Yes, Most Vicious," and "Yes, Lord Vicious" rang out.

Vicious looked at Hideous. One of his eyelids fluttered. A low groan struggled to escape a chest full of broken ribs. "And you will never have the honor of speaking to me directly. You will speak to another who will speak to me. Do you understand?"

He waited. "Oh, yes, forgive me. Blink your good eye if you understand." He waited. "I'll take that as a blink. Good. We are all in agreement. Now, I must speak to my servants. Get to your feet. It is time for you to carry my hat."

It took several minutes for Hideous to rise. He finally stood, supporting himself on the leg that wasn't crushed. His broken body was stooped in pain from head to toe. He looked through the one eye that he could barely see out of and stretched out the arm that wasn't crushed.

"What if I were not a patient master?" said Vicious. He took off his hat and acted like he was going to give it to Hideous and threw it on the ground several yards away. "Go get my hat, Hideous."

In all this, the demons had not broken formation or moved an inch. But their eyes were straining at the corners to see the humiliation of their former master.

"Hideous is history. Look at me."

All eyes fixed on the new master.

"I stand in the presence of the Council of Hatred of All Women. Believe it or not, your former master now carries my hat because I just happened to be in the region when a friend of a friend requested a favor. So you can thank fate for your good fortune.

"This dog woman, Myra, is insignificant. A nothing. A nobody. But this Josiah character, he's not a nobody. He's a prayer warrior. This friend of a friend doesn't like the idea of him stirring up trouble in his jurisdiction.

"You never know with these types. Intercession—the kind they tell me he does—starts off with helping one person. Next thing you know you've got an uncontrollable mess on your hands. And who wants that?

"The thinking is the quicker we can get rid of this woman, the quicker this Josiah guy can turn his attention somewhere else. Presumably, somewhere in another jurisdiction other than this one."

Vicious looked with disdain at Hideous as he slowly crawled toward the hat. "I read the report of your activities, Hideous. Pathetic. You've had more than enough time to hurt this woman beyond repair." Vicious took quick strides to his right. He pointed at Gluttony. "You. No, the fat one. Get up here."

Gluttony got up there as quickly as he could, which was slow.

"You are all failures because your former master is a petty crook. He's good at snatching purses, but he couldn't rob a bank if his life depended on it. We don't have time for small minds and limited talent."

Vicious peered at Gluttony. "Which leads me to you. Just what exactly are you doing here? Are you going to beat her to death with a jelly donut? Strangle her with a pasta noodle?" He didn't wait for the profusely sweating demon to answer. "Get out!" he snapped. "Get your snacks and get out of here."

Vicious called out several other demons he considered worthless and gave them the boot, too. The first demon on the first row commanded, "Fill the ranks." Demons in the back filled the holes in the front left by the vacating demons.

Vicious smiled at the formation, then looked at Hideous. He was just now turning to crawl back toward Vicious. "I bet they never showed this kind of discipline under you."

Hideous would never have admitted it, but it was true.

"We have one objective. Destroy this female dog. It is not to make her feel bad. Do you understand me? It is about destruction. And I have no intention of being here long. The work will be quick.

"I have assigned a demon of compulsion who specializes in anxiety to cover this dog. He has already successfully done so. The demon, Exhaustion, has proven his worth by working with Compulsion to cause the woman to injure herself. Each of you will prove your worth, or be severely beaten, or if you're lucky, run off.

"My own fighting demons, specialists, and support demons are in route to make sure this job is completed and completed quickly. You will do whatever they tell you to do."

Chapter 31

Vicious stood several yards from the garbage the enemy called woman. He could barely tolerate her female smell without throwing up. She was a worthless dog. A rotten pig. A horrible reminder of how God had outsmarted them and sealed the eternal doom of hundreds of millions of courageous angels.

How could the Son of God enter their world through the body of this vile creature? Ovaries. Fallopian tubes. Uterus. Vagina. Breasts. *Repulsive*. As far as Vicious was concerned, this was the most offensive and humiliating of God's many tricks and injustices.

He watched her in silence and seethed with a fury that could not touch God except by touching this dog whom he had unjustly honored with his physical birth. Watching women, gazing and peering at them with memories and imaginings of base acts and cruelties committed against them, was his custom. His eyes were utterly locked on the woman with insatiable hatred.

He could enter her if he so desired, but he had no need and no desire to dirty himself with such intimacy—yet. Unlike demons of the lower classes, he had no humiliating and groveling need for a human body to express himself or to lessen the discomfort of his curse.

But it was undeniable that even for angels of his stature, personally inhabiting a human could provide advantages and pleasures that were not otherwise available to a spirit who operated from the outside.

His wicked mind wandered in thought. There was nothing like personally squeezing a woman's soft neck and looking into her bulged, terrified eyes as he strangled her. Or tearing away her genitalia in the name of a human custom. Or of beating and raping one of these dogs.

Yes…yeesss, he thought, as his pleasure neared the heights of a dark spiritual orgasm.

"Lord Most Vicious, we have a problem."

Vicious peered several more seconds at the woman, enjoying the pleasure of his thoughts, before turning away from Myra to face the demon. It was one of his own. A trusted and capable fighter and tactician. "What is it, Bludgeon?"

"It must be the African. The chippers can't get inside of the woman. There's a wall of fire."

Vicious looked at several dimensions of the woman. "I see no wall of fire. Take me to it."

They walked several yards before Vicious stopped and looked back at Hideous hobbling with his hat. "Bludgeon, he's not going to be able to keep up."

"Yes, Lord Most Vicious." The large demon pounded his heavy feet back to Hideous. "Protect your master's hat," he ordered. He wrapped his large hand around the crushed ankle of the now physically small demon and yanked him off his feet and dragged him to Vicious.

"Yes, it must be the African," said Vicious.

Bludgeon's strides were long as he effortlessly pulled his master's hat carrier. Hideous fought desperately to stifle his groans, battling his excruciating pain as he kept the hat from touching the ground.

"There," pointed Bludgeon.

Vicious looked at the scene. "Hmm." He took a seat on a boulder and rubbed his chin in thought as he rested his elbow on a knee.

Thousands of tiny demons carrying hammers and chisels moved left, right, up, and down in unison. Each time they did a wall of fire moved before them, blocking their path. Oddly, the wall of fire didn't completely surround the woman.

Vicious looked at the obvious apparent openings leading to Myra. Chipper demons were exceedingly effective at what they did. They were also exceedingly fixated. No matter what happened around them, they would not separate themselves from the lead chipper. But the lead chipper was so surrounded by chippers that he couldn't see the openings.

Vicious was curious. "Bludgeon, take some of the chippers and toss them toward the openings."

The demon threw Hideous's leg to the ground. Hideous gritted his teeth at the pain that shot up his leg. Bludgeon took a handful of chippers and threw them toward Myra. There were as many sparks and popping sounds as there had been chippers.

"They're toast," said Bludgeon.

"Indeed they are," said Vicious, pondering. "They smell horribly burnt, don't they?"

Bludgeon grunted agreement.

Vicious thought out loud. "Some of the enemy's fire is seen, some unseen. He is often working where he appears to be absent." This brought back stinging memories of when he and the other fallen angels had discovered this truth too late and were suddenly kicked out of heaven."

He continued. "Zechariah," he said. He was exceedingly proud of his knowledge of that wretched Bible. A good strategist had to know his enemy. And he was a great strategist. "I myself will be a wall of fire around her."

"That African has prayed a wall of fire around this dog," said Bludgeon.

Vicious watched the chippers going back and forth looking for an opening and leaving the path to the invisible fire alone. "Maybe chippers aren't as dumb as we think they are. Distract the African. Hurt him if you can. I will get the woman to give the chippers permission to enter."

"How will you do that, Lord Most Vicious?" Bludgeon did really want to know. He also knew the benefit of stroking his master's ego.

"I will get her to curse herself."

Bludgeon waited for the rest.

"Her lovely family," said Vicious. "Her very lovely family."

Bludgeon hit the inside of his massive palm with his club. "I will go after the African."

Chapter 32

One week later and the weight hadn't left. It had increased. Myra was now three-tenths of a pound heavier instead of two tenths. A fifty percent increase from her starting point. She was going in the wrong direction. How was it possible to exercise as much as she was exercising and to gain weight instead of losing it?

It's never coming off.

It's never coming off.

It's never coming off.

In six months, your closet will be filled with plus size clothes.

The only way to stop gaining weight is to try harder.

This was turning out to be the most mentally and physically grueling week in Myra's life. She had never been so absolutely exhausted. She could barely sit at her cubicle without falling asleep. Her work productivity and quality were being affected. Plus, she could barely move. Every muscle ached from overtraining.

Then there were the skid marks on her face from her first fall on the treadmill. (She had fallen a second time, but luckily the contract lady hadn't seen this fall.) She wished she could go back to only being ugly. Now she was ugly, fat, and disfigured. Things were going from bad to worse, even though she was trying harder than she had ever tried in her life.

Call your mother.

The recurring thought to call her mother was back. This was as ridiculous now as the first time it had come to her. Call her mother for what? Reassurance? Encouragement? *Love?* And with these marks on her face? There was no way she was calling her mother.

Myra stood in the hallway before her apartment door and did nothing. For some reason, ever since Allison had returned from visiting her sister, she'd go through these episodes of asking her uncomfortable questions. She was too tired to go through that, and she liked her too much to hurt her feelings. *Oh, Allison, not tonight,* she thought.

Myra closed her eyes and let out a long and slow breath that felt so, so, so good. She opened the door and went inside. Allison was sitting on the sofa, legs folded beside her, looking at her laptop, which sat on a cool, small table with a long, bendable neck. She wore shorts and a sleeveless shirt that had *Be Hopeful!* written across the chest. Myra hadn't seen that shirt before.

"Hey, Allison." The plan was to get to the bedroom as quickly as possible. She hoped Allison would speak and continue looking at her laptop.

"You really beat it out of there today," said Allison. "If I didn't know any better, I'd say you have a mystery man."

"Yeah, well, if this mystery man's name is LA Fitness"—Myra mentally kicked herself—"then I guess I do."

"Didn't you go to the gym this morning? You went again?"

Myra wished she had a lie ready, but she was blank. "Yeah."

"What are you trying to do? You ever heard of overtraining?"

"I'm not overtraining."

"Is that why you've been walking like you're ninety years old and falling to sleep at your desk?"

Myra's eyes widened. She sat on the matching loveseat. "Someone saw me sleeping?"

"Uhh, it's more like *everyone* saw you sleeping."

Myra whispered a curse word.

"Jarrod didn't see," said Allison. "So all is well. Your boss didn't see you sleeping." She paused. "But your three direct reports did. Don't worry. We're not going to write you up. We appreciate you volunteering to bring in bagels...and coffee," she said, with an opportunistic smile. "But good to know you're not overtraining." Allison gave Myra time to share. When she didn't, she said, "Are you okay?"

She snapped out of her thoughts and smiled to deflect the question. "Yeah."

"Well, you don't look okay."

"I am."

Allison nodded disbelievingly. "You know how me and my sister always get into it, right?"

Myra nodded.

Allison shook her head. "She surprised me. She really did. She was the last person I wanted to see when my therapist killed herself. I didn't want to give her a platform. But I needed to get out of here." Allison thought of her trip to Colorado. "I've got to give her credit. She's not as nuts as I thought she was."

Myra wondered where this was going.

"There's obviously something going on. Maybe you should talk to your mom."

Myra's expression didn't reveal how ridiculous this was. But as she looked at Allison, she understood how Allison could say this. She had lost her mother at such a young age. She had a hole in her heart that would be healed if only her mother had lived. But that wasn't her story. Allison couldn't understand that sometimes a mother's presence could cause as much pain as her absence.

"I'm glad your trip back home went nicely," Myra said, politely. "I'm going to hit the sack early." She started walking toward her bedroom.

"Give it some thought, Myra. I really think you should talk to your mom."

Myra kept walking.

Vicious kept peering...and calculating.

"And try that new cream I told you about for your face," Allison yelled out. "You don't want those scars to become permanent. Life is hard enough."

"It's about to get a lot harder," said Vicious. "Bludgeon," he said, "have someone visit her father."

Chapter 33

Three Days Later

Myra listened to Cornelius with alarm. "Fell down the stairs? How is he?" she asked, afraid to hear the answer.

"You know Dad. He's not going to tell you if something's hurting him. He's all banged up and sore. He broke his leg. Hit that hard head of his, too. They kept him overnight just to make sure."

"Kept him overnight? When did this happen?"

"It happened two days ago. But like I said, Dad's Superman. Or at least he thinks he is. He didn't tell Mom."

"Cornelius, how'd he cover up a broken leg?"

"I don't know. Gifted I guess. Look, everyone's been by to see him. I went by last night. He said the only one of his children who hadn't come to see him..."

"I didn't even know until now."

"I know," Cornelius chuckled. "He did the same thing to me. Man breaks his leg and pretends like it never happened, but falls to pieces if you don't go see him immediately. Just go by and see him so he can stop whining."

Vicious smiled. "That's right, dog. Go see your daddy."

***

It wasn't until the door to her parents' home opened, and her mother looked at her with aghast and said in slow melodrama, "What...in the hell...happened to you? You've got marks—*on your face*," that she remembered the marks on her face. How could she have forgotten them?

Her mother hadn't spoken loudly, but apparently there was something mystical about the words *marks on face* that echoed throughout the house and pulled her sisters down the hallway and to the door as though the house was on fire.

Her mother and sisters studied her face in silence. Their mouths were closed, but their faces spoke volumes.

Lauren said, "I couldn't live with that." She turned and started down the hallway. "That is a mess. I'd just slit my wrists."

I'd just slit my wrists.

Your sister's right. You should slit your wrists.

"Don't listen to her. What happened?" asked Tina.

"What difference does it make?" said Elizabeth. "This kind of disfigurement is defining. Come in," she said, unaware of the disgust in her voice.

Your mother is disgusted with you.

"I didn't lose an eye, Mom. I just fell down," she apologized.

"Fell down?" said Elizabeth. "How does an adult fall down. Were you not paying attention?"

She thinks you're stupid.

"Yes, I was paying attention. I was on a treadmill."

"Treadmill?" Elizabeth looked pleased. She looked her up and down. "Are you trying to get your weight under control?"

Myra felt that whatever answer she gave would be the wrong one.

Tina filled the silence with what she thought was encouragement. "She's only a little overweight, Mom."

"Just exercising," said Myra.

The wall of fire was still there blocking the chipper demons with their hammers and chisels, and pickaxes, but the heat wasn't as intense.

Tina took Myra by the hand to pull her to safety. "Dad's in here."

"Aww, the prodigal daughter has finally come to see her dying father?" said George, as he looked over his shoulder. "Lauren says you had a car wreck."

"I didn't say *had* a car wreck, Dad. I said *is* a car wreck. Look at her face, Daddy."

"Oh, boy," he said, looking at her face with concern, "as if it weren't hard enough fitting in with these three beauty queens. But who said life was fair? What happened, baby?"

There are these three beauty queens...and then there's you.

"She fell down on a treadmill," Elisabeth answered for her. "You and your father. Falling down like toddlers."

"I'm telling you, Liz, it was like somebody pushed me down the stairs," said George.

"If you say so, George. At least Myra's not blaming her faults on the invisible man."

"Well, if you fell on the treadmill, at least you were trying to better yourself," said Lauren.

Did you hear how she said that? "Trying" to better yourself. She knows you're hopeless.

Myra didn't waste breath responding to Lauren. She had lived with her sister's tongue for most of her life. It wasn't changing. It wasn't discriminatory. It wasn't going anywhere. It was a stubborn weed being what it was. Only Mom and Dad were beyond its reach, and others who weren't afraid to use their tongues like razors. Lauren could give it better than she could take it.

"There are better ways to fight obesity than to disfigure your face," said Elizabeth. "Are you taking anything for it?"

Obesity? thought Myra. Disfigured face?

George shifted himself in his recliner. "You may be able to get a skin graft."

"A skin graft, Dad? I fell off a treadmill."

"Yeah, but you don't want something like that hanging around too long." He laughed before he delivered his joke. "This could be the uncle who comes to visit and doesn't go home. You want to look like Gorbachev the rest of your life? That Russian fella's got a map of the world on his forehead. Skin graft."

"That's not a bad idea," said Elizabeth. "They can take it off your butt."

You heard how she said that? It's not like you'd miss it.

"Less treadmill time," said Tina, innocently.

"I'll make the phone call for you," said Lauren. She wasn't joking.

Myra said as resolutely as she could, "I'm not getting a skin graft."

Her mom and Lauren looked shocked. "You're not?" they both said.

"No, I'm not getting a skin graft."

"Look, this girl came here to see her poor 'ole daddy," said George. "She didn't come to be harassed by you beauty queens." He studied the scars again. "It doesn't make a difference what you look like, you'll always be my little girl."

It doesn't make a difference what you look like.

Myra heard mocking laughter in her mind.

Tina stretched her neck and face into a half-smile, half-grimace. "Geez, thanks, Dad...for the moral support. I think that's what that was. Right?"

"Aww, Myra knows we love her," he said.

"What's wrong with your face, Auntie Myra?"

Myra looked to the right. Her mouth dropped open. "Ohhh, look at you," she gushed. "What a beautiful dress. And your hair." Myra bent down. "Come here, Lizzy. Give Auntie Myra a hug."

Lizzie took obviously choreographed steps, one foot landing precisely on the imaginary straight diagonal line in front of her. The other following and landing precisely on that line. Myra turned her head to the side in a puzzled grin as she watched her niece.

"Be careful when you hug me," she said, holding her face away from Myra. "I don't want my lashes or makeup to come off."

Myra's head popped backward. "Lashes? Makeup?" she said, looking her over, then looking around, waiting for someone, anyone to answer why Lizzie was wearing lashes and makeup—and heavy makeup at that!

No explanation, but many silent smiles as they looked at Lizzie. Apparently, Lizzie was the one with the answer.

"I am going to enter and win the Atlanta Little Miss Peach beauty pageant. I will exhibit superior beauty, poise, and charm. Yet this is only my sunrise. My sun will not set before I follow in the footsteps of my beautiful grandmother, my beautiful mommy, and my beautiful Auntie Tina. I will win a state beauty contest."

Myra was horrified. How many times had her mother made her recite this same empty mantra almost word for word? Until she had finally given up hope that her not-beautiful- enough-daughter would ever win another trophy beyond the age of nine.

"Lizzie's going to enter a beauty contest?" Myra could almost throw up.

"You're looking at a future Miss Michigan," said Lauren, smiling widely at her daughter.

Elizabeth beamed. "Oh, it doesn't have to be Miss Michigan."

"That would be something, though, wouldn't it, Daddy?" said Tina. "Mom, Lauren, me, and one day, Lizzie."

"What are you going to do, Lauren?" said George. "Move back to Michigan so the girl can win beauty pageants in Michigan?"

"It doesn't have to be Miss Michigan," Elizabeth repeated. "I'll accept Miss Georgia."

"That's the plan. One day," said Lauren. "Mother has set a high bar for the Hansen girls. It wouldn't be right not to emulate her accomplishments. That's in the Bible, isn't it, Mom?"

Elizabeth may have said Miss Georgia would be an acceptable title, but she was glowing with satisfaction at her daughter's words. "That's right, Lauren. 'To whom much is given, of the same is much required.'"

This was the only Bible verse she knew. And she knew this one only because her mother had made her memorize it, and because she had convinced her that Almighty God expected her to use her remarkable beauty to get ahead in life. Beauty pageants were the logical first step.

"Did you hear what your grandmother said, Lizzie? That's the word of God," said Lauren. "It's in the Bible. There's a reason He has made nearly all of the Hansen girls so pretty."

Whoop. Whoop. Whoop. Whoop. The sound of the large axe spun through the air toward Myra. Axe head. Handle. Axe head. Handle. Axe head. Handle. Axe head. Handle. Until the axe head hit her between her breasts and burst her chest open.

Myra looked at Lauren. Lauren seemed to have already forgotten the horrible words that had just come from her mouth. Myra looked at the others one after the other. All had heard and not heard the insult and were moving about and talking as though Lauren had just said Arizona had hot summers. *Why, of course, Arizona has hot summers. And, of course, Myra is not as beautiful as the other Hansen women.*

Myra could have pressed past her fear to confront her family, but even if she were able to gather the courage to do so, what would that accomplish? These weren't deliberately mean people. They weren't deliberately cruel people. They were simply incredibly shallow and insensitive people. People who happened to be her family.

Myra had felt small and insignificant in their presence many times before. But this time she felt something different. She *really* did not belong here. She didn't belong in this family. She didn't belong anywhere.

Vicious waited for his moment with a tightly closed mouth. Each of his deep and long breaths released rage that refused to lessen. The dog was only moments away. He could feel it.

Myra staggered through her visit the best she could without breaking down and crying. When she got to her car, however, she cried as though she was a woman with no hope. Then she said it. "Why was I born? I hate myself. I wish I was dead."

Vicious closed his eyes. He opened his mouth and let out grunts of deep satisfaction. "Now you are mine."

The wall of fire disappeared.

The chippers covered Myra from head to toe and feverishly swung their pickaxes and hammered their chisels. It was only a matter of time now before this dog's very life was in the hands of Vicious Hatred of All Women.

Special Representative of the Council of Hatred of All Women.

Chapter 34

"What just happened, Commander?" asked Aaron-Hur.

Mishnak found what he saw hard to believe. "How does she keep standing? She's full of arrows and spears and darts and axes. They split her open."

"She has no armor," answered Jezrael. "If she were an obedient daughter of God, she would have protective armor. And she would be able to fight back. She would even be able to go on the offense. She could take the fight to the demons."

"What kind of armor?" asked both angels.

"In the blessed book, it is written, 'Therefore take up the whole armor of God, that you may be able to withstand in the evil day, and having done all, to stand. Stand therefore, having girded your waist with truth, having put on the breastplate of righteousness, and having shod your feet with the preparation of the gospel of peace.

"Above all, taking the shield of faith with which you will be able to quench all the fiery darts of the wicked one. And take the helmet of salvation, and the sword of the Spirit, which is the word of God."

"The axe that split the woman open," said Mishnak, "the breastplate of righteousness would have prevented this." It was part question, part statement.

"Not by itself, Mishnak. The armor works as a whole. This is why the Scripture says, 'Take up the *whole* armor of God.' When the Spirit moved upon God's servant, Paul, to write these Scriptures, Paul was thinking of the Roman soldier. Successful warfare begins with knowing the enemy. That is why Paul began by identifying the true enemies."

"Satan and his demons," said Aaron-Hur. His tone carried his hatred of the dark powers.

"Yes," said the commander. "No matter how well-equipped a soldier is, if he doesn't know who his enemy is, his equipment will be useless."

"The woman doesn't even know there is an enemy," said Mishnak.

"And if Satan has his way, she won't find out that he exists until she dies." The commander continued. "Once you know your enemy, you can prepare for him."

"She's a sitting duck," said Mishnak.

"What do you mean, 'a sitting duck'?" asked Aaron-Hur.

"Have you attended familiarity classes?" asked the commander. "I've noticed your use of their language."

Mishnak brightened with holy pride. "Class and field observational studies. But this is my first on the frontline in hostile conditions."

Aaron-Hur gawked at Mishnak. "I haven't had such opportunities."

"Have you asked for them?" said Mishnak.

"No."

"You have not because you ask not," said the commander. He looked at Mishnak with a smile, and looked at Aaron-Hur. "Ask, or angels like Mishnak here will take your slot."

Aaron-Hur shook his head, finding it hard to believe he had overlooked something so obvious. "I've never asked."

"If someone is like a sitting duck, it means he is a defenseless target," said Mishnak.

Back to business.

The commander said, "The servant of God must be in *the* truth and be a person *of* truth. Her heart must be protected by the righteousness that comes from believing on Christ. She cannot have faith in her ability to establish her own righteousness. Nor can she live as a hypocrite. The righteousness she trusts in will produce righteous behavior. If it does not, it is not real. God is holy."

Mishnak and Aaron-Hur said, "Blessed be the name of the Lord. God is holy."

Jezrael continued. "Her shoes are the gospel."

Aaron-Hur asked, "Is this evangelism?"

"It was understood in Paul's day that the one who received the gospel had an obligation to share the gospel. So, yes, it includes evangelism. The gospel message destroys strongholds. But for the individual, shoes protect your feet...which give you a sure foundation."

Aaron-Hur looked at Myra and gestured strongly. "And the shield of faith could have blocked these weapons."

"Yes," said Jezrael. "Do you know why the apostle said, 'above all, taking the shield of faith'?"

"Aaron-Hur answered quickly. "Because none of the armor works without faith."

The commander's expression was serious as he pointed sympathetically at the woman. "Faith in God could have blocked every one of these weapons."

All three angels silently watched Myra's bloodied spirit stagger and fall repeatedly. Large puddles of blood gathered each place she fell. Mishnak turned away. Watching this bleeding woman fall down and struggle to her feet only to fall down again and again was too much.

"Look at her, Mishnak," ordered Jezrael. "Frontline angels don't have the luxury of turning away from the realities of spiritual warfare, no matter how uncomfortable it makes us."

He didn't try to explain. "Yes, I apologize, Commander."

"There is more," said a voice that came from everywhere.

All three angels looked around for the voice, but saw no one. Then they felt the majesty and power of the infinite Creator. Each of them dropped to their knees and shook in delightful awe. Jezrael struggled a whisper. "Lord...God."

The Voice said, "In the holy Scriptures it is written, by faith the elders obtained a good report. Abel. Enoch. Noah. Abraham. Sarah. Isaac. Jacob. Joseph. Moses. The prophets. These were all imperfect people. Yet I was well-pleased with them because of their faith. They entered my rest because of their faith. Faith makes all things possible. Teach my servants, Commander Jezrael."

Several minutes after the angels were certain the manifest presence of the Almighty God had lifted, they remained on their knees. Each had seen the Creator from a distance many times. They had heard His voice many times in the great assembly. They had felt His presence many times. But He was so vast and powerful and glorious and infinite and holy that it was impossible to get used to Him.

He could be fully experienced, but never fully explained.

Finally, the angels stood.

"Aaron-Hur, your eyes are about to pop out of your head," said Jezrael, in an attempt to get the focus off him.

"The Creator called you by name," said Aaron-Hur.

Jezrael sniffled and breathed heavily, rubbing his hand over his nose and mouth. "Yeah." He wiped his face dry of tears.

"Teach us, Commander. The Creator said, 'Teach my servants,'" said Mishnak.

Aaron-Hur and Mishnak waited for the commander to stop wiping fresh tears from his face.

"The helmet of salvation," he began, exulting in the pleasure of hearing God say his name, "is worn on the head. The blessed book teaches that this is the culmination of salvation. It is the coming of the Lord and the resurrection of the body. It is called the blessed hope.

"If a child of God is filled with this hope and meditates on this hope, it will give her an eternal perspective on all things, which will produce wisdom, and it will protect her mind from the evil values of this world. This is why the enemy attacks the doctrine of the second coming."

"The woman doesn't have this," said Mishnak. "She has only the hope that this world offers."

"Which, in her case, is nothing," said Aaron-Hur.

"That is the case for all who trust in this world," the commander corrected. "Not just her."

"Thank you, Commander, for teaching us," said Mishnak.

"Yes, thank you," said Aaron-Hur.

"There is one more piece of armor," said Jezrael. "It is the sword of the Spirit. When a child of God skillfully uses the word of God, it acts as a sword."

"How is this done?" asked Mishnak.

Commander Jezrael, teach my servants. He said my name. He called me Commander. He trusts me as a commander and teacher of his angels.

"Commander?" said Aaron-Hur, noticing the commander's difficulty to speak.

Jezrael looked at both angels. His mouth opened. His expression followed the wonder and honor of the Almighty's acknowledgement of him.

"Commander, are you well?"

Jezrael could contain it no longer. He lifted his hands and face toward the heavens and yelled as loud and long as he could before falling to his knees. "My Lord and my God," he said, before falling onto his belly and crying with sobs of gratitude that shook his body.

Glory fell upon them all. Mishnak fell to his belly. Aaron-Hur danced and sang.

An hour later the three angels looked at one another with smiles and wet faces as they sat on the ground.

"I may never finish this teaching," said Jezrael.

"You must. The Lord told you to teach us," joked Mishnak.

Jezrael raised a palm. "Mishnak, don't. Are you trying to bring down the glory again?"

"Actually, Commander, it was you," said Mishnak.

The commander smiled. "Okay, it was me."

"You were about to tell us how children of God skillfully use the word of God as a sword," said Aaron-Hur.

Jezrael said, "It is written in the blessed book, "The word of God is alive and powerful, sharper than a two-edged sword, piercing even to the dividing of soul and spirit, joint and marrow, and is a discerner of the thoughts and intents of the heart.

"The best example I can give you also comes from the blessed book. You remember when our blessed Lord was tempted by the evil one in the wilderness."

Aaron-Hur snarled his words. "That traitor and usurper tried to make the Creator stumble in his humiliation. I will never forget. His day is coming."

"Yes, it is," said Jezrael. "Each time the enemy tempted the Lord, he spoke the word of God against him."

"But, Commander," said Mishnak, "the accuser, he also used the word of the Lord."

Aaron-Hur got even angrier. "That is right, Commander. That accuser tried three times in the wilderness to use God's own word against him. 'He shall give His angels charge over you, to keep you.' Think of it! Trying to use a promise of the Lord to get him to jump off the temple roof. This evil spirit is a lunatic. He is crazy."

Aaron-Hur looked at the commander and Mishnak. "I am sorry. I do not mean to get off track."

"No apologies necessary," said Jezrael. "The accuser *is* insane, and he is a criminal. But he is also wise in darkness. He was unsuccessful against the Lord. But he is usually successful when he uses this tactic on the people of God."

Aaron-Hur and Mishnak looked at one another as though this was an impossibility.

"I will explain," said Jezrael.

Chapter 35

The Lord knows the word," said Jezrael. He hesitated long enough for his statement to sound awkward to his students.

Aaron-Hur and Mishnak looked at one another. Mishnak agreed with a nod to be the one to say it. "Respectfully, Commander, of course the Lord knows the word. He is the Word. How can he not know it?"

Jezrael said, "What I'm implying is that you must know the word for it to be effective as a weapon. If you don't know it, or know it well enough, you can't use it to combat Satan's lies and accusations. You also won't know when he's twisting the word to deceive you."

Aaron-Hur's face showed great bewilderment. "Commander, I admit to my shame that I do not know the words of the blessed book as I should…"

The commander prodded him. "Yes?"

"But I am an angel. I live in heaven. There is no evil in heaven. It's God's home." The angel shook his head. "There is no danger to me. But it sounds like you are saying that even the people of God don't know the words of the blessed book, although their very lives depend on it."

"It is true," said Jezrael.

"Aaron-Hur is correct," Mishnak added emphatically. "This makes no sense. They are behind enemy lines. The accuser is a formidable enemy. A great deceiver. He seduced angels out of heaven. He seduced Adam and Eve out of paradise."

Aaron-Hur blurted, "How can they face such a threat and not read and cherish the very book that can save their lives?"

"Some are busy. Some are lazy."

"Some are *busy?*" said Aaron-Hur.

"And others are *lazy?*" said Mishnak.

The two angels shared expressions that progressed from surprise to anger to disgust, and finally to discouragement.

"I share your feelings," said the commander. "It is a tragedy."

A long, heavy silence fell upon them.

Slowly, a determined grin formed on the commander's face. He said, "I've read the blessed book many, many times. I do not claim to understand it all. No angel does. Its deep secrets are reserved for the sons and daughters of God. We learn from their discoveries."

Aaron-Hur and Mishnak heard something hopeful in their commander's voice.

He continued. "One thing is clear to all. To the sons and daughters of God. To the angels of the Lord. To Satan and his demons."

"What is that, Commander?" asked Mishnak.

"God wins." He smiled confidently at both angels. "The sons and daughters of God win."

Aaron-Hur smiled. "We win."

Mishnak pulled himself from the exuberance of the moment. The commander had been right earlier. He should never have turned away from the woman. Now he turned away from the angels and looked pitifully at her. Bleeding. Staggering. Under the weight of sin and injuries to her spirit and soul. This was one whom the Lord of glory had lived and died for.

A tear coursed down his face. "What about now?" he said. "What about her?" He added, "Myra."

Commander Jezrael brightened with the angel's show of emotion for Myra. She was becoming less of an observation to him and more of a person. Mishnak was growing. This would go in the commander's report.

"Let's talk about her.

Chapter 36

"This demon who comes from the Council of Hatred of All Women," said Mishnak, "he is worse than the demon, Hideous. Hideous is a beast. He behaves as a beast. But this one, this so-called Lord Most Vicious, his hatred for Myra doesn't come from animal instinct. He is driven by something deeper."

"And he is a thinker," said Aaron-Hur.

"You both are correct," said Jezrael. "Most high-ranking demons like this were high-ranking angels before the great rebellion. They are twisted versions of what they once were. I do not know who this demon is, but he was surely once a great angel. My guess is that he gets his great hatred of women from feeling peculiarly slighted by them."

"But what could a woman have ever done to him?" challenged Aaron-Hur. "He is in trouble because of his own foolish decision to rebel against the Creator. This is no woman's fault. It makes no sense."

"Don't try to make sense of demons," said Jezrael. "They blame everyone but themselves for their troubles. They will drive you crazy trying to make sense of them. They are not rational. Their reasonings are dark. They have no light."

"This Vicious spirit, he orchestrated Myra to go to see her father," said Mishnak. "He has stated that he wants her hurt or dead. He brutalized Hideous for making her feel just bad. Now he is doing the same."

"He did something that Hideous did not do?" said Jezrael. "He convinced her to curse herself."

"I did not hear a curse," said Aaron-Hur.

"Neither did I," said Mishnak.

Jezrael said, "When Myra said, 'I hate myself. I wish I was dead,' she cursed herself."

"But she did not mean to curse herself," said Mishnak. "It is a figure of speech. I have heard this saying many times. They don't mean it."

"It doesn't make a difference whether they mean it or not. Satan is a legalist. He will use any opening he is given. Besides, the same creative power the Lord shares with His people through their words works to bless or to curse. 'I didn't really mean what I said' is not a defense."

"That is why the wall of fire disappeared and those tiny demons were able to swarm Myra?" said Mishnak.

"Yes."

"I am confused, Commander," said Aaron-Hur. "The demon that Vicious calls Bludgeon...he pushed Myra's father down the stairs. How was he able to do that? I thought only angels could enter the human dimension."

Mishnak added, "And that only with permission from God Himself. Is this not correct, Commander? Why would Vicious work indirectly against Myra through her family if he has power to touch her directly?"

"Very good questions," said Jezrael. "Demons need special permission to directly interact with people in their dimension. But this permission can come from God or from people."

"How can a person give authority that only God has?" asked Aaron-Hur. "The ungodly would unleash an unstoppable force of demons!"

The commander's eyes were sharp. "God is gracious beyond our ability to understand. He shares more than any of us can understand why." He paused. "But nothing He does and nothing He shares will ever stop Him from being God."

Aaron-Hur and Mishnak bowed their heads and said, "Blessed be the name of the Lord God. He is sovereign."

"People may yield to ungodliness, or they may actively invite Satan's presence. This can open the door for special manifestations of the evil one in the human dimension. Myra's father has an open door in his life that allows these manifestations."

"What is that door?" asked Mishnak.

"No one in this family serves the Lord," said Aaron-Hur. "Shouldn't they all have open doors to the enemy?"

"Yes, Aaron-Hur, this is true," said Jezrael. "It is written in the blessed book, 'To whom you yield yourselves slaves to obey, his slaves you are to whom you obey, whether of sin leading to death, or of obedience leading to life.'

"Satan has considerably more access to his own servants than to God's servants. But Myra's father has a different kind of open door in his life."

"What is it?" asked both angels.

"Witchcraft."

Neither angel had to be a frontline angel to understand the implications of this pronouncement. Witchcraft demons had once been exceptionally close to the Lord. They had been constantly in His presence. Their influence among the ranks and societies of angels had been enormous.

Mishnak stared at the ground, pondering the severity of this revelation. Aaron-Hur turned around with his mouth wide open, with his hand on his forehead, and his face skyward.

"He asked witchcraft to come into his life," said Jezrael.

Aaron-Hur spun around. "He asked a witchcraft spirit to come into his life? Why, I don't understand. What am I missing? He doesn't appear to be any more wicked than the rest of the family."

"He isn't any more wicked than the rest of them. He didn't know what he was doing. He did this when he was in university."

"Did he sacrifice an animal?" asked Aaron-Hur.

"Was it a ceremony? I attended a lecture once," said Mishnak. "A ceremony can—"

"It wasn't a ceremony," the commander interrupted. "And George would never have sacrificed an animal. He went to a psychic."

Mishnak and Aaron-Hur looked at one another puzzled and underwhelmed. "What's a psychic," asked Mishnak.

"Another name for witch," said Jezrael. "At least in the eyes of the Lord. He used to play basketball for the university. He wanted to know whether he would be drafted to play professionally. That's when he went to the witch."

Mishnak spoke in almost a whisper. "I have heard rumors that the Creator has destroyed many for consorting with witchcraft. Even whole civilizations."

"That is correct, Mishnak. And that is when the curse of the Lord came upon this man." Jezrael answered the question in the angels' eyes. "He has terrible headaches and nightmares. And sometimes he has short bouts of confusion. He has never told his wife about the confusion."

"He has gotten off easy," said Aaron-Hur, looking at Mishnak, "if what you say true."

"He also picked up a spirit," said Jezrael.

"He has a demon?" said a wide-eyed Aaron-Hur.

Jezrael said, "The man has many accidents. It is written, 'He who seeks to save his life shall lose it.' He cursed his basketball career when he asked the witch to tell him whether he would be drafted. At that point, he began to have frequent accidents. I learned all of these things before I was assigned here."

"A demon who causes accidents," mused Mishnak. He looked at Jezrael. "And what of the tiny demons? What are they doing to Myra with those chisels and pickaxes?"

The commander couldn't hide his concern for her. "They are called chipper demons because they chip away at the person's peace. I believe the plan of Vicious is to chip away at Myra until she is compromised enough to go into deep depression and more dangerous levels of bondage. He wants to make it impossible for her to say no to him."

Mishnak's heart clenched. "Myra...in the hands of such a wicked spirit."

Aaron-Hur's face registered fear, too, but for a different reason. He pointed toward the horizon. "The angel of death appears to be closer."

Chapter 37

In human terms, the demon was morbidly obese. But this was not the kind of fat spirit that Vicious hated. (He couldn't put his finger on why he detested fat spirits.) It was the kind he loved. For the extra weight of this demon had nothing to do with food. No, this demon's weight was simply weight. Heaviness.

Vicious was like a general looking out over the battlefield. His hands were perched on his sides under his coat. His hat carrier on one knee beside him, head bowed and holding up his hat. He imagined how he looked to his demons. He knew it was a good look.

The fat spirit had been given no instructions and didn't need any. He knew what to do. He wrapped his sticky fatness around Myra, totally covering her.

"Wait," ordered Vicious. "Put the isolation helmet on her," he ordered another demon.

Helmet was not an accurate description of what the demon had in his hand. It was actually something akin to a tight, rubbery mask with no openings that snugly covered the entire head and face. The demon put the mask on Myra's head and pulled downward.

It appeared too tight to fit. But that was how it was designed to fit. Tight and smothery. He jumped two feet in the air and hung onto the sides of the helmet as he came down, holding his feet in the air to let his weight help pull the mask down. The mask resisted, then slid down and cupped tightly under Myra's chin. The demon checked the fit and gave a thumbs up to his master.

Vicious looked at the fat spirit.

The demon resumed his job. He squeezed Myra until he was firmly fixed to her body.

***

Myra sat elevated above the trees in the still rocking chair and looked at the sunrise from the long and wide elevated porch. It wrapped around the entire small Blue Ridge mountain cabin. She didn't see the beauty of the sunrise or hear the chirping of birds. Nor did she feel the cool breeze against her skin or smell the freshness of the trees.

She wasn't here to enjoy nature. She was here because Allison had been given strong hints by Myra's boss, Jarrod, that she should convince her friend to take a vacation and come back to work refreshed and ready to work.

Myra no longer felt embarrassed for missing two task deadlines and being asked to take a vacation, although she knew she should feel embarrassment. She no longer felt the surprising revival of fresh humiliation for losing badly in her last three child beauty contests and being told by her mother that it was a waste of time to enter her in beauty contests because she didn't have a chance of winning.

She also no longer felt the sting of the resurgent memory of overhearing her mother years later discuss how disappointing it was that her daughter, meaning her, had grown out of her beauty. And how fortunate she was that she still had two daughters with exceptional beauty.

All of those troubling memories and their accompanying feelings had rolled upon her over the past week and a half with all of the relentlessness of angry ocean tides. That, coupled with her growing anxiety over her weight, and her exercise program, had contributed to her feeling overwhelmed.

But now she felt nothing.

Only heaviness and isolation.

There were seven and a half billion people in the world. And, yet, truly there was only one. That one was sitting on a porch in a cabin in the beautiful Blue Ridge mountains—in solitary confinement.

Chapter 38

The horrible feeling was beyond words. It was beyond description. Whatever *it* was, it was more than a feeling. It was a miserable state of being that was so real that she actually *felt* encased in something. Like a mummy. Only her wrappings were invisible.

She felt it all over, but on her head the worst. Myra ran her hands over her head, exploring for...*what?* She didn't even know where to begin imagining what this was and what was causing it. No one could understand how she felt.

Tears rolled down her grimaced face. She felt so heavy. And whatever was on her head was unbearably tight. Myra frantically rolled her hands back and forth over her face and head unable to grasp this invisible thing that was beyond her touch. "What is this?" she screamed.

Myra felt worse by the minute. An hour later, she left the rocking chair and went inside. Maybe a change of location would do something. She went to the living room and sat on one of the two sofas. The misery accompanied her.

A big, black cast iron fireplace was in a corner of the room. Her eyes slowly followed its long black neck to the ceiling and back down and fixed on the glass of its black doors. There was no fire within. Only darkness, which was fitting.

For she would not have seen the fire's light had there been a fire. Her empty eyes looked to the tabletop before her. Magazines. Maybe flipping through their pages would help get her mind off how she felt.

***

Vicious sat on the opposite sofa with a leg folded over the other as he peered at Myra. His arms spread atop it as he rolled the fingertips of both hands in anticipation. His grin was slight and fixed with certainty. He let his eyes drop from her to the wood table before her. His demons had placed the proper magazines all over the cabin.

He wondered about Bludgeon and the African as he waited for Myra to open one of his magazines. She picked up all three. Vicious thought of a few Scriptures from the enemy's book and smiled, amused at his own commentary on God's word.

> *I will set no wicked thing before my eyes:*
> *I hate the work of them that turn aside; it*
> *shall not cleave to me* (Psalm 101:3).

"The dog doesn't know the magazines are wicked. She thinks they're innocent. Foolish, foolish girl, anything that promotes the lust of the eyes, the lust of the flesh, and the pride of life is wicked. And my power shall certainly cleave to you. It's the tradeoff. Your desire for the world's approval is my power."

> *Bad company corrupts good morals,* (1
> Corinthians 15:33).

"I certainly agree with your morals, loser Myra, but they can always be worse. That's where bad company comes in. Enough exposure to evil and I can ruin anyone. Get on with the magazines. I have much to say to you."

***

Myra picked up a magazine and looked at the cover. Its dark effect was immediate.

The magazine was one of the Council of Hatred for All Women's most successful women's publications. Prominently on the cover was the large closeup of a beautiful white woman with immaculate skin. No lines. No blemishes. No bumps. No moles. No marks. Perfectly flawless.

Myra's eyes squinched from the tight pressure in her face as she looked at the manipulated standard of beauty. It didn't make a difference that the model was twenty-one years old. It didn't make a difference that post-production corrections, another term for digitally removing the model's skin flaws, had been meticulously done to create what didn't exist and to erase what did.

What did matter was the message that Vicious was powerfully and repeatedly screaming into her soul. *"This is how your skin should look!"*

Myra stared at the model's absence of imperfections until she had to shut Vicious's mouth by turning the page. But the picture on the next page, and the caption above it, kept his mouth running.

This time it was another white woman. Young. Beautiful. Glamorous. Sophisticated. Long and full hair. Long and thin arms and legs. Short, sleeveless dress. Both arms were covered with luxury watches. The caption above read *Perfection loves perfection.*

Vicious ran his mouth.

Myra flipped page after page. Whether the model was white, black, or otherwise, the message was clear. They were beautiful. She was not. She had lost her beauty at nine years old. Myra took the three magazines and flung the indictments at the fireplace.

Vicious smirked. It was time to take the opposite approach. It wasn't in his nature to say anything encouraging to a female, irrespective of strategy. "Exhaustion," he beckoned.

The perfectionist spirit made his way through and finally out of the dark corridors of Myra's mind. He couldn't hide his nervousness as he approached his master. The master hated fat spirits. No one knew exactly why. But he felt it may have something to do with them being slow. Exhaustion wasn't fat, but he was slow.

"I like your work," said Vicious, "but I don't like your speed. I had almost forgotten that I called for you."

Exhaustion futilely wished he could answer the master without breathing so hard and rapidly. "Lord...Most Vicious, I...apologize for...my curse. It is not for...demons of your level—"

"Yeah, yeah, yeah," said Vicious. "Put her to work. I want her drugged up."

Drugged up? "I'll get right on it," said Exhaustion, proud to have answered in one breath.

"Look at your former master," said Vicious. The demon obeyed. Hideous was a mess from fresh beatings. "I do not tolerate insubordination or the memory of insubordination." He looked icily at Exhaustion. "I do not tolerate failure. I want this dog put down."

Chapter 39

Exhaustion was taking no chances. He wasn't going to end up like Hideous. He looked his two friends in the face with an expression that pleased Worry immensely. "Worry and Insomnia...we have to...do this quickly. If we fail...Lord Vicious...will do to us...what he did...to Hideous. Maybe...worse."

The smile left Worry's face. *He was now worried.*

***

Myra sat on that same spot on the sofa for fifty minutes before she realized she had gazed at the fireplace for nearly an hour. She needed to get up. For what, she didn't know. But she couldn't sit in one spot the whole day and just stare. That's the kind of thing you saw on television when someone was in a psychiatric hospital. The person just sat deathly still—and stared.

No, thought Myra, I'm not going there. I'm not crazy. This is temporary. I have to get up.

But she was so heavy.

Maybe if I rest...take a nap. Maybe then I can get up, she thought.

Worry walked back and forth in her mind, wringing his hands and shaking his head. He had long, frazzled, unmanageable white hair that stood up in places, laid down in others, and hung loose in others. He looked like an old man, demon orchestra conductor who was on stage before a crowd and couldn't figure out what was wrong with his sound.

"No, no," he said, "you can't sleep. There's too much to think about. Your life's a mess. Your face is a mess. You're fat as all darkness. No, no, we have to think this thing through."

Exhaustion competed between huffs and puffs. "Try...harder. You have to...try harder."

Insomnia sat on a cushy sofa of lies. He had the easiest job of the three. All he had to do was wait. Once she was filled with worry, he'd have access to her brain. It would be impossible for her to go to sleep.

Myra thought about her job. Jarrod was going to fire her. She knew it. Why else would he make her take a vacation? Had he really seen her sleeping? Or had one of her direct reports told him? Maybe they even showed him her sleeping. What if Allison showed him? No, Allison wouldn't do that. But what if she did?

Pelican legs.

Why did Daddy always call her pelican legs? She'd told him more than once she didn't like it, and he did it anyway. Did she really have pelican legs? But Mom and her sisters thought she was fat. How could she have pelican legs and still be fat? But she had put on weight. Three-tenths of a pound. *Almost half a pound!*

"What's going to happen when you put on more weight?" asked Worry. "How will you ever get it off? Look how difficult it is to get off three-tenths of a pound. How will you be able to lose forty or fifty pounds? Because that's where it's going, you know."

Myra thought this over. If she was this fat at three-tenths of a pound over her normal weight, what would she look like at forty pounds over? What size would she wear? An eighteen? A twenty?

"Can you imagine what your mother and sisters will say?" asked Worry.

"It doesn't...have to...come to that," said Exhaustion. "Not if you...exercise more...and eat less."

Worry raised his long bony hands and shook them and his head with closed eyes. "And that face of yours. It's ugly and marked. You've been ugly since you were a child. And those marks are permanent. I know they are."

Exhaustion said, "Get that skin graft." He rested. "If not...at least more makeup."

"You can't fix ugly and you can't hide the marks. You're screwed," said Worry. "Oh, what are you going to do?"

Myra's mind was in a race with itself. The faster one part ran, the faster the other part expended energy to keep up. One moment, she could fix herself if she tried harder. The next, she was doomed no matter how hard she tried.

This race went on nonstop for hours. It lasted all night. It was there the next morning. It was there that evening. And the next day. Days later the nonstop race was as furious as ever. Myra had forgotten how long she had been at the cabin. She was dead tired, but so wired up with worry that she couldn't sleep. Then she felt something like a fuse in her mind pop.

Chapter 40

Actually, there were two pops. One was the sound of the chipper demons as they broke through the last of Myra's resistance. The other was the cork coming off the champagne bottle as Vicious celebrated the victory.

Exhaustion would have peed on himself when Vicious got behind him had he had the equipment to do so. His master placed one large hand on his left shoulder and dug sharp claws into it as he poured the champagne into his glass on his right side.

"Have you ever tasted *Sulphurin Black*, Exhaustion?" asked Vicious.

Exhaustion winced and stared across the long table at a demon who appeared quite amused at his predicament. "No, Lord Vicious."

"Hmm, I suppose not. I save it for celebrations," he said. "There wasn't much to celebrate with your old master, was there?"

"No, Lord Vicious."

Vicious now stood behind Worry. Worry did have the equipment to pee on himself. He did just that. *He's going to beat me like he beat Hideous. No, worse. He's going to—*

"What about you, Worry?" Vicious interrupted his thoughts, pouring champagne into the frightened demon's glass.

"I have never tasted any kind of black champagne."

Vicious finished pouring. "Pity. The way you and exhaustion work together—you've worked together before, haven't you?"

"Yes, Lord Vicious, many times."

"You would think there would have been many occasions to celebrate," said Vicious. He finished pouring for all his guests and took his seat at the head of the table. He looked to his right at

Hideous. The former lord was on one knee holding his master's hat. "And what about you, Hideous? Have you ever had *Sulphurin Black*?"

Hideous began to tremble.

The expression of the face of Vicious didn't reveal whether he was delighted at the demon's fear or disgusted by it. "How forgetful of me. You do not have the honor of speaking directly to your master. Exhaustion, are you willing to speak to such a loathsome creature as this?"

Exhaustion hesitated. Vicious may have been setting him up.

"You do well to think it over, Exhaustion. Such a loser is unworthy of the lowest of honors."

"If you desire...I will speak to him."

"Provide your answer to Exhaustion," ordered Vicious.

Hideous had been so repeatedly beaten for the slightest of reasons, and often for no reason at all, that he could hardly gather his thoughts. "I have never drank *Sulphurin Black* champagne," he lied.

"Now honor Exhaustion for stooping so low to speak to you."

Honor Exhaustion how? Hideous braced himself for another beating.

"For some reason, I am feeling kind," said Vicious. "Perhaps it is the moment. Kiss the back of his hand, and that will suffice."

Exhaustion held his hand out. As much effort as Hideous put into crawling to him, it seemed to Exhaustion that it was taking forever for his former master to reach him. Hideous raised himself from his belly at Exhaustions's knees and kissed his hand.

Vicious clapped his hands once, startling Exhaustion, and nearly killing Worry. "Now, I'd like to offer a toast." He lifted his tall glass. Every demon followed his lead. "To myself, for bringing order and the honor of the Council of Hatred of All Women to the pathetic shack that my hat carrier called a stronghold. To the chippers, for doing what they do best—turning this dog into a shell of her formerly disgusting self."

Vicious turned his raised glass toward Exhaustion and Worry. He eyeballed Insomnia. "You did nothing but sit on your butt and show up after the hard work was done. Be grateful that I allow you to sit at my table."

He looked again at the other two demons. "To Exhaustion and Worry, for giving the woman hope," Vicious raised a hand, "and snatching it away," he said, with a tightly balled fist. He raised his hand. "Giving..." He clenched his fist. "And taking. The dog is so exhausted and worried about how she looks and who is saying what about her that she doesn't know whether she's coming or going."

He drank the entirety of his large glass and slammed the glass to the floor. He walked slowly and stood behind Exhaustion and Worry. He placed his hands on both of their shoulders.

"A special, celebrated demon is on the way. Quite the magician. Self-Hatred's his name. Not the run-of-the-mill self-hatred demon. He specializes in women, and he works fast. He will open the door for demons who will take this dog's life. She is not adequately prepared for him yet. But I anticipate her problem with drinking will produce the self-loathing necessary for this demon to do his work."

Vicious looked around the room of demons, his hands still on Exhaustion and Worry. "You may be thinking, 'But the woman doesn't have a drinking problem.' Is this not the question some of you are thinking?

"Exhaustion—" No, he changed his mind. He didn't have all night to wait for this tired spirit to get his words out. "Worry, ask your lord about the woman's drinking problem."

Worry responded immediately. "Most Vicious, the woman does not have a drinking problem. From where will she get such a problem?"

"She will get this problem from you. And Exhaustion." Vicious's tone turned menacing. He dug his claws into both of their shoulders. "She will get this problem before Self-Hatred arrives. Otherwise, his trip is meaningless."

"Most Vicious, self-hatred usually comes before the drinking problem," said Worry.

"Usually is not always," said Vicious.

"Most Vicious," said Worry, "may I ask when this demon will arrive?"

Vicious squeezed harder, his claws now buried an inch into both demons. "Soon."

Chapter 41

Myra looked up at the ceiling. How could blinking her burning eyes take so much energy? She was on her back in the upstairs hallway. Gravity was trying to pull her heavy body through the hardwood floor.

Somehow she had made it up the stairs. She didn't recall going up the stairs. Nor did she know why she had done so. And most disorienting, she had no idea when she had come upstairs. Was it an hour ago? A day ago? Or more? And how long had she been at the cabin?

Worry looked at Exhaustion.

"What's wrong?" asked Exhaustion.

Worry looked to be on the verge of a nervous breakdown. "What's wrong is there's no alcohol in this place. Even if there were," he jabbed his finger at her, "look at her. She can't get off the floor. If by some chance in darkness we could get her up, she wouldn't make it to that store without going off the side of the road. Did you not see the curves on that road?"

Exhaustion looked at this nervous wreck of a demon. Why hadn't he thought of that? His eyes narrowed in wonderment at Worry's empty head. It had come out of his own mouth and he hadn't understood the great opportunity that was before them.

"Worry," said Exhaustion.

"Yes, I'm worried. I have good reason to be worried. Look at—"

"Worry, stop!" yelled Exhaustion.

Worry looked startled that Exhaustion was capable of yelling.

Exhaustion took a few moments to recover. "All of this...is so...Lord Vicious can kill...the woman. If she crashes..."

Worry's eyes widened. "We'd get credit. That's a brilliant idea." The light left his eyes. "But so much can go wrong. What if she doesn't crash? What if she crashes, but doesn't get hurt? What if...?"

Exhaustion ignored Worry's endless *What ifs* and went to work. "You can do it...Myra. You just...need something...to help you...sleep. You haven't tried...alcohol."

***

Myra wasn't too exhausted and disoriented to push back at the crazy thought of trying to drink herself to sleep . A social drink or even two was one thing. She knew her body. There was a thin line between being relaxed and being compromised. She didn't like being chemically compromised.

She thought of Michael Jackson. He hadn't drank himself to death, but his story was close enough for discomfort. He had taken a drug to help him go to sleep and he never woke up. Myra wasn't a fool. Alcohol was as much a drug as whatever killed Michael.

She shook her head, barely. *No*, she thought.

"It's only...one time, Myra," said Exhaustion.

She resisted. Again and again she resisted.

Exhaustion was at his wit's end. His nature told him to keep trying. But his fear of Lord Vicious convinced him it would be better to ask for help and share the glory with someone more qualified at lying than himself. Under no circumstances could that Self-Hatred demon arrive before the woman had a drinking problem. He'd get the help of a professional liar.

***

"Good afternoon." The demon lowered his voice into a whisper. "I was told to look for a spirit full of vigor and energy, with handsome and exquisite features." He looked in the direction of Worry, who was pacing back and forth, murmuring to himself. He snickered. "Surely this is you. You are Exhaustion, are you not?" he said with a mischievous, sideway smile.

If Exhaustion was not in such danger, he would have found the demon's attire, speech, mannerisms, and obvious lie hilarious. The curses imposed upon the losing side in the great rebellion against God seemed endless.

This demon actually had two faces, one behind the other. The face on top was transparent and was what the humans would consider beautiful. The one beneath it, awful. Rotten and maggot-infested. He carried a bag and wore an immaculate black and white tuxedo and spoke with exaggerated and lyrical pronunciations. *Oh, what had become of the great armies of Lucifer!*

Exhaustion followed the tuxedo down to the demon's feet. He fully expected to see black patent leather shoes. *Why not?* What he saw were no feet at all. He had none. He hovered just above the floor. It made sense. It was a lying spirit. You didn't hear him coming.

"Yes...I am Exhaustion."

"Of course you are," he answered. "It is tiring work, isn't it?" He didn't wait for a reply. "I do appreciate the invitation. With the state of mind she's in, I'll have her on the road in no time."

"Do you really think...you can...do it?"

The demon turned his face sideways and wiggled his face. "Have you heard of Ananias and Sapphira? The story's in God's book. They're the ones who lied to the Holy Spirit. God killed them on the spot. That's my work," he lied.

Exhaustion said nothing. Spirits were always padding their resumes with lies. He turned away, cursed, and said, "I'm...doomed."

Worry looked across the distance at Exhaustion and stopped pacing. "We're doomed," he yelled.

The lying spirit smiled at them both. He had been underestimated before. He took out his dancing shoes and placed them on his feet. He looked at the tired, despondent demon and said softly, "Just because you can't see them, doesn't mean they're not there. Time to go dancing."

Chapter 42

The demon stood sideways and slowly drew his right arm high and backward at the same time that he jutted out his left arm and left leg. He stood motionless, with his chin close to his chest. He jerked, then danced his way to where Myra was lying on her back on the floor.

"My name is Whatever You Want Me to Be. But that can be a bit cumbersome. So, I go by Lies. I'm told you drink, but not too much. That's where there's a problem. You have a fear of losing control when you drink. But we need you to overcome your fear and to drink.

"A lot. We can start with a little. In fact, I always start people off with a little. If you don't believe me, I can give you the names of thousands of alcoholics."

He chuckled at his own joke. Then his face, the good-looking one, took on a snarl. The toying playfulness of his tone turned into a hiss. "Your fear is for nothing, Myra. There's no one here but you. There's absolutely no danger to you getting yourself some alcohol to help you relax. You want to go to sleep, don't you? It's the wisest thing you can do."

Myra thought about the demon's argument.

A voice said, "Wine is a mocker, strong drink is raging, and whoever is led astray by it is not wise."

Lies jumped and moved in a tight circle when he heard the voice. His sword was ready for battle. "Who said that? Show yourself," he challenged.

The sword appeared first. Its point was just beneath his chin. Then appeared the angel who held it. Both of Lies' faces showed terror. *Ambushed!*

He looked into the angel's angry eyes, waiting for the sword's blade to separate his head from his body. It would happen so quickly it would be painless. The pain wouldn't begin until he entered the dark prison, where demons destroyed in this dimension went to be tormented until the final day of judgment.

This staring contest had gone on long enough. "What are you waiting for, angel? Go on. Do it."

The angel's sword inched upward until its tip felt like a pin's prick under Lies' chin. But he went no farther. Lies narrowed his eyes in thought. He examined the dim glow emanating from the angel's skin. It was fire. A smirk slowly formed on both of his faces.

"Of course. The little Scripture routine." He mocked, "'Wine is a mocker, strong drink is raging...' You're an angel of truth." Lies slowly pushed the sword away from his face. He backed away with two grins. "You have no power here unless the woman gives you power," he said, enjoying his leverage.

The angel disappeared.

The sword didn't.

Lies didn't know what to make of this. What was this truth angel up to? A flame erupted on the sword. Lies gasped and jumped back. "What is this?" The conniving angel was breaking the rule? Was he supposed to fight a sword?

The sword elevated over Myra, then disappeared down her throat.

Both of Lies' faces went through a series of silly expressions. But he found nothing funny about this disappearing sword. Why would a truth angel put his sword in a daughter of darkness? She had no right to use the word of God. It made no sense at all.

Lies sensed a trap. He backed away farther and kneeled on a knee and watched. Finally, he followed his compulsion and began his lies. It wasn't long before Myra was convinced that alcohol could help her. She convinced herself that she would drink just enough to take care of her insomnia. Afterwards, she'd go back to her practice of only taking an occasional social drink.

Lies was elated. Both faces were smiling. The woman would soon become one of his testimonies.

Chapter 43

Myra's head was foggy. She wisely kept her hand on the rail of the outside stairs as she made her way down toward her car. She had maybe slept eight hours in four days. She felt awful. The thought had not been lost on her that there was a danger of falling asleep at the wheel. She'd turn the music up loud and try to freeze herself awake with the AC blowing as cold and high as it could get.

She'd have to navigate three miles of winding mountain streets to get to the highway that would take her to the store she had passed. Myra was wide awake after two minutes of loud music and frosty air.

"Look at her...eyes," said Exhaustion. "I think she's...falling asleep."

"You think so? You think so?" said Worry.

Myra's eyes closed. Her head slumped. The car veered to the left. There was no guard rail. Over five hundred feet of air awaited her to become airborne.

"She's sleep," Exhaustion celebrated.

Worry still wasn't convinced. "Something's going to go wrong."

The car crossed the line and went to the street's edge. It bounced off something and slowly went to the right. Exhaustion was surprised that the woman hadn't gone over the cliff. She was still asleep.

But before he could finish his questioning, he readied himself for the car's crash on the right. The drop wasn't nearly as far. It probably wouldn't be deadly, but she'd be badly hurt. That was something. And who knows, maybe she'd hit a tree. She wasn't wearing a seatbelt. *Right through the windshield!* he hoped.

The car's right front tire left the ground. Exhaustion's mouth dropped open when the car hit something invisible and slowly righted itself before veering back to the left only to leave the road and instead of going airborne, it again hit something invisible and went in the opposite direction.

Exhaustion watched this mystery in morbid fascination. This couldn't be happening. Worry, however, wasn't surprised.

"I knew it," he said. "I knew something like this would happen. This is why I worry. So much can go wrong."

"I don't...understand," said Exhaustion. "Why didn't the woman...go over the cliff? She belongs to darkness. We have rights...to her."

"I've seen it before," said Worry. "I've seen it all before."

"Seen what?"

Worry's voice was shaky. "Prayer. Someone's praying for this woman. It's a losing battle. We're doomed."

Prayer? thought Exhaustion. It made sense. As if I'm not in enough trouble.

***

Myra's eyes fluttered. She gasped and jerked her head up with wide eyes, fully expecting to find herself plummeting through the air. But instead of seeing a see of trees racing toward her, she saw a man coming out of a building.

Myra stared at the man, then looked to the left and right. She looked back at the building. She was parked in front of the liquor store. How had she gotten there? Was she so tired that she couldn't remember the drive?

She shook off the question and the oddity of her making a special trip to buy alcohol. Thank goodness she was out of town and didn't have to worry about running into someone she knew. It wasn't like she was in a grocery store and could mask her purchase with a loaf of bread. She was at a liquor store. People went into a liquor store for one purpose.

Out of town or not, Myra looked around before exiting the car and walking through a crowd of demons. She opened the store's door and entered the thick darkness of the stronghold of addiction to make her purchase.

***

Myra jumped. She lifted her head in the alertness of fear. She looked around. It had happened again. The last thing she remembered was struggling to keep her eyes open as she started the ascent up the base of the mountain road.

Now she was parked in the driveway of her cabin. *How did I get here?* she thought. After a minute of wondering, she cradled the bottle in her arm. She looked around as though someone she knew could pop out of nowhere and say, "Hey, Myra, what's in the bag?"

A couple of hours later, Myra was back on the sofa. This time she wasn't numbly staring at the fireplace. She was deep in a drunken sleep.

***

Exhaustion almost cried when Myra took the first sip. When she passed out, a funny sound emitted from his closed mouth.

"What was that?" Lies asked. He sounded angry.

"Just happy." He turned his head away from Lies and pinched the moisture from his eyes.

Lies came around and planted himself directly in front of Exhaustion. He stretched his neck down. His expressions of both faces left no question. He was definitely angry. "What was it that you conveniently forgot to mention, Exhaustion?"

"About what?"

"I had a visit from an angel, Exhaustion. He popped out of nowhere. No, let me get the facts straight. His sword popped out of nowhere. It popped directly under my chin. Then the angel appeared."

"What has that...got to do...with me? Angels of truth...always...harass...lying spirits."

Lies was incensed at the duplicity. "Not *always*, Exhaustion." He peered accusingly at Exhaustion, as though he was waiting for an admission of guilt.

Exhaustion wasn't confessing anything.

"Seldom do I run into truth angels when I am lying to children of darkness. Unless..." It was a hanging accusation.

"Unless what?"

Lies yelled, "Unless someone's praying. Why didn't you tell me this woman had prayer support? You could've gotten me sent to the dark prison. I tell you what, you worthless little asthmatic weasel. My work is done. I'm out of here." He stormed off, dragging his bag of tricks behind him. He yelled over his shoulder, "And this is the last favor I do for you. Don't ever call for me again."

"He's right, you know," said Worry. "She's drinking, but someone's praying. You saw what happened to the car. I guarantee you angels kept that car on the road. We're in big trouble. Either Most Vicious is going to get us, or prayer's going to get us."

Exhaustion looked at the sleeping woman. *Maybe not, if he tried harder,* he told himself.

Chapter 44

She had tried to go to sleep without drinking alcohol. It just didn't work. The insomnia was relentless. How long would this go on? She couldn't rely on alcohol forever. But she also couldn't afford to chance being awake all night either. Falling asleep at work again or being too tired to produce was no longer a matter of embarrassment. It was a matter of continued employment.

Still, it had been a month of being dependent upon alcohol to get to sleep. It was bad enough taking alcohol to go to sleep. To make it worse, the quality of her rest was horrendous. It was a vicious cycle. A dilemma of rotten choices with no way out. How long would it be before she'd become an alcoholic? Fear raced throughout her body, causing her to shiver. *What if I'm already an alcoholic? No, you can't become an alcoholic in a month.*

Myra shifted the marketing campaign folders on her desk. There was no need to do this except nervousness at possibly being caught surfing the web at work. She pushed against the floor. Her chair rolled backward to the cubicle's entrance. It was clear.

Myra looked up *How long does it take to become an alcoholic?* She scanned several articles. Everyone said it depended on a bunch of variables. Genetics. Environmental factors. Depression. Mental illness. Parental use. Etcetera.

Basically, it was a flip of a coin whether you were more predisposed to alcoholism than someone else. You could drink a long time and not become an alcoholic; you could drink a short time and become an alcoholic.

That was scary enough, but what alarmed her the most was learning that alcoholism wasn't as cut and dry as having or not having cancer. With cancer, you had it or you didn't. But this wasn't the case with alcoholism. They didn't use a microscope to diagnose alcoholism. They used behavior graded on a spectrum.

The American Association of Psychiatry graded alcoholism by its severity, and they called it Alcohol Use Disorder, or AUD. Myra pushed her chair back to the cubicle entrance again, scanned quickly, then returned to reading.

You were in the early stage, chronic stage, or end stage. And you were rated as mild, moderate, or severe, based upon how many of the official signs you had within the past twelve months. Myra read the official eleven signs of alcoholism. Two of the signs caught and held her eyes like a hook in a fish's mouth.

According to this thing, I'm an alcoholic! she screamed inside. The American Association of Psychiatry's designation of her as only mild provided not an ounce of relief. These people had diagnosed her as an alcoholic!

Myra stared at her future in a daydream of bloodshot eyes, trembling hands, and dried vomit on her clothes. Had it come to this? *I'm just trying to get some sleep,* she thought.

"Myra," someone called.

Myra flinched and minimized her computer screen. "Allison, what's up?"

Allison hesitated. The truth angel said something to her.

"The Johnson account, right?" said Myra.

"Yeah, Jarrod's doing his panic thing."

"Calm him down, Allison," Myra said, with feigned playful confidence. Confidence about the job she had done with the account was real. Confidence that people couldn't see past her pretense that all was well was fake. "It's done. He's going to love it. I'll be right there."

"Not going back to his office without you," said Allison. "Orders."

Myra got the Johnson folder. She looked at Allison with a smile and stood. "Come my child. You'll want to take notes."

"Oh, so we are full of ourselves, are we?"

When they got to Jarrod's open door, Allison said, "I'll be right back. I'm going to the restroom."

Myra stepped inside of Jarrod's office.

Allison did go to the restroom, but only after she had doubled back to Myra's computer and pulled up several minimized screens.

Chapter 45

Sitting behind a steering wheel provided little relief.

Myra felt the ache of rest deprivation. It was in every muscle. It was in every bone. Not sleep deprivation. Rest deprivation. The alcohol was helping her get to sleep. But she was never able to enter it fully.

She felt like a starving woman on the verge of death from malnutrition and being slowly fed a watery soup through an eyedropper. The drops added up. They were enough to keep her alive, or at least to give her hope that she may not die, but they were not enough to give her strength.

Myra navigated her car as she thought of her predicament. She could drink and sleep and be a functional zombie—and keep her job. For how long, she didn't know. Or she could stop drinking and...

This is where she found that she was lost in the deep jungles of her thoughts. Danger was in the bushes.

And...*what?*

What would happen if she stopped drinking? How would not sleeping at all be better than going to sleep and waking up feeling like her body had rejected eighty percent of her sleep? A hundred percent sleep and twenty percent rest was better than one hundred percent insomnia and zero percent rest.

There was something else in the bushes that troubled her more. It jumped on her like a wild tiger. *What if I can't stop drinking? Just accept being an ugly, disfigured, fat alcoholic?*

Myra entered her apartment complex garage and drove to the third level and parked. For about a minute, she didn't move. She hadn't heard the voice that used to harass her about being ugly in over a month.

It was a sick thought, but she longed to go back to her old bondage. Back to when her torment was limited to only hearing voices and feeling ugly. Now even though the voice was gone, she felt worse.

Physically, she felt as though something had her in a tight headlock, and that she was carrying a three-hundred-pound load. Psychologically, compared to how awful she now felt about her appearance, she could facetiously say she used to feel beautiful. And then there was the feeling that termites had eaten her soul away. That she was adrift on the ocean's wave, being carried wherever and having no power to resist.

And the alcohol? What if I can't quit? She shook her head. I have to prove it to myself. I can quit. I'm not an alcoholic.

Deep in her soul, however, she knew this would be like trying not to breathe air.

***

Myra opened her front door. Good. Allison wasn't in the living room. She went to the left, down Allison's hall. Her door was closed, and light was coming from under the door. But this didn't mean she was in there. Her door was always closed. And sometimes she did forget to turn her light off.

But just in case, Myra walked with light, hurried steps to the right of the living room and down her own hall. She entered her bedroom and closed the door. *Safe.*

The first thought that came to mind when the door closed was *Get a drink.* A drink was actually two drinks in a tall glass. This was Myra's way of not admitting that she was drinking more now than when she first began a month ago.

Myra tossed her bag onto the bed and sat on its edge. Just a minute to unwind. She closed her eyes and took long, slow breaths. They felt good.

Get a drink.

A few more breaths and she opened her eyes. She looked at her gym bag. She unzipped it and took her clothes out. It was almost laundry time. "And you are going to the cleaners," she said to her blouse.

She thought of the cleaners and how they had messed up a skirt a couple of weeks ago and huffed. This cleaners was so conveniently located. She didn't want to find another one.

Get a drink.

She recalled another cleaners that was closer to her job. It was on a corner. Myra thought of the location of the driveway and the traffic flow. It wasn't ideal. Maybe she should just give these guys another chance. This was their first time messing up something. And who's to say the next cleaners wouldn't make a mistake?

Get a drink?

Myra looked toward her closet. There was a giant magnet in there. She was a piece of metal. Her eyes watered in submission after an emotionally violent minute of staring at the door. Yet her legs allied themselves with the residue of her will.

Until it was time to obey.

Her treacherous feet moved. The magnet slowly pulled her up and toward the door. She stretched forth a palm as though saying no, all the while her feet were saying yes. She touched the knob with the very tips of her trembling fingers and paused. Then finding no will to resist, she gripped it.

She watched the door open as though she were a spectator of someone else's unfolding tragedy. *What was going to happen next?* But this wasn't someone else's drama. It was hers. She knew what was going to happen next. She was the star of the show. The magnet was about to make inevitable contact.

Myra looked into the corner and noticed something amiss. She got on her knees and thrust her hand inside of the dirty clothes basket. Her angst eased when she felt the bottles. She pulled out one and went wide-eyed. She thrust the other hand in and pulled out the other bottle.

She stared at the empty bottles, wondering. Her face was frowned, her mouth open. *How could I have drank all of this?* She stretched for an explanation. *Maybe one,* she thought, knowing though that last night there was at least half a bottle left. *But the other one hadn't even been opened yet.*

Myra put both bottles close to her face as though alcohol would appear if she stared hard enough into the emptiness. Had she mistaken? Had there been less in the opened bottle than she had thought? That still left her with the new bottle. She shook her head, unwilling to admit the only possibility left. That she had drank so much alcohol in so little time. Was that even possible? If she had, maybe her memory *would* be impaired. Deep down, she wasn't buying it.

Myra stuffed the bottles back under the clothes. She didn't have answers for what happened to her liquor, but she did know where to get more.

Myra headed for the front door. She was reaching for the knob when Allison spoke from the darkness of the dining area. "Where you going, Myra?"

Myra flinched to a stop. "Allison?" she said, looking into the darkness.

"Where you off to?"

Pause.

"I..." another pause.

Allison spoke from behind a large plant on the table. "You know, when I saw Coke and ginger ale in the fridge, I thought, 'Now why would Myra start drinking sodas? She doesn't like soda, and she's trying like a freakin' maniac to lose weight.' It didn't make sense. But now it does."

"What are you talking about, Allison?"

Allison's eyes drilled into Myra's eyes as she reached back and slowly turned the dimmer up. "Where are you going, Myra?" she asked again, like a parent waiting for the child to make matters worse by telling an obvious lie to get out of trouble.

Chapter 46

The question may have been uncomfortable, but innocent had it not been for Allison's tone and theatrics. What was going on with her that she felt she could speak to her this way? She'd never behaved like this before.

Myra went on the offensive. "You know, Allison, ever since you came back from your sister's—"

Allison cut her off. "At least you're a top-shelfer."

"What? Allison, I don't know what you're going through—"

Allison cut her off again. "Your rum. It's top shelf. The crap's on the bottom shelf. That's where you're going, isn't it? To replace your rum."

Myra's mouth and throat went dry. She mustered up enough saliva to push the cotton ball down her throat. She looked at Allison disbelievingly. "You?" She took several steps forward and met Allison's hard expression with one of her own. "You went rummaging around my room? What were you doing in my room? I have never violated your space."

"You. Are missing. The point," said Allison.

"No, I don't think I missed anything. You went into my room—"

"You need to sit down," Allison ordered.

Myra's neck went back in surprise, then returned in anger. "As far as I know, you don't have any children. And I'll be just—"

"You'll be just what? Damned? Well, at least you can see where this is headed."

"What?" Myra snapped.

"I said you need to sit down. You are not going to like what I have to say."

Myra snatched the chair from the table and sat down hard. "I'm...sitting," Myra said, angrily. "Now you tell me why you went into my room? I thought we were friends. Friends respect boundaries."

"Obviously, you and I have different understandings of friendship."

"Obviously," said Myra.

Allison stood up from the back chair and took a side chair. She sat down and scooted the chair closer to Myra. The stares were intense. "I grew up with an alcoholic. You think I don't know the signs?"

Alcoholic.

Myra saw that she had missed the point. She was protesting Allison violating her space and had somehow not connected the dots that this argument wasn't about privacy. It was about something far more serious.

Hearing someone else put her and alcoholic in the same sentence was a gut punch. Her anger drained into nothingness. Her lips trembled. Her eyes watered. "I'm not an alcoholic, Allison."

"You're also not original. Now what would have been original is if you had admitted to being an alcoholic. But alcoholics don't admit to being alcoholics until they're forced to admit it."

Myra wiped a tear from her face. "I haven't been able to sleep for a month. It's the only way I can sleep, Allison. That's why I drink. But I'm not an alcoholic. Alcoholics can't stop drinking. I can."

"Oh really?"

"Yes."

"Okay, so you're on your way to the liquor store because you can do without it? You had two standard bottles of rum, Myra. Fifteen hundred milliliters. What person needs fifteen hundred milliliters? Do you know how much alcohol that is?"

"I know it's a lot. I thought it would be better to buy that much so I wouldn't have to go back for a long time."

"A long time? What's a long time, Myra? I'm going to tell you something. The sister I said was crazy with all of her weird Christian stuff. You were the one who told me when I was having a hard time with Dr. Brown's suicide that I should go to my sister's house. You said to ignore her church stuff and just chill. You remember that conversation?"

"Yes."

"I did it. It was a trade-off. I put up with her in exchange for a bedroom with large windows with an incredible view of beautiful mountains. My niece was a bonus. I left there no longer believing that she was crazy. Actually, well, to be honest, I gave my life to Christ while I was there."

Myra shifted a couple of times, thinking about this. It made sense. The odd questions. The new way she was handling pressure. Even the new messages t-shirts she had been wearing. But it was still shocking. Allison was as cynical about religion as a person could get.

"But you're an atheist," said Myra.

"Oh, don't be ridiculous," said Allison. "We didn't pop out of nowhere. Atheism was my default. It served its purpose." She ended that conversation. "I started to tell you, a few times actually, but I didn't want you to look at me the way I looked at my sister. She used to really piss me off talking about God all the time."

"That's where you've been going on Sundays? To church?"

"Yeah. I guess I shouldn't have been such a coward and said something. Eternal life is not something you should be ashamed of."

"Why are you telling me this now?" Myra was leery that Allison was about to use her sleeping situation as an excuse to pressure her into going to church.

"Because you said you bought two standard bottles of booze so you wouldn't have to go back to the store for a while."

"That's right."

"No, Myra, that's a lie. Two weeks ago my ex-crazy sister tells me of a dream she had." She looked at Myra as though she had irrefutable evidence she was about to disclose. "You want to hear it?"

Myra did not want to hear it. She kept her mouth shut and hoped for this conversation's end.

"She said you were in serious trouble."

"She doesn't know me."

"Well, she actually said my roommate was in serious trouble. You're my only roommate. It's you."

"Allison, I told you why I'm drinking. Your sister's dream is a dream," she stated. "People have dreams all the time."

"That wasn't all of the dream, Myra." She paused for effect. "She also said there was a bomb in a basket in your closet."

Allison let that statement continue to speak as she silently watched Myra think about this. She continued.

"I could have ignored it. Really, that was my first thought. I thought maybe I was right about my sister the first time and wrong about her the second time. But what better way to prove it was just a dream than to go to the closet and see if there's a bomb in a basket. Right?"

"Wrong," said Myra. "Your sister's dream doesn't give you the right to search my room."

Allison pointed an index finger upward. "Uuh, I said *bomb*. And it wasn't a search. I walked directly to that basket and looked inside. I was fully prepared to call my sister and tell her off. You would've never known I was in your room. I didn't find a bomb."

"Of course, you didn't find a bomb," Myra protested. "This conversation is over, Allison." Myra was in the midst of rising when Allison's words sat her back down.

"That is, unless we look at a handle of Bacardi Gold as a bomb. Myra, now I know you're good with numbers. That's fifty-six ounces of alcohol. The bottle I saw was nearly full. A week later it was almost empty. You know what that tells me?"

Myra felt as though she was sitting before the FBI, and they had just shown her an exceedingly clear picture of her face as she robbed a bank. A weak and embarrassing grunt emitted from Myra's throat.

Allison continued. "It tells me you've been drinking like a fish. What is wrong with you? And don't you dare tell me you're taking this for insomnia."

Myra sat there immobilized by so many things. Being found out. Allison's transformation into a bossy sheriff. The sense that her life was spiraling out of control—in public. The accusation of being an alcoholic. The tightness of her face and head. The heaviness that was pushing her down.

"Myra, I wish someone would have stepped up to the plate with my drunk of a father. If nothing else, it would have saved me a lifetime of therapy. They didn't. I'm going to give you one shot at answering this question. If I get the wrong answer, I'm taking matters into my own hands."

Myra's eyes widened in fear. "Allison," Myra's voice tremored, "I...what are you going to do?"

"Are you an alcoholic?"

Myra's insides trembled. "Allison," Myra tried to reason.

"Are you an alcoholic," Allison repeated.

Myra panted nervously. Tiny beads of sweat formed on her tingling forehead. She rolled her tongue over her bottom lip before nervously swallowing. "Allison, please believe me. Maybe I drank more than was necessary for my insomnia. But I am not an alcoholic."

Allison moved her chair close enough to Myra to clasp one of her hands with both of hers. She looked at her friend with a softness that masked the resoluteness of her heart. "I love you, Myra. Really, I do. You've been there for me when I've needed you. But wrong answer."

"Wrong answer," Myra pled. "What...what...Allison...just wait."

"That was the mistake they made with my dad. They waited. You're my friend. I'm not waiting. There's going to be an intervention."

This struck Myra like a lightning bolt. "Intervention?"

"Yes. You sent me to my sister. I'm calling your mother."

The most terrifying scenes of ten thousand horror shows formed in the frozen expression on Myra's face. "You cannot do that?"

"Oh, yes I can. I still have her number. And I'm calling her. Now."

Chapter 47

Myra's expression changed to mimic a shell-shocked soldier on a battlefield, staggering without any sense of where he was, and looking dumbfoundedly at the talking person in front of him, but hearing nothing except terrible ringing in his ears.

Myra would have welcomed such ringing. Better still would have been the bomb's direct hit. For oblivion was ten thousand times better than what Allison had just threatened.

"I can see you're not taking this well," said Allison. "But you need help."

Myra was able to finally shake herself out of her gaze. "You can't do this, Allison."

"I'm sorry, Myra. I'm not going down the path of doing nothing. I can't turn my head when I see a friend, a good friend, destroying herself." Allison felt sympathy pulling at her heart, trying to get her to change her mind. Her eyes watered. She shook her head and said, "No. No, I am not going to be a part of this. You destroy yourself, you do it by yourself. I am not going to empower this self-destructive behavior."

"Allison, please."

Tears flowed freely down Allison's face. "I'm going to be here every step of the way with you, Myra. But I can't provide the kind of support that only a mother can give. And the rest of your family," she added. "You've got family. That's what families are for." She stood.

Myra stayed seated and grasped both of Allison's forearms. She looked at her with desperately pleading eyes. "You don't understand, Allison. If you tell my family..." Myra couldn't articulate her horror at thinking what life would be like were Allison to give her family one more thing to criticize her for.

"It's humiliating," said Allison, with difficulty. Seeing her friend in such a compromised and frightened condition tore her heart. She felt the pressure of her friend's desperate plea, but she had learned from her own life. Sometimes you needed someone to step in and do what needed to be done.

"Yes, but it's more than that," said Myra. "They *can't* know about this."

Allison strengthened herself. "I *can't* leave you like this, Myra. I won't. How much longer do you think you're going to last like this? You think no one at work knows there's something strange going on?"

Myra looked shocked.

"Myra, people aren't stupid."

"They know?" asked Myra.

"They don't know you're drinking—yet. But they know you're not right. You can't keep something like this a secret forever. Sooner or later it catches up with you. For you, it's sooner." Allison thought of her own father. "Which is probably a good thing." She looked down at Myra with a grimace and said softly, "Let me go, Myra. We need to do this."

When Myra didn't let go, Allison pulled her arms free and turned to walk away. Myra panicked. She spoke quickly. "There's someone else who can help me. You don't have to call my mom."

"Who?" said Allison, seeing this as a stalling tactic. She'd seen it all before with her dad.

"My brother's friend. Josiah."

Allison's face and tone were steadfast. "Myra? This is the same guy you blocked from your phone?"

"Yes."

"The same guy you said was a nut?"

"Yeah, that's the same guy."

Allison put her hands on her hips and let out an exasperated breath. "And now all of a sudden this nut, this low-level stalker, is qualified to help you? Myra..." she huffed in irritation. She turned around without finishing the sentence and started to walk away.

Myra blurted out desperately, "He can help me. He's like you."

Allison spun around. "The *nut* is like *me*?"

"I don't mean it like that. He's a Christian."

Allison studied Myra.

"He is," said Myra. "He's like your sister. He believes in miracles and stuff. He says he's an intercessor. He calls it a prayer warrior."

Myra looked intently at Allison. Allison was thinking.

"He tried to talk to me about God. He said God was telling him in dreams that I was in trouble—just like your sister."

"He told you that he had a dream you were in trouble?" Allison didn't sound convinced.

"More than once, Allison." *Please, Allison, you can't bring my family into this,* Myra pled inside. "I think he can help me." She wasn't really lying. Keeping her family out of this would help her.

"Is he a therapist?"

"No, he's into network security."

"Network security. Myra, even if he is a Christian, how can a network security guy help you with your drinking problem?"

"The dreams." She didn't believe there was anything to Josiah's dreams. And she couldn't explain Allison's sister's dream, even though she was sure it wasn't God. But Myra *needed* to win this concession. These dreams were her only hope of keeping her family out of her business. "Your sister had a dream, and here we are. Josiah had a dream. Maybe there's something to his dream, too. I mean maybe the two dreams are not a coincidence."

Myra watched Allison shift uncomfortably as she thought this over. It was like watching the hangman decide whether he was or wasn't going to pull the lever.

Allison made an expression as though she'd just remembered something. She had. It was how her father would make promises to her mom whenever she put the heat on him to change. It was all a sham.

"You don't need a network guy. You need someone invested who can walk you through this mess no matter how long it takes. I'm calling your mother." She turned away and left Myra sitting alone and stunned.

The doorbell rang.

Myra turned in her chair. Allison stopped and looked at Myra. "Are you expecting someone?"

"No, maybe it's your boyfriend," said Myra.

"He'd call first," said Allison. "Anyway, I introduced new rules he couldn't live with. We're history," she said, as she went to the door and looked through the peephole. "It's a black guy. I don't know him."

Myra stood up. She walked to the door. "What guy?" She looked into the peephole, then stepped back. She looked at Allison, her mouth open as if to speak, then she looked down shaking her head in wonderment. Should she be furious or overjoyed?

"Do you know him?" asked Allison.

"Yes. That's the nut. That's Josiah."

Chapter 48

Myra opened the door widely. "Josiah," she said, in a whispery voice that baffled him. She looked and sounded happy to see him. The exact opposite of what he had expected. "Please, come in."

Josiah looked at Myra. He looked at the other woman. She was studying him. Why did he have the foolish thought that they had been talking about him? He slowly entered the apartment. He had rehearsed his apology and reason for coming to her house a hundred times. But Myra's surprising demeanor made it seem unnecessary.

"So, you're Josiah," said Allison.

They had been talking about him. "Yes. I'm Josiah."

"I'm Allison. Myra's roommate."

"Hello, Allison."

"Did Myra call you? Hello," she added awkwardly.

It was obvious now. Something was going on. "No, Myra did not call me." He looked at Myra.

"How could I call him, Allison? You were right here with me."

Allison said to Josiah, "So Myra didn't call you at all? At any time? Asking you to come here?"

So, the apology rehearsals hadn't been for nothing. "I must apologize...to both of you," said Josiah.

"It's okay, Josiah. You came at the perfect time," said Myra.

Josiah's brow bunched. "I did?" He turned his questioning expression from Myra to Allison. She folded her arms. It didn't appear that she shared Myra's perspective. "I would never invite myself to anyone's home—especially a female. And especially after having been told"—he was totally off script and showing every bit of the discomfort he felt—"to not contact you." He said these last words looking at Myra.

"It really is good timing, Josiah. Really, it is," said Myra.

Allison unfolded her arms, shifted to the other leg, and refolded her arms the other way. If Myra had called this guy, they were putting on a good act to convince her otherwise.

Now Myra's brow furrowed. "How did you get my address?"

"You didn't give him your address?" Allison asked warily. If this guy looked her up on the internet and then popped up unannounced, then Myra was right. He was a nut.

Josiah anticipated Myra's response. His voice didn't carry the certainty he felt in his heart that he was doing God's will. "I was praying," he said to Myra, waiting for her to put two and two together.

And what? thought Allison.

Myra's eyebrow raised when it hit her. She shook her head disbelievingly and let out several irritated half-chuckles before saying, "You're telling me you got my address in a vision?"

"No, I heard a voice."

"Was this voice attached to a body?" Allison asked cynically.

"No, it wasn't an angel. I heard it inside of my spirit."

Voices. Angels. Spirits. Allison threw her hands up and held them there as she walked away, saying, "Okay, I've heard enough. This is your company, Myra. You can talk about voices and spirits. I've got a phone call to make."

"Wait," Myra pled. "Isn't this what I told you? I told you he's like your sister. She had a dream, right?"

Allison stopped and turned around. She looked intrigued, but not convinced.

"You thought your sister was crazy, right?" pled Myra. "And she wasn't."

"So, what are you saying, Myra? That I should leave you in the hands of this guy because he dreamed about you?"

Josiah's lips parted. His eyes widened. He turned his head sideways in curiosity. "Leave Myra in my hands? What is this you are speaking of?"

"No," said Myra to Allison. "I'm just saying we're standing here now because your sister had a dream about me." Myra's eyes widened as she spoke with her hands. "Josiah had a dream about me. They're both Christians. Maybe these dreams are connected. Maybe God gave them the dreams."

Myra regretted her last sentence as soon as it hit her own ears. She had dove into a deep pool of hypocrisy with no water below awaiting her. Allison's expression said she also knew the pool was empty.

"Myra, you now believe in God?" Josiah asked hopefully.

She looked at Josiah. She looked at Allison.

"When did this happen?" Josiah asked.

She looked back at Josiah.

"Yeah, Myra, when did this happen?" asked Allison.

She looked back to Allison. "I never said I didn't believe in God."

Allison shook her head. It was her father all over again. Say anything to get off the hot seat. "Okay, tell you what, Myra. You obviously fear me bringing your family into this—even though it's for your own good."

"Into what?" asked Josiah. "Maybe I can help. The voice told me to help you."

"Allison," said Myra, asking with her eyes that she not tell Josiah all.

"It's him or your family, Myra."

Myra sighed a long breath of defeat.

Josiah frowned at Myra's dejection. "What is going on here?"

"Myra has a drinking problem."

Myra lowered her head and looked into her soul. This was an intervention. Her best friend was doing an intervention on her. She tried to convince herself that Allison was overreacting because alcohol abuse had played such a large role in her own painful childhood. Her conscience wouldn't cooperate with the act. Yet, her mouth did.

"I have insomnia. I can't sleep. I've been drinking a little at night to help me fall asleep."

A little, thought Allison. *It's always a little. One drink. A couple of beers.* She looked at Josiah, who was staring at Myra with his lips slightly parted and apparently frozen in place. When he looked at Allison, he saw the unbelief in her eyes.

"You don't believe her," he said to Allison.

"It doesn't take a bathtub of alcohol to fall asleep," said Allison. Allison saw Myra prepare to defend herself. She cut her off, speaking directly to Josiah. "This isn't about insomnia. It's about addiction and lies. It's about hurting people who care about you. It's about..."

Josiah waited for the rest.

Allison's lips trembled. Her watery eyes looked at Josiah, but saw only the pain of a little girl abused, abandoned, and abused more.

"It is about what?" said Josiah.

Allison blinked hard a couple of times and pinched the insides of her eyes, cutting off the tears. She looked at Myra. Her friend was humiliated and broken. But being humiliated and broken wasn't the same as being honest.

But Allison couldn't hold this against her. Myra wasn't yet capable of honesty about her condition. Hopefully, it would come in time—with her family's help.

"Allison," said Myra softly, "it's not pride. That's not why I don't want my family to know."

Allison pushed past her compassion. This wasn't about feelings. "You'll thank me later, Myra," she said, hoping this was true. She turned away.

An angel of truth stretched forth his hand and placed the tips of his fingers into Myra's closed mouth and touched her tongue.

"Josiah, I have a drinking problem and I need you to help me. It started with insomnia, but it has turned into something else. I feel like something is making me drink. Something's out to get me."

Allison stopped dead in her tracks at Myra's words.

Myra was shocked at her words, but especially that last statement. It was true. She did feel like this. But why in the world had she told them? *Oh, goodness! I've gone from alcoholic to crazy alcoholic. Allison's definitely going to call my mother now.*

Allison looked at Myra with eyes widened with surprise. "You admit it," she said, hardly believing this breakthrough. "You admit you have a drinking problem."

"Yes, Allison. I have a problem with alcohol," she answered, then immediately wondered again at her own surprising words. What was she doing?

Allison looked at Josiah. She had tried unsuccessfully to get Myra to admit her problem, and this network security guy shows up and she comes clean.

Josiah looked into Allison's eyes. She was thinking something. He was thinking something, too. He had thought God's assignment was to tell Myra about Jesus. Now it had turned into something else. Alcoholism and... *What does she mean that something's out to get her? Did God show her the tiger?*

"You said God told you to help my friend, right? A voice," said Allison.

"Yes, and dreams and a vision," said Josiah.

"That's right. Dreams *and* a vision," said Allison.

"Yes."

Allison looked into Myra's wide, waiting eyes. "Good," she said, before looking back to Josiah. She pointed to the sofa. "You can use the sofa or the floor. Your choice."

"What are you saying?" asked Josiah.

"You want to help Myra, right? God told you to help her."

Josiah's face twisted in confusion.

"You're a network security guy. You get paid big bucks to find and connect dots. My friend needs help."

"You want me to spend the night?" Josiah asked in shock.

Allison's expression answered.

Myra shared in the shock. "Are you serious?"

"You're not spending the night," said Allison.

"Bless the Lord, oh my soul I am not spending the night," Josiah said, resolutely.

"You're moving in," said Allison.

"I am *what?*"

"He is what?"

"For two people who have no problem with voices, you sure are having a problem with mine. Maybe it's the fact that my voice has a body." She stared a few seconds into each of their eyes and stretched out the phone and began with Josiah. "You pop up here and tell us that God spoke to you and told you to help Myra. Right?"

"Yes, but—"

She shut him down. "No buts. God told you to help Myra. That's what you said." Allison looked at Myra. "I tried to get you to see you had a problem and you denied it. This network guy who you said was a nut shows up and you're confessing to him like he's the Pope."

"A nut?" said Josiah.

"Shush!" Allison told him.

"But move in, Allison?" said Myra.

"Have it your way, Myra. It's late and I'm not riding this merry-go-round all night. I have to work tomorrow." She swiped the phone with her finger.

"Okay," Myra exclaimed in defeat. "He can move in."

"It is not okay," Josiah yelled. "Are both of you insane? I am not moving in with two women."

"You have to, Josiah," Myra pled. "You said God told you to help me."

Josiah grabbed both sides of his head. "Help you, not move in with you."

"If that's what it takes, that's what it takes," she pushed weakly.

"What are we doing here, prophet?" said Allison. "Did you or did you not tell God that you would do whatever it took to help Myra?"

Josiah flailed his arms up and down and grabbed his head, shaking it. "Oh Lord, I cannot believe this. What have you gotten me into? I am holy and pure, and you make me move in with two beautiful women. This is insane. This is totally insane."

"Would it be easier if we were two ugly women?" said Allison.

Josiah looked at her, mouth open in silence, his face stiff in twisted confusion, like a disfigured, dried out sponge

"Good," said Allison. "It's late." She pointed. "There's a half bathroom down Myra's hall." She started walking toward her own bedroom. "No key. You two will have to coordinate. And unless Myra changes it, you don't have to worry about staying holy and pure."

Allison had not slammed her door. Yet, the sound of it closing softly behind her was uncomfortably loud. For both Myra and Josiah. It froze them both in place. Josiah looked warily at Myra.

"You don't have to look at me like that," said Myra. "I didn't want this."

"Oh, you sounded very much like you wanted this."

"Well, I didn't."

"Here is the deal, Myra. I am not going to stay here one moment longer than is necessary. You are going to be delivered, and I am going to get out of here."

"Fine," she said.

"Fine," he said. A couple of seconds passed. "You will do as I say."

"Excuse me."

"You will do as I say..." he waved the back of his hand at her and finished the sentence without looking at her, "or your roommate calls your family."

Myra shook her head. "I can't believe this."

"You can't believe this? I can't believe this. It is totally inappropriate." Josiah grabbed the sides of his head, his fingers digging into his flesh as they slid down his face. "Lord, you must free this woman speedily!"

Chapter 49

Vicious Hatred of All Women had one leg folded over his thigh as he sat on his throne, impatiently rolling the fingers of both clawed hands. He had been through this before. There was nothing he could do but wait it out.

He could hear the panic and aimless movement of the idiot demons he had inherited from Ugly. In contrast, he pictured his own disciplined and expertly trained demons. Still and alert.

The deafening sound of the ram's horn finally lowered into silence. The thick, blinding fog that had filled Myra's spirit and soul and mind slowly thinned until he could see again.

Vicious stopped rolling his fingers. He gripped and squeezed hard on the throne's arms as he peered at the threat outside.

So that's what the fog and horn were about? he thought. I send Bludgeon out against you and he doesn't return. Vicious peered at the man and tapped the long claw of his index finger several times. But you do.

"Lord Vicious," said one of his own demons.

"I know," he said. "It's the African."

"I am not here about the African, my lord."

Vicious stopped tapping.

"It's Bludgeon."

Vicious felt his spirit rise. His trusted warrior and assassin had not been destroyed after all. He was alive. But the African was in Myra's living room. He had questions for Bludgeon. "Where is he?"

"He's at the south gate."

"Get him here now."

"And he's at the east gate, Lord Vicious."

A chill went over Vicious. "He's at the south gate. And he's at the east gate. Since when do I like riddles?"

"His head has not been located."

"He's in pieces and his head is missing," Vicious said drily.

"We all know how fond you were of Bludgeon. He will be missed."

Vicious pushed his thick back against his throne. A short assignment conducted for a friend had turned into a great military and political embarrassment. Bludgeon was admired by many and had other friends in high places. Very high places.

Soon Vicious would be standing before some ruler or prince's throne to give an accounting of this loss. He had to be ready for them. He thought of his options.

The head of this African would serve as good insurance, but that would be a long-term proposition with no guarantee of success. And he'd be certain to suffer even more embarrassing losses.

No, the smart thing was to be professional. Forget about emotions. Forget about trying to trap a new animal. Go after the one already caught in the snare.

"Find the rest of Bludgeon," he ordered.

"My lord, we have—"

"Find—the rest—of Bludgeon."

The obedient demon turned and went his way. Vicious sat for several minutes and pondered his position. It was as simple as war would allow. The favor for a friend had turned into a fight for his reputation and political life. He *had* to destroy this woman.

"Get me Self-Hatred," yelled Vicious.

Chapter 50

Vicious stroked his chin with his fingers as he looked approvingly at Self-Hatred. It was remarkable that such a lethal demon could appear so *un*remarkable, so *un*imposing, so *not* dangerous.

"You're late. I was expecting you weeks ago." It was not an accusation. He knew there must be a good reason for the delay. Besides, he and Self-Hatred had briefly worked in close proximity on a few projects. And if the truth be told, he liked this demon. They had much in common.

"What can I say, Most Vicious? The perils of being good at what you do. The council gets what the council wants."

"No way to run a war," said Vicious. "I'd rather you said you were delayed by angels."

"I was. Unfortunately, they were our angels. Communication with the field has never been the council's strong point. But as much as I'd rather not, I must admit that this time the lack of communication was due more to distraction than to imperial dismissiveness."

This piqued Vicious's curiosity. For as much as he enjoyed the banter of deriding the Council of Hatred of All Women, he knew it was exceptionally good at what it did. "Oh, and what might that distraction be?"

"A number of things, actually. That pest, J. Lee Grady, is still running around exposing our hatred of women and freeing them of sexist and religious bondage. Lots of them, too. He's a real pain in the darkness.

"Then there's that Joyce Meyers. The only thing worse than someone helping women on such a large scale as this is that this someone is a woman. The council's put in a request for headquarters to do more with demons of feminism in the church.

"Feelings are if they can get more Christian wives to rebel against God's authority in their husbands, there'll be a backlash against all women. They can use it to discredit female ministries. Shut them down."

Vicious looked at the demon as though this plan was wishful thinking.

"Well, that's the sentiment," said Self-Hatred. "Maybe they can shut up some of them."

Vicious felt his temperature rising. He hated J. Lee Grady, but he hated the woman more. She was a *woman.* "She should never have recovered from what we did to her."

"It's a tragedy for sure," Self-Hatred agreed. It was obvious that Self-Hatred had more to say.

"And?" said Vicious.

"This woman, Myra."

"What about her? She's insignificant."

Self-Hatred smirked with a raised eyebrow. "You don't need me to remind you of the enemy's words."

Vicious's face grew thoughtful. But God has chosen the foolish things of the world to put to shame the wise, and God has chosen the weak things of the world to put to shame the things which are mighty; and the base things of the world and the things which are despised God has chosen, and the things which are not, to bring to nothing the things that are.

"You're in Corinthians, aren't you?" said Self-Hatred.

"Yes."

"I know where you're at. That 'God chooses the losers of this world' biz, right? I hate that passage," said Self-Hatred.

"So do I," said Vicious. "And why does the council think the enemy has his eyes on this dog? She's being stalked by an angel of death. Sounds like she's about to be history."

"Oh, Most Vicious, the angel of death is hardly news. You know as well as I that everyone who rejects Jesus Christ has the sentence of death hanging over them. No, I think the council's concern has something to do with Bludgeon," said Self-Hatred.

"Bludgeon? What has he to do with this?"

"He's in pieces, is he not?"

"How did you know? I've just found out myself."

"Most Vicious, my friend, Bludgeon has been in pieces for weeks."

"For weeks? They just found him at the gates today."

"You found him at the gate today because the angels put him at the gates today. He's been salad meat for weeks. Pieces of him are scattered all over the place." Then he said as though he were sharing a coveted secret. "They found his club, you know. Had an inscription on it. King of kings and Lord of lords."

Vicious cursed, taking the Lord's name in vain. "No, I didn't know."

Self-Hatred said, "How much you want to bet that the angel who carved that into Bludgeon's club wasn't talking about our illustrious leader? They chopped him up. They didn't have to humiliate him, too."

Vicious thought of his political predicament. "Bludgeon's gone."

"Bludgeon has been in many great battles," said Self-Hatred.

"Ferocious battles," added Vicious. "Against terrible odds."

Self-Hatred's dark eyes stayed fixed on Vicious as he lowered his head. He raised an eyebrow as he waited for Vicious to say it.

"He made it through all of that without becoming a shish kabob," said Vicious.

"Salad meat. Shish kabob. Point is he was whole until this woman," said Self-Hatred.

Vicious yelled and slammed his heavy fist on the throne's arm. "But she is so utterly nothing! How could she be the cause of Bludgeon's destruction?"

A few moments of dark silence.

Self-Hatred spoke first. "I've examined the woman."

Vicious heard the mumbling of Self-Hatred's words, but continued in his silo of fury. His yellow eyes fixed in a trance of hatred.

"Someone's not in a very good mood," said Self-Hatred. "You will be. Shortly. Those chipper demons did a number on this trash.

They're like piranhas. They barely left anything for me to get her to hate."

Vicious didn't move or change the focus of his eyes as he spoke. "How long?"

Self-Hatred's confidence slowly grew into a smile. "It won't be long. Like I said, the chippers did a good job." The demon let out a heavy breath of satisfaction. "And I wouldn't worry too much about that African and those other angels. We get rid of the woman, he's gone."

Vicious dismissed Self-Hatred and watched him walk away. Demons were now cracking jokes about the formidable Bludgeon now being salad meat. How could he not worry about the African?

Chapter 51

Self-Hatred was wasting no time. He stood next to the woman's bed. This way he could fully see the next notch on his belt of victory. His unassuming face was expressionless, not revealing the smirk of his heart.

Most Vicious had certainly lived up to his reputation in ripping this woman to shreds. The stronghold in her mind was impressive. Perhaps it was already impregnable. Self-Hatred thought of the enemy's resources. *Perhaps not.* It was a coin toss.

Self-Hatred wasn't a gambler. Coin tosses were for those with compromised positions. For those demons forced to trust in something that may prove fatally untrustworthy. Now the smile crept onto his face.

That's what he did, was it not? And it was why his services against women were in such high demand by the higher powers. He removed the uncertainty.

Self-Hatred slowly walked around her bed. Unlike Most Vicious, his hatred of women did not blind him to their beauty. She slept on her back. This gave him a good look at his victim. Her lips were luscious and inviting. He imagined their taste.

Her long brown neck begged to be licked. His rough tongue swished involuntarily around his nasty mouth. Her eyelashes fluttered ever so slightly. Pressure rose in the demon's chest. He would have loved to have seen her eyes again. Sad, hopeless eyes, yes. But beautiful, nonetheless. He would have loved to have felt the warmth of air escaping her delicate nose.

He gazed on all that unfair spiritual rules would allow him to see. Which wasn't much! That wretched dictator of a creator. Incubus and lust and witchcraft demons could see all of them and often touch them. Why can't demons of my class see and touch them? His thoughts were angry.

Funny how this works, he thought. Most Vicious hates you because you're ugly. I hate you because you're not ugly...because I can't have you. You're beautiful. You're so exceptionally...beautiful.

The demon bent over Myra. He stretched forth his hand longingly to her face. It passed through it. *Oh, that I could touch you.*

"That would make it easy, wouldn't it?"

Self-Hatred turned in surprise at Most Vicious. "I must admit, it is hard not to let my mind wander into thinking of how it would feel to snap her neck." He flipped his hand. "Well, it is what it is."

It wasn't that much of a secret that some in Self-Hatred's class of demons were like some men. They hated what they lusted after and could not have. Why a demon would desire such an ugly, loathsome creature was a mystery to him. But Most Vicious saw nothing to gain by outing Self-Hatred. "We play the hand we're dealt," said Most Vicious.

"I prefer to play the hand I deal myself," said Self-Hatred. "Once I raise my army, you'll be able to do anything you want to her. Sickness. Disease. Depression."

"I want her dead," Vicious said, impatiently.

"I wasn't through," said Self-Hatred. He looked at Vicious with a raised eyebrow and slight smirk. "Anything includes suicide and a host of other possibilities."

Chapter 52

Myra leaned heavily on her bathroom counter. She didn't want to look into the mirror. But she had to look. Something inside of her made her look. She lifted her face against the heaviness that made her head feel like it weighed a hundred pounds.

The voices were back.

The heaviness was heavier.

The desire to lose weight was deeper.

The urge to fix her ugliness was greater.

The futility of someone so totally disgusting and ugly was final in her mind. There was nothing she could do to undo the ugly creature she was. Still, there was an unexplainable something inside that would not even allow the rest of surrender. It demanded she fight a battle it told her was impossible to win.

Myra started her examination with her too big lips. Then her too small eyes. Next, it was her too big, too wide nose. Finally, her too dark complexion.

I have to do something, she lamented.

Self-Hatred looked approvingly at the tired demon called Exhaustion and whispered ever so slightly into the untouchable woman's mind.

She saw no sense in the thought. Nor did she look forward to the physical drudgery of dragging herself to do it. But whatever was inside of her was determined to go. She didn't have the energy to find out whether she could successfully fight it.

"Myra, are you okay?"

Josiah, she thought. His voice sounded muffled.

What he really means is, Are you back there drinking? said a demon. His first day and he's accusing you. Get rid of him.

She couldn't get rid of him. It was him or her family. Myra heard him call out again. She slowly opened the bathroom door. "Don't worry," she said with a tired voice. "I didn't sneak any alcohol in here. I need to go somewhere. I need a few more minutes."

"A few more minutes? You've been in there almost an hour," he said. She didn't hear him, and he had not intended her to hear him.

Josiah was in deep, but barely audible prayer when she finally came out of the bathroom—ninety minutes later. It would have been longer had she been alone.

He raised his head from his sitting position and forced his eyes not to widen. Or so he thought. He had never seen so much make-up on a woman in all his life who was not a professional entertainer.

"Where are we going?" he asked, wondering what destination would make her do that to her face.

"Did you see his eyes? How he looked at you? I told you. You can't cover the kind of ugly you have. It's a waste of time," a voice said inside.

Another competed with, "You should've put on more makeup. Cover that bad skin. And those marks are getting worse. Darker."

She looked at him with resignation. He had to go with her. She had no choice. Allison was watching her at work. Josiah was watching her at home. That was the deal. "Barnes and Noble," she answered, and walked toward the front door.

Josiah looked at her disbelievingly. "Barnes and Noble? Myra, I don't plan to be here long. We don't have time for you to go look at books. We have to get you delivered."

"You can't deliver me after I go to Barnes and Noble?"

"It's not a question of can God deliver you before or after going to the store. It's a question of priorities. You have no sense of urgency. God is not a waiter or a bellhop."

That something inside pressed her to leave.

Myra's face tightened. "I do have a sense of urgency, Josiah. I *have* to go to the store." She opened the door and looked at him, waiting.

Josiah's mouth dropped open. He looked at her for an explanation that didn't come. "You *have* to go to Barnes and Noble?" he asked disbelievingly.

Myra felt vulnerable and ashamed. She didn't know what was wrong with her. Was it a nervous breakdown? Could a nervous breakdown turn her into an overnight alcoholic? Could it cause paranoia? Could it make her feel like something was inside of her? Whatever it was, it was making her feel crazy. And now this man was going to find out she had more than a drinking problem.

"Yes," she said, a tinge of regret and shame in her whispered voice, "I have to go to Barnes and Noble."

Josiah looked into her eyes for a long questioning moment. The longer they looked at one another, the more he saw fear and helplessness in her eyes. He walked slowly toward her, not letting his eyes drop from hers. "You're afraid," he said, softly. "Let me help you."

Her heart spoke instead of her mind, and before she could object. "Please," she said. She pressed her lips together and hoped she'd not be further betrayed by the tears forming behind her grimace. Were her lips trembling? Did he see them trembling?

Please.

One word.

Josiah didn't think. He acted. The only way he could. She was in trouble. He stepped forward. "Don't be afraid. I am here."

Myra kept her lips pressed and nodded silently.

"Let's go," said Josiah. "I'll drive."

Chapter 53

Honestly, Josiah didn't know what he felt as he watched Myra. Curiosity? Yes. This was bizarre. Irritation? He knew this wasn't right. It wasn't the spirit of Christ. But, yes. He was irritated. He had been forced by God and hijacked by Myra to move into her home to help her, and instead of crying out to God for help, she was here flipping through a stack of magazines.

He studied her face as she turned page after page of magazine after magazine. Her fingers whipped through pages as though she were looking for something specific. She'd stop and gaze longingly at a picture, then snatch through more pages until she found the next one.

It was like one of those amnesia movies where the woman looks desperately at pictures, trying to jar her brain into remembering her identity. Whatever irritation Josiah had melted away into pity. *Myra, what are you doing?* he wondered.

***

Self-Hatred knew exactly what she was doing. She was following the path of many of his victims. "That's right," he coached, as he smugly looked at the angels in the distance. He knew he was well within his rights. "Get those images burned into that weak mind of yours. We need an army that no amount of angels can stop."

***

"What does that demon mean, no amount of angels?" asked Aaron-Hur. We can gather many more angels than they can demons."

The captain looked at Aaron-Hur and Mishnak. They needed this to sink in. "Seldom is it only a matter of numbers...of power...of who is greater. Who is greater than God?"

"There is none greater than God," said Mishnak.

"No. No one," agreed Aaron-Hur.

"If it was only a matter of power, the great rebellion would never have happened. The great fall would never have happened." Jezrael widely waved his arm backward. "None of this would have happened," he said, meaning the effects of sin.

The two angels waited for the captain to explain further.

"This kind of demon, one with his experience and skillset, specializes in raising armies that..." The captain's voice trailed off into a sad memory.

Both angels saw that Jezrael's mind had drifted onto something uncomfortable. Neither pressed for details.

"She's losing control fast," said Jezrael. "Her compulsions are spreading and growing stronger. He's pressing her to fill her mind with images of that which she believes she does not have."

"Covetousness? Envy?" said Mishnak.

"This is no different than what Vicious was doing to her with his magazines at the cabin in the mountains," Aaron-Hur.

"It is different. Vicious is a different kind of demon," said Jezrael. "He is a master at butchering women. He is not a master at getting them to butcher themselves. Self-Hatred is."

Aaron-Hur said, "But magazines are magazines."

Jezrael shook his head. "No, with this Vicious demon, the hate comes from the outside-in, from him to her. But with Self-Hatred, the hatred comes from within her."

Aaron-Hur said, "But Myra feels hatred whether it comes from Vicious or Self-Hatred."

"Aaron-Hur," said the captain, "Vicious can make her feel hated by *someone*. Like people who are paranoid that someone's out to get them. But Self-Hatred can make her feel hated by herself. She becomes her own worst enemy."

Mishnak looked here and there, trying to make sense of this. "This Vicious...and that council."

"The Council of Hatred of All Women," said Jezrael.

Mishnak's face turned up. "That one. You said that's what they do—get women to hate themselves. The beauty industry."

"That's true, Mishnak. That's one of the things they do. Create discontent among the masses of women. But that is done so demons at the lower, tactical levels can have something to work with. Discontent is an open door for demons. That is why the blessed book says, 'Godliness with contentment is great gain.'

"Given enough time, Vicious could beat her into hating herself— probably. But he doesn't have time. And he can't take chances. That's why he called in a specialist. Self-Hatred makes it certain."

"Certain?" Aaron-Hur blurted. "Captain, why is this certain? Angels of truth can—"

"Angels of truth can do nothing that God Himself cannot do," said the captain. "God cannot make someone freely accept truth, and neither can angels. Myra must decide."

"What about this man, Josiah?" asked Aaron-Hur. "He is here to help her."

"We can only hope that his knowledge is as great as his zeal," said Jezrael.

After a moment of silence, Mishnak asked, "Then how long before this demon's army arrives?"

The captain looked at Myra. "The army is has arrived."

Chapter 54

Josiah had thought it would be polite and helpful to give Myra space as she looked at her magazines. Now he was convinced it had been more polite than helpful. He stood ten feet away flipping through *PC Magazine* with no interest at all in its pages. His interest was in Myra's intensity and now her mutterings.

He approached and stood over her. She didn't look up. Probably didn't even see him. He broke into her mutterings. "Myra." Her eyes remained fixed on the glamour model. Josiah looked at the page and wondered what in the world she found so fascinating about a nearly naked woman wearing more make-up than a circus clown.

"Myra," he repeated a little louder.

She didn't acknowledge him.

"Myra," he said, louder.

She flinched. "Why are you yelling?"

"I am sorry. You are in a trance. I had to yell to get your attention. We have to go."

"I can't. I still have some magazines I haven't—"

"The store is closing, Myra."

She looked around as though the store's closing would be a crime against humanity. "They can't close."

Josiah said nothing, wondering at her behavior. Then he said, "You can purchase them."

The suggestion cut through Myra's alarm. "Yeah, that's right. I can purchase them," she said, as though this was a brilliant thought.

Josiah watched her scoop up the stack of magazines. "You don't have to restock them. You can leave the ones you're not purchasing on the table."

"I'm buying all of them," she said.

"You're buying thirty magazines?" Her embarrassed expression made him feel as though he had opened the restroom door as she was using it. "That's...really none of my business."

Myra faced him, hugging the magazines to her chest, but not looking at him. She closed her eyes and inhaled and exhaled a long breath before looking at him. She couldn't explain it to him this moment. Yet, it was inevitable. She'd have to explain it to him soon. She wanted to tell him. All of it. But what was *it?*

"It's okay, Josiah." Horrible word choice. She knew nothing was okay. "I admit it's a bit odd. You're not going to out me on social media, are you?"

Her try at humor was unexpected. Josiah appreciated it. It took some of the edge off the moment. "No, of course not. I was thinking billboards and flyers."

She smiled. "Going old school on me. I thought you were a tech guy."

He joined her smile. "Some things are best done slowly."

Her expression turned mischievous. "Oh?" she said. "You're into slow?"

Josiah's eyes widened. He started stammering out an explanation.

"Don't swallow your tongue, Josiah. I'm just trying to laugh to keep from crying." There, she was opening up to him.

This didn't remove the nervous itch that had suddenly broken out all over him, especially his face. He hadn't meant it like that. *Some things are best done slowly.* Oh, Lord, it did sound like he was flirting with her.

Myra welcomed his innocent discomfort. It was cute. And funny. As cute and funny as something could be to someone with a terrible toothache. Her toothache was the incredible heaviness she felt trying to push her to the floor, and the anxiety that made her feel as though she was literally coming apart.

"Really, I was just kidding, Josiah. I'm going to go pay for these." She took a couple of steps and stopped and looked back at him. "Do you mind carrying these for me?"

"What? Oh, yeah. Of course."

"I feel really drained."

They walked slowly to the counter. When they arrived, the cashier asked, "Are you okay?"

Myra didn't answer.

Josiah looked at her and instinctively placed his arm around her waist to keep her from falling as he put the magazines on the counter. Some fell to the floor.

"I can get those," said the cashier, hurrying around the counter.

"I'm okay, Josiah. I just feel very heavy."

"I can call 911," the cashier offered.

"No, that's okay," said Myra.

"You sure?" the young lady asked.

"Josiah, if you could just get me home."

He paid for the magazines. "Will you do me a favor?" he said to the cashier.

"You want me to call?"

"No. If you could take the bag—"he swooped Myra up in his arms as though she were light as a life-size doll—"and set it on top of her."

Myra was unbelievably heavy and coming apart at the seams. She was having a nervous breakdown. But she wasn't crazy yet. She knew this man had just swept her up in his arms, and that he was solid. He felt like iron wrapped in flesh. She wrapped her arm over his opposite shoulder and laid her face onto his neck and shoulder and rested.

"You smell really nice."

Josiah tried unsuccessfully to ignore her words and her face snuggling deeper into him.

The young cashier's mouth was slightly opened. Her eyes twinkled at the sight of witnessing a romance novel in real life. She put the bag atop Myra and said, "I'll get the door for you."

When they got to the car, he buckled her in, let her seat back, and trotted around to his side. Before he could start the car, she said, "Josiah."

"I am here," he said.

"I can't beat this by myself. I trust you. I'll do whatever you tell me to do."

Whatever was just below *stunned* was what he was. How could a person change so quickly? "I—that is good to hear. I know it is hard to admit you need help." He smiled reassuringly. "Alcohol must bow its knees to the mighty power of God."

"Josiah, it's not just alcohol."

He shivered. "What else is it?"

Chapter 55

"Let's go home, Josiah." Talking drained her even more. "We'll talk there."

Myra's eyes were closed. Josiah knew the peaceful expression of her face masked a deeply troubled soul. He resisted the urge to consciously ponder her beauty. The Bible said to "flee fornication."

So he had kept his eyes and mind disciplined, his running shoes always on, laced, and tied. This practice had kept him sexually pure when so many others he knew had fallen.

He wasn't accusing her of being Bathsheba, conveniently taking a bath where the king could see her. But neither was he volunteering to be King David, conveniently being on his balcony where he could accidently look down and see Bathsheba bathing. The best antidote for a snake bite was not to get bitten.

Nonetheless, against his will (or was it really?), he found himself enchanted by Myra's words. *Let's go home, Josiah.* It was more like a prophecy of the future rather than a request to go back to her apartment.

He was mentally several hundred yards away, tumbling head over heels, before he realized he had been swept away by a flash flood of pleasurable thoughts of life with Myra.

Courtship.

Presenting her to his family.

Marriage.

Children.

He hit a rock.

His eyes popped wide. *Dear God in heaven! What is this foolishness?* He looked around as though his unruly thoughts had been caught on camera. He rubbed imagined sweat off his guilty forehead while blowing out air.

This woman is not even a servant of the Lord. It is impossible, he told himself, trying to ignore how it had felt to carry her in his arms and feel her face against his neck.

Her words. You smell nice.

Why would she say such a thing? That had been quite unnecessary. He drove the rest of the way praying inaudibly for her deliverance and wondering how much longer he would have to stay at her apartment.

How could this possibly be of the Lord? Had he allowed himself to be cajoled into this because deep down he had something for this woman? Maybe that's why she thought he was flirting with her—because he was.

The possibility of him using God's name to follow his own desires was troubling. Desires that he thought had been lain at the feet of the cross.

Lord, forgive me. That is not what I desire, he thought. *I will fix this.* He'd take her home, pray with her, and this would be the last time he'd ever set foot in her apartment. He glanced at Myra. She was still sleeping.

But Myra wasn't fully asleep. She was somewhere between consciousness and being trapped in a nightmare, struggling desperately and futilely to scream for help.

Monsters were everywhere.

Chapter 56

Josiah drove to the front gate of Myra's apartment complex. "Myra," he said. Her head moved slightly. He decided against shaking her. He had touched her enough. "Myra," he said, again.

A low groan rolled deep within her throat.

"Myra—" Josiah began.

Myra's eyes popped open at the same time she lurched forward screaming. Josiah's back slammed against his own door. He recovered almost immediately.

"What is it?" he said.

Myra stared straight ahead, panting heavily. When her breaths returned to a semblance of normal, she said, "Monsters. Stabbing and slashing me. I couldn't get them off. They were everywhere. On me. Around me. In me." She yelled the last word. "*Everywhere!*"

Josiah looked behind to see if they were blocking anyone. "Let's get inside and we'll talk. A car is coming."

Myra's left hand gripped the side of her seat. Her head was bowed into her other hand. She breathed tremulously. "The card is in the side pocket of my purse."

Josiah hesitated. He really hesitated. Then he went into the pocket. He tapped the card against the card reader and the gate opened. He parked the car thinking about Myra's purse. He switched his thoughts. "You want to talk about it?"

Myra's answer was whispery and immediate. "There's something wrong with me, Josiah."

He waited.

"The alcohol—it's not—there's something deeper. Before the alcohol." She shook her head in frustration.

"We are in no hurry, Myra."

"I can't believe I'm telling you this," she said.

"Your secrets are safe with me. Who'd believe me anyway? I'm a nut, remember?"

Somehow Myra found the strength to briefly smile through her torment. She looked at him. He had a slight smile. "You are a nut, Josiah. A beautiful...chocolate nut." She dropped her eyes and paused in thought. "But I'm a nut, too. Only more."

Silence.

Did she just call me beautiful? And chocolate? "Why do you say you're a nut?" asked Josiah.

Myra thought about her answer. I hear voices. Loud, tormenting voices. I've heard them all my life, and they've gotten louder and more tormenting. Oh yeah, and something's out to get me—someone's out to get me. And it's inside of me. And I hate myself. And I wish I was dead. She thought cynically, But I'm not crazy, Josiah. Just having a bad day.

If she told him, if she were honest, there'd be no turning back. There'd be no way to erase his memory. She settled for a safe "I've been depressed for a long time."

"About what?"

"I don't really know."

That wasn't much to go on. Josiah asked, "How long have you been depressed?"

"I don't know exactly. Several years." Myra wasn't intentionally being evasive. At least not entirely so. It was true that she couldn't be precise.

"And there was nothing that happened?"

"No. It's not like one day I was happy, and the next day sad. It happened over time."

"And nothing happened to cause this?" Josiah asked, trying to use words to mask his feeling of impotence.

She didn't answer.

"God can help you," said Josiah.

"How?"

"He can give you joy?"

Joy. Myra wondered at the concept. "I'd love to be happy," she said.

"Joy is deeper than happiness, Myra. Happiness comes from how you feel. Joy comes from who you know."

"If I knew God, I'd have joy?"

"Yes."

"Just like that?"

"Yes. Just like that."

"Okay." Myra let her seat back a little.

Josiah looked at her closed eyes and wondered what had just happened. "You want God?"

"Yes. I want joy...and peace."

Are you kidding me? he thought joyfully. *Just like that!* His lips parted in surprise. He hardly knew what to do he was so excited. "Okay," he said. He quickly explained the death and resurrection of Jesus from the dead. "Do you believe this, Myra?"

"Sure."

Myra's eyes were still closed. Josiah wondered at her answer. It was anticlimactic. Underwhelming in its lack conviction. Like she was agreeing to one brand of table salt over another.

"That He died for your sins?"

"Um-hmm," she answered, without opening her mouth.

A barely discernible grimace pushed onto Josiah's face. He'd never experienced such disinterest from a person who was supposedly coming to Christ. Hope abruptly rose in his heart. *Maybe it's the depression and not her.*

"Myra, do you want the Lord's joy in your life?"

"Yes. I'm desperate, Josiah. I'll do anything you say. I need peace."

Josiah couldn't explain it. She was saying all the right things. Why did her words deflate him? "I would like to pray with you," he said.

Eyes closed. Voice weak. "Please pray for me," she said.

Still, Josiah couldn't shake the trouble in his gut. What was wrong?

Chapter 57

Vicious watched the African and the woman from the assembly area of the stronghold. He didn't try to shake the trouble in his own gut. What would be the point? It wasn't going anywhere until this African was out of the way. He barked out his orders again. This was too important for some trigger-happy demon to try to make a name for himself.

"Stand down! No one does anything. No attacks. No manifestations. Nothing. Total silence. Our advantage is darkness. Do nothing to turn on the light."

He looked down at Hideous with his freshly broken bones and snatched the back of his neck, sinking long talons deep into his flesh. He dragged him as he spoke. "The demon who exposes our presence will join this wretched creature."

Vicious slung Hideous to the ground. He turned slowly in a full circle, peering at his demons. Thinking. Strategizing. This development with the African wasn't his specialty. He needed a demon who could tell him exactly what was going on.

"This Josiah character has just led the woman to give her life to the enemy," he yelled. "Why is there no activity from the angels? Why are we not under attack? Is this a ruse? A trick? Is there not one among you who desires to be promoted? Not one among you with this kind of experience?"

"I can...help you. Lord Most...Vicious...you need—"

A crowd of demons parted for the demon who was slowly making his way through them. Vicious stretched his neck to the right and gazed. *I do not believe this,* he thought, when he saw who it was.

"—a seducing spirit. Religious...has to be...religious. Preferably...antichrist."

"Antichrist!" yelled Vicious. "Where am I going to get an antichrist spirit in this nation? They're all busy. And why antichrist?"

"The woman...the reason...we are not...under attack," Exhaustion inhaled deeply and slowly exhaled, "is because—"

"Because what? Spit it out."

"Repentance. No repentance."

"What do you mean?" Vicious demanded. "I heard her. He led her in the sinner's prayer. She believes in Jesus. She said all the right words."

Exhaustion finally made his way to Vicious. "Where's the attack?" he asked.

Vicious's mind searched possibilities.

"No repentance...no attack," said Exhaustion. "Words don't save. Jesus saves." He rested. "She doesn't want...God. She wants...peace."

Slowly a smile formed on the face of Vicious. "Of course," he pondered. "The man wants so desperately to rescue her that he skipped the one thing the enemy demands. No repentance—"

Exhaustion finished the sentence. "No attack."

"Excellent," said Vicious. He turned to leave.

"Most Vicious," said Exhaustion.

"I'll think of something to give you for your service," said Vicious, without losing a stride.

"The antichrist spirit," said Exhaustion.

Vicious spun around. "What about him?"

"We need him."

"Why? You've told me all I need to know. The woman is a false convert. There is no danger."

Exhaustion didn't know how long this conversation would last. It was entirely too exhausting to continuously speak loudly. He slowly walked toward his clearly impatient master.

Every slow step of the tired spirit made Vicious want to scream. How could such a slug be so valuable? "Well?" said Vicious.

"There's always the threat—"

"Of her truly going to the Lord? Denying herself? Taking up the cross? Following Christ? Et cetera?"

"Yes. The antichrist demon...will keep...that from happening. He will give her...something...instead of...the real thing."

"I will say this again, and for the last time. Where. Can I. Get. An antichrist spirit? It's not like they're swinging on hammocks waiting for something to do."

"There must be...one church ruler...that can spare—"

Vicious cut him off. "I don't have time. I need to deal with this woman now. Self-Hatred has raised an army."

Vicious saw in Exhaustion's eyes that he wasn't convinced. Not that he had to convince this tired spirit of anything, but he said, "An antichrist spirit would give her something instead of the real thing. Right? I don't have an antichrist spirit, but I do have something. I'll relieve just enough torment to give her reason to believe she's free. Then I'll strike at a moment of my choosing with overwhelming devastation."

Vicious bent over to get nearer the small demon's face. "Does that meet your approval, Lord Weary?"

Exhaustion dared not answer.

Vicious walked away, speaking to Exhaustion without turning around. "If I had an antichrist spirit, I'd use him. I don't have one. We'll do it my way."

Chapter 58

"How do you feel?" Josiah asked, Myra's watery eyes giving him hope that God had truly touched her heart.

Myra dabbed at the tear rolling down her cheek. "Lighter."

"Lighter?"

"Yes. I felt really heavy before. And my face..." She stretched her face in different contortions. "Oh, my goodness."

"What?"

"The mask. The helmet. Whatever it is. It's gone!"

Josiah's eyes danced with joy and questions.

Myra sat up. She touched her face and head as though discovering them for the first time. She started crying. "I think it happened, Josiah. I think I'm free."

Josiah laughed. "You are? Really?"

"I think so," she exulted.

"Oh, precious Jesus," said Josiah. "That's the weight of sin. He took it from you."

Myra grabbed both sides of her face and laughed and cried at the same time. "Oh, Josiah, I can't believe it. All this time— I could have been delivered just by saying a prayer."

Josiah's joy bag sprung a leak. His smile remained, but with difficulty. "Yes. All who call upon the name of the Lord shall be saved," he said.

Myra was shaking her head and repeating softly, "One little prayer. One little prayer." Each time she said it, a wave of nausea rolled through Josiah's gut.

"I feel like I can fly, Josiah. Like a butterfly. Like a beautiful butterfly."

"I must admit, this is..."

"Wonderful!" said Myra.

"Yes, it is," said Josiah, with fifty percent certainty.

"What?" asked Myra.

"Nothing," he said, with more enthusiasm than he had. "Here is what you do now, Myra. You must be baptized in water. The old life is gone. You must bury it. I will present you to the church."

Myra looked at him oddly. "I was baptized as a child."

"Baptism is for disciples of the Lord. Were you a disciple of the Lord Jesus?"

"What do you mean disciple? They asked me if I believed in Jesus and wanted to go to heaven when I died? I said yes and they baptized me."

"A disciple is a follower of Jesus. Did you follow Jesus after you were baptized?"

"I was a child, Josiah."

"That is what I am getting at, Myra."

"What? Children can't be disciples?" Myra looked at him as though he made no sense. "This is the best thing that has happened to me in a long time." Their eyes locked for a few seconds. "Maybe the best thing ever. This is what you wanted. Right?"

How could he answer yes and no? He hesitated. "Yes."

It was obvious he had something else to say. "What do you want to say, Josiah? Just say it."

He breathed heavily.

"I don't understand your reaction, Josiah." She took his hand and sandwiched it between both of hers. "But I feel great. You delivered. I'll deliver. I promised I'd do whatever you asked. Right?" She smiled and bounced as she said, "Set it up. Set up the baptism."

Josiah placed his free hand atop hers. "I apologize for my behavior. Sometimes it is hard for me to stop running once the race is over."

Myra beamed. "You can stop running, Josiah. Both of us can. Let's enjoy the victory, okay?"

"Let's enjoy the victory," said Josiah.

"Can I have a hug?" said Myra. "Or is that crossing a line. I wouldn't want you to melt in my arms like butter."

This made him chuckle. "I am not butter."

"I am not butter," she said, playfully mocking his accent.

They hugged.

As they did, he thought, I have to call Mama and Papa. Something is terribly wrong here.

When their embrace ended, which Josiah felt was quite long, she looked at him with a face that radiated gratefulness—and beauty. She was the most beautiful woman he had ever seen. He dropped his eyes and turned away when he was sure she was reading his mind.

She had read his mind. She grinned and flipped the car's sun visor down to look at what had so mesmerized Josiah. To see the new Myra. An arctic chill swept through her body.

She was as ugly as ever.

Chapter 59

"Hello, Mama?"

"Josiah? Boy, what are you doing calling here at three o'clock in the morning? Is everything right?"

"I am sorry, Mama. Everything is right here."

"If everything is right there, we will talk in several hours."

"Mama, wait."

"What is it boy? Papa and I were casting out demons all night. We are not in heaven yet. These bodies must rest."

"It is a woman."

Mama's eyes popped wide. She sat up in bed. "What is this about a woman?"

Josiah pondered where to begin.

"Why do you say nothing? Did you lay hands on this woman?"

Now Papa rose up in bed. "What is this? Who are you speaking to?"

"No. Of course not. I would never do that."

"It's Josiah," said Mama.

Papa took the phone. His large eyes open wide with this shocking news. "Boy, what is this I hear? Have you laid hands on a woman?"

"Papa, no. I have n—"

"Why does Mama say you have laid hands on a woman if you have not laid hands on a woman?"

"Papa, give me back the phone. I did not say the boy laid hands on a woman. I was asking him if he laid hands on a woman."

"Why would you ask my son such a thing? What are you not telling me?" Papa looked at the face of the small alarm clock. "Three-thirteen! Tell me what has happened."

Mama knew she wouldn't be getting the phone back any time soon. She went to the kitchen.

Josiah laughed quietly. This was why he had hesitated to find the right words. Papa, and Mama to a lesser degree, but only slightly lesser, was prone to jump to conclusions. He could be like a wild, bucking horse once he got a hold of part of a story. You couldn't get him to listen to the rest of the story until he got tired of kicking and jumping all over the place.

Josiah waited a few minutes until Papa had reminded him of how he and Mama had raised him to honor God and women. And besides, how could he bring such reproach on the church and the family name? He was the only child of seven to do such a thing. Papa took a breath.

Josiah snatched the opportunity. "Papa, I did not lay hands on a woman. I led a woman to the Lord. But I am not satisfied with the outcome."

There was a pause.

"Oh," said Papa, "you did not lay hands on a woman?"

"I would never behave in such a way without a holy covenant."

Papa yelled to the kitchen. "Why did you say this boy had laid hands on a woman? He has done no such thing." He waited, but got no response from Mama, who chose instead to roll around the avocado and smoked fish in her mouth without comment. Papa spoke into the phone. "I do not know why Mama stirs things up the way she does. I tell her often to listen, but you know Mama."

"Yes, Papa."

"Now why is this matter so urgent?"

Josiah hadn't anticipated this question. He had to have known they would ask it. He braced himself for another round of Papa. *Just get it over with,* he told himself. "She asked me to get something out of her purse." Josiah heard a gasp and a long, *"Whaaaat?"* He lied flat on the bed with a smile and with his eyes closed.

"What did you do?"

"I went into her purse."

"Mama, get in here," Papa yelled, as though needing help. "You must hear this development. A woman asked him to go into her purse."

It's not a development. It's me getting a gate card out of a woman's purse, thought Josiah. He slowly shook his head. Round two. He heard Mama in the background.

"Josiah."

"Yes, Papa."

"You are on speaker. Tell Mama about this development. It is a woman, Mama."

"A woman?" said Mama. "Tell me of this development."

"It is not a development, Mama. I led a woman to the Lord. We were—"

Mama interrupted. "Papa said this woman asked you to go into her purse."

Oh, if only the good Lord would let him lie just this once. "That is right, but—"

"Then she has designs on you," said Mama.

Josiah exhaled through his mouth. "She does not have designs on me." He wondered if his protest sounded as phony to his parents as it sounded to him.

"Did you do it? Did you go into this woman's purse?" Mama pressed.

"Yes, Mama, but—"

It was plain as day to Mama. "Then you have designs on this woman."

Papa in the background began spitting out the evidence. Mama took the evidence as though she were finishing up a double play to win the baseball game.

"Did your Papa go into my purse?"

"That is what you said, Mama."

"That is not what I said, boy. It is what happened. What about your uncles?"

"I remember Andrew—"

Papa jumped in. "Andrew, Danso, Kafui—"

Mama added, "Your sisters… Yomawu and Mawusi—remember how they joked about the magic of the purse last Easter?"

There was his escape. "We are Christians. We do not believe in magic. You and Papa have always preached against believing in superstition."

"We are not talking about magic and superstition," said Papa. "Magic and superstition are nothing. We are talking about women and purses and marriage. This thing works all over the world."

They weren't going to let this go. He'd have to try a sharp curve. He stopped himself and considered how much he should tell them about Myra. Against the grain of what he was willing to admit, he thought, *Just in case there is truth to this purse business.*

"Papa, her name is Myra. I led her to the Lord, but I am not satisfied. I told her she must be baptized."

"This woman loves the Lord," Mama exclaimed in triumph and relief.

Papa said, "Of course, she loves the Lord, Mama. Josiah wouldn't get into a development with a woman who doesn't love the Lord."

"Has she been baptized?" asked Mama.

"No."

Papa's eye twinkled. "You are planning to bring her here for baptism?" Before Josiah could answer, Papa said, "Then this is serious."

Mama said, "This will require much planning. This is more than a baptism. Everyone must be here for this occasion."

"Wait, Mama and Papa, we are getting ahead of ourselves. I only called to get advice about discipleship for Myra." Surprisingly, there was silence on the other end of the line. "Papa, I led Myra in the sinner's prayer for salvation."

There was still silence. Josiah wondered and continued. "Something remarkable happened when we prayed. The weight of sin dramatically lifted off her. She's happy and radiant and joyful."

Papa spoke. "So what is the problem? I feel a problem."

"The problem is"—he still didn't know what the problem was—"I don't have assurance of her salvation."

"It is not your salvation," said Mama. "It is her salvation. The assurance must be in her heart. You said something remarkable happened when she prayed. You said God lifted the weight of sin, and she's full of joy. What else do you want?"

He thought about it while they again were surprisingly quiet. "Holy fruit," he said.

"When did she turn to the Lord?" asked Mama.

"A few hours ago."

Papa and Mama burst forth into talking to one another and to themselves. Finally, Papa's loud voice took the lead. "What is this, Josiah? The three-hour discipleship program? You plant a seed at twelve o'clock and you want to eat the fruit at three o'clock? You were wise not to become a pastor."

Mama said, "Papa is right. The good Lord is faithful to His word. He said, 'All who call on the name of the Lord shall be saved.'"

Something clicked. Josiah said, "Uuhhh..."

"What is this uuhhh?" said Mama.

"Eyeeeee don't know if she really called on the name of the Lord," said Josiah.

There was silence.

Papa said, "What do you mean you do not know? You were there. You are the one who led her to Jesus?"

"Papa, I am wondering now if I really led her to Jesus."

Papa said, "If a man shaves his face, he does not say, 'I wonder if I shaved my face.' Boy, it is very early in the morning. You talk to Mama and—"

Mama said loudly, "Ah, ah, ah, ah. Papa, I think I understand this boy. Josiah, you said you led this girl in the sinner's prayer? Are you talking about that foolishness the American evangelists preach to our people in the big crusades?"

Josiah was ashamed to answer.

Papa couldn't wait any longer. "Josiah, is this true?"

"Of course, it is true," Mama answered for him. "That is why his lips do not move."

"Boy, is that why your lips do not move?" asked Papa.

"Papa, I made a big mistake. I had been praying mightily for her salvation. She had problems. I think I led her to receive God as her problem fixer, but not as her Lord."

"There is no such thing. Papa, do you hear this?" said Mama. "Your son told this woman that Jesus is a waiter. Boy, you need to fix this."

"Mama is right. I do not know what got into you to think you could bring this girl here for baptism. Did you talk to her about her sins? About living holy?"

Josiah didn't answer.

"Boy, you have made a mess," said Papa. "We are going back to bed. Give that woman the true gospel. She must repent of her sins."

Josiah said his goodbyes and ended the call. It was hard to believe he had done something that he had heard his parents preach against all his life. What a dumb mistake!

But this realization left him baffled. Something good had definitely happened to Myra when they had prayed. If she had not received salvation, what had she received? He lied down with a heavy heart and a mind racing with questions.

Oh, God, I think I have created a false convert. Please help me to fix this mess.

Chapter 60

Myra sat on the edge of her bed in a painful stupor. It was like the heartbreaking news story she had recently read. An unmarried couple were on vacation in Tanzania. They had an unbelievably romantic cabin that had a bedroom fully submerged under water.

The guy swam to the large bedroom window and pulled out a ring and proposed to his girlfriend, who was inside looking out at him and laughing with surprised delight. She ran giggling upstairs to meet him with her answer of *Yes, I'll marry you!* only to find that he never reached the top. Her dream of happiness had turned into a nightmare of grief in one tragic, fluid-filled moment.

Myra was there herself beside that woman.

Yes, I'll marry you!

My God, he's dead.

Josiah's prayer was like the proposal. Full of magical promise. A new life of beautiful sunrises.

And the first sunrise had happened. Immediately. The darkness had vanished, and in its place a brightness and warmth that were truly magical.

And perhaps as premature and unlikely as it was to entertain such a thought, maybe she had seen in the horizon of this new sunrise a future with the man who had delivered her from her troubles.

The way he had looked at her. With such desire. It was impossible to resist such a hope.

But when she had looked in the mirror, water filled the lungs of her hope and drowned it. Gravity pulled it into the blackness of the depths below. Forever destroying even the unreasonableness of a desperate attempt at a miraculous resuscitation.

The sunrise vanished. Darkness returned in mocking triumph. All she had now was a gutted soul, an echo chamber in her mind filled with familiar voices telling her she was ugly, and a bed covered with fashion and diet and exercise magazines.

The insane compulsion to look at the magazines was demanding attention. She tore into the magazines with even more energy than she had shown at Barnes and Noble, while she simultaneously pondered odd and troubling feelings.

One, she somehow knew the ravenous hunger to look at images of beautiful women was insatiable. It would never and could never be satisfied. And yet...

Two, she also knew, but had not an inkling of how it was so, that this monstrous desire was tearing her apart—literally. It was like she was breaking up into a million pieces.

It made no sense.

***

Self-Hatred congratulated himself with a wide, closed-mouth grin. It made perfect sense to him.

Chapter 61

Josiah watched Allison make her way to the door.

"I'll be back in a couple of hours," she said. "I hope you have a good talk. I'll give Myra a call when I'm on the way."

"Thank you," said Josiah, as the door closed.

He hadn't told Allison about Myra's conversion. *Good thing,* he thought. *It was probably fake news anyway.* Then it dawned on him that Myra and Allison had been together at work all day and Myra had apparently not said anything to Allison about her becoming a Christian.

Despite his own doubts of her salvation, it chafed him that she had not mentioned to Allison that she was now a Christian. *More proof that she was not in God's family.*

He repeatedly rehearsed what he would say to her. This discussion was too serious not to know exactly how he would proceed. Thirty minutes later Myra opened the front door.

Josiah was seated on one of the living room chairs. He looked at her purse. He thought of his sisters, Yomawu and Mawusi, speaking of the magic of the purse. It was foolishness, of course. Still, his mind went absolutely blank.

"Oh, hey, Josiah."

Josiah was puzzled. Her mood was exactly opposite of what it had been the night before. Not only was there not the slightest sign of joy. Her face was nothing but sadness covered with a sheer, limp smile. "How are you feeling? Is everything well at work?"

"Josiah," she said.

He waited through her long pause. He looked into her eyes and saw fatigue and defeat. They begged him for help. In a moment, he was off the chair and standing before her. "Tell me what it is," he said, softly.

"It's back, Josiah."

"What's back?"

"Everything." Before he could ask for more, she said, "I have to sit down."

They sat.

Josiah was unaware that he was holding her hand. "Tell me everything. I want to hear."

The impulse for Myra to smile at Josiah's interest and tenderness could not break through the granite of the weight that was crushing her. "The depression is back. Last night when you prayed for me—"Myra tried to recall how free she had felt less than twenty-four hours ago; she couldn't—"it was magical. Everything just stopped. The heaviness. The helmet. They were just gone."

Helmet? He thought. "And now they're back?" he asked.

"Yes. I did what you said, Josiah. And I was serious about allowing you to baptize me again. Why did it return? Why would God do something like that? Why would He give me something only to take it back? I don't understand."

"I think I do understand."

"You do?"

"Yes, I think I am the cause."

Myra's heavy eyelids parted wider.

"Myra, I made a grave mistake. I wanted so badly for you to enter life that I widened the road."

"What do you mean widened the road?"

"Jesus said, 'Broad is the road that leads to destruction, and there are many who go that way. But narrow is the road that leads to eternal life, and there are only a few who find it.' I made the road to eternal life wider by leaving out the most important part, and I said nothing of the wide road of destruction. I must make this right. I must share with you the true gospel."

Chapter 62

"Okay, this is it," said Self-Hatred, his voice carrying the confidence of past victories, but also a hint of caution. You just never knew what God would do. He could be arbitrary and unfair in the extreme.

Most Vicious took his intense eyes off Josiah. "I requested you to make this victory certain."

Self-Hatred kept peering at the woman. "*My* work is certain, Most Vicious. But I cannot account for you know who."

Vicious's eyes narrowed. "Mercy angels?"

Oh darkness! Thought Self-Hatred. Every muscle in his body contracted him into a frozen position. Only his widened, terrified eyes moved, searching for the big-headed cannibals.

"What is wrong with you?" demanded Vicious.

Self-Hatred remained hopefully frozen in safety for several more seconds, ignoring Vicious. When he saw that the dignitary's movements hadn't ended in a violent, gooey, black mess, he slowly turned his head in every direction.

Vicious was appalled and intrigued at the demon's terror. "What is it about mercy angels that command such fear in your ranks?"

Self-Hatred might have tried to protect his ego, but there wasn't a tactical demon anywhere that would not have responded the same way. "Lord Vicious, I am certainly not among your class. However, I would humbly suggest that you do be careful with your use of the words," he lowered his voice, "mercy angels. They can be quite demoralizing."

"This stronghold is—"

Self-Hatred raised his palm. His fingers stretched and spread apart. "History—the moment mercy angels show up."

"There are rules," Vicious stated forcefully.

Self-Hatred's smile was without humor. "That they don't follow."

Vicious eyed him as though they had no history together. Self-Hatred could feel the dignitary's blood beginning to boil. He'd have to be careful how he explained the way things worked at the tactical level.

"Lord Vicious, I have heard from friends...well, really friends of friends of rulers that it is a rare thing for mercy angels to trespass into the higher realms. But here, on this level, mercy angels can pop up at any time." He flicked his hand. "Bite off a head here...rip out an organ there...whatever scratches their itch. They're really quite volatile. And rules? I doubt they can even spell the word."

Lord Vicious didn't stop seething, but Self-Hatred sensed that the special demon's anger was no longer directed at him.

Vicious mumbled the wretched Scripture contemptuously, "Mercy rejoices over judgment."

"Exactly," said Self-Hatred. He added, "Unfortunately for us."

Lord Vicious could hardly wait to get out of the muck and mire of wallowing around in the mud with tactical demons. He was a strategist, not a street sweeper. "So we do all of this and mercy angels can just march in and do whatever the darkness they want," he snapped.

Self-Hatred said, "Of course, if we had spirits of unforgiveness that would significantly lower our risk. They're the only kind of demons I've ever heard of taking on," his voice lowered, "mercy angels and living to tell the story."

Vicious had a disgusted look on his face. "Is there anything *else* I need to know?"

"I think we're okay," said Self-Hatred.

You think we're okay, thought Vicious. "And what about this African? He's about to explain the true gospel to this woman. What happens if this dog repents and believes the gospel? What about this army of yours? Where is it?"

"I believe we are in superb shape, but..."

"Another last-minute fox hole revelation?" said Vicious.

"True salvation can produce unanticipated consequences." Self-Hatred looked into those evil eyes and wondered what Vicious was thinking. A demon of his stature wasn't used to the changing whims of low-level warfare. "At least that has been my experience. I think it would be wise to sound the alarm."

Vicious could hardly keep from screaming. He held his menacing voice low. "Self-Hatred, the more you peel the fruit, the more I see it is rotten."

"Lord Vicious, with all due respect, I've peeled the fruit given to me."

"Your army!" snapped Vicious.

"My army is ready."

Both demons whipped their head around when Myra lifted her hands and said, "Lord Jesus, please wash away my sins. I'll do whatever you want. I'm tired of the life I'm living."

They watched her burst into tears and sob so greatly that her body shook. She slumped to her knees. Vicious spat on the ground when she got on her face and pressed her forehead into the carpet and screamed, "Jeeeeesus!"

Self-Hatred was sure he knew what was next. He was on the move, getting out of the courtyard meeting area and hurrying toward the tunnel leading inside the formidable structure. He looked over his shoulder. "Lord Vicious," he yelled, "we have to find somewhere safe."

"What's that sound I hear?" said Vicious. "Do you hear it?"

Self-Hatred yelled again, "Lord, you have to—"

The demon's mouth gaped open for a split second as he stopped and stared at the wall of water rushing their way. He snapped out of his suicidal trance and glanced at Lord Vicious. *A regal deer in headlights,* he thought, as he shot through the arched opening.

Chapter 63

Vicious was indeed like a deer staring at oncoming headlights. It was absolutely fascinating. He didn't often see these types of things at his level of warfare. Actually, rarely was he ever this close to see anything. It was mostly strategy behind closed doors, and only occasionally was he able to experience the thrill of being close to battle.

The glistening white wall of rushing water contrasted brilliantly against the backdrop of the violent ceiling of thunderous, rolling black clouds. Each flash of lightning and booming of thunder heightened his exhilaration. He braced his back foot and pushed against the strong, hot wind gusts that threatened to knock him over backward.

What is this? he wondered.

A voice spoke from the clouds. "It is written, 'The Lord has His way, in the whirlwind and in the storm, and the clouds are the dust of His feet.'"

That's Nahum, he thought, in inexplicable near giddiness.

Vicious was like a young child at a concert who had just been called to the stage by his teen idol. Had he just heard the voice of the Lord? Then it dawned on him that the voice, whoever it belonged to, had read his mind. Vicious didn't realize that his mouth was wide open. Or that the wall of water was almost upon him.

It was the searing blast of hot air and the explosion from the lightning bolt striking the center of the meeting area that unlocked him from his own trance. He jumped back with bulging eyes. "Darkness!" he gasped. He turned to run.

Hideous.

Vicious turned back around. His footstool was looking longingly at the wall of water. Vicious ran to him and grabbed him by an ankle and ran toward the tunnel. "Your miserable life isn't over until I say it's over," he said to the groaning demon.

In a moment, the white water smashed the stronghold and covered it in thick dark clouds and fire.

Chapter 64

Josiah was elated. This is what had been missing. A revelation of her own sinfulness. She wasn't using God as a waiter. She was bowed before Him in brokenness and true repentance. Josiah wanted to drop to his knees beside her and give her support. He told himself no. He would not interfere with the work of God.

Finally, Myra helped herself to her knees. Josiah looked at her nose and hurried to the restroom. He returned with a handful of tissue.

"Thank you," she said, and blew her nose.

Josiah struggled not to say anything. His expression was nondescript, but he was turning cartwheels inside.

Myra blew her nose again and remained on her knees. Her head gently shook side to side as she spoke. "I've never felt this clean in all my life. I feel like I've been washed inside. Like a river has run through me."

She sat back on her calves and tilted her face upward. Her eyes were closed. A beautiful, peaceful smile rested lightly on her face. "I saw something, Josiah."

His eyes widened excitedly. "What did you see?"

"I saw..." She shook her head a couple of times as tears rolled down her cheeks and dissolved into the corners of her closed lips. Her chest bounced as she cried inwardly. In a few moments, voiceless pants of emotion pulsated from her mouth.

Josiah wiped his eyes.

"I saw a wall of water. A tsunami. And dark clouds and lightning and thunder. They all came upon me. But they didn't hurt me. They went inside of me. The water cleansed me. There was fire, too. It burned so much. I could feel things inside me disappearing."

"You had a vision," Josiah said, with glee."

"Two," said Myra.

"You had another one?"

Myra laughed and cried. She opened her eyes. They glistened with tears and sparkled with joy. "This thing was stalking me. It was really a person, but not human. It was like—I had the feeling it was an angel. But it was coming to kill me."

"That is not good news," said Josiah.

She searched for the right words. "It didn't really *want* to kill me. It was more like it *had* to kill me. It was a deputy or a bill collector or something. It was like I owed someone something I couldn't pay. He was coming to collect. I don't know. It's hard to describe." She paused. "But when the fire burned away the junk, and the river washed away the garbage, my debt was gone. I was innocent. That's when I heard the voices."

"What voices, Myra? Tell me."

"Someone said, 'And what of the woman?' Then a really deep voice, a voice that seemed to fill the universe, it said, 'She has passed from death into life. Myra is my daughter.'"

Josiah was leaning forward almost off the chair. "A really deep voice? It said Myra is *my* daughter? Myra, that was God," he said, in awe.

"I guess so, Josiah. He did say *my* daughter. He didn't say His daughter or God's daughter."

Josiah silently and motionlessly stared at. Did she understand that the Almighty God had spoken to her?

"Josiah, you look more surprised than I am." She smiled. "You really should start believing that God answers prayer."

He smiled widely and sat back in the chair. He bounced his body forward and backward as he tapped on both chair arms. "Two visions. Ha-haaaaaa... You know what you are, Myra?"

She looked at him with a closed-mouth smile and waited a couple of seconds. "Tell me," she prompted.

"You had not one vision, but two. And you heard voices. One of them was the Almighty. Myra?"

She waited, smiling.

"You are a nut."

She looked at him, but thought upon the fresh memory of the visions and voices. Her soul was so clean and free. "Yeah, I guess I am. And you know what, Josiah?"

"What?"

"I like it. I like being God's nut. I'll be anything He wants me to be." Josiah's words came back to her mind. *And you heard voices.*

Myra's smile remained. As did the incredible joy and lightness she felt. But now she found herself wondering about voices. The other voices.

Chapter 65

Vicious was face down on the ground in a puddle of mud when his fluttering eyes finally opened. He tried to breathe and coughed when the mud clogged his mouth and nostrils. He lifted his face and immediately felt horrible pain. It was his back and butt.

Before he could shake the confusion and explore his pain, to the left a ball of fire caught his eye. A demon—a very slow moving demon—was on fire. What an odd spectacle? How could any demon be on fire and still—?

Wait a minute, he thought. "Exhaustion? Is that you?"

Exhaustion continued his slow-motion sprint to nowhere, stopping and turning and slowly waving his arms as he studied where to go.

"Roll on the ground, you dumb slug," barked Vicious. But Exhaustion was trapped in panic. He hadn't even heard Vicious. *What an idiot,* thought Vicious.

The pain in his back and butt was now unbearable. He placed his hand near his butt and snatched it away. He looked behind him and saw flames. His butt was on fire!

Vicious jumped to his feet and looked behind. It wasn't just his butt. His back and legs were on fire, too. Panic gripped him. He knew he should do something. The signal in his brain was bucking up and down like a rodeo bull ferociously trying to kick out of the stall. But he couldn't think straight. The fire deep in his spiritual flesh commanded every ounce of mental activity. He bounced around, flapping his arms, trying to pat the fire out.

Self-Hatred watched the entertainment from the inside of the stronghold. He surveyed his knee with his hand and grimaced through his smile as he stayed fixed on the dignitary. Self-Hatred was battered and bruised, but he wasn't on fire like the master strategist down there.

He shook his head with a condescending smile. *At least take the coat off,* he thought. Then he said, "With geniuses like this running the show, there's no wonder we've got reservations for the lake of fire."

Self-Hatred made his way, moving debris and stepping over demons to get outside. He looked at Lord Most Vicious, Special Representative of the Council of Hatred of All Women, hopping around and flapping like an idiot and chuckled.

"Roll on the ground!" he shouted, as he, with much deliberate effort, dramatically hobbled toward Vicious. "Roll on the ground," he shouted again and added under his breath, "you idiot," as he emphatically pointed to the ground.

It clicked. The rodeo bull burst from the stall.

Vicious spotted the puddle he had gotten out of and ran to it and jumped on his back. He groaned as the muddy water quenched the flames.

"You're lucky you made it," said Self-Hatred.

Vicious was unaware that his continued groans of relief were anything but dignified. The pain finally lessened enough for him to realize he was lying in the mud and relishing it like a hog.

He looked up from his shameful posture into the face of Self-Hatred. The demon's amusement wasn't evident on his face. But Vicious knew inside he was laughing hysterically.

With difficulty, He slowly came to his feet. He wanted terribly to rub his butt, but he knew this event was certain to hit the gossip highway. He didn't need to add butt-rubbing to the humiliating story.

"We lost a lot of demons." Self-Hatred pursed his lips nonchalantly. "To be expected, I suppose."

To be expected? thought Vicious. He tried to mask his question as a statement that any demon at his level would ask a tactical demon. "You were expecting this?"

"As they say, what goes up must come down. Or another way of putting it is, you sow like the wind and reap like the whirlwind. One of the few Scriptures I know," said Self-Hatred.

"It's 'they sow the wind and reap the whirlwind,'" Vicious corrected.

"Oh, there's no like in it?" said Self-Hatred. "Hmm. I added to the Scripture, didn't I? Anyway, I wouldn't expect this type of thing to happen at your level. But it's a danger we deal with all the time. Someone turns from darkness to light," the demon looped his long arm as though he were releasing a bowling ball down the lane, "and here comes the fire and water."

"This happens every time?"

Self-Hatred deeply nodded once. "Every. Single. Time. The fire burns the garbage. The water washes it away. Every time."

Vicious eyed the structure. It was horribly damaged. He involuntarily reached for his butt and stopped when he saw Self-Hatred intently looking at his hand.

"Looks even worse inside," said Self-Hatred.

A slow-moving demon ablaze in a ball of fire moved within ten yards of them and collapsed face down.

"Isn't that the asthma demon?" said Self-Hatred.

"It's Exhaustion," said Vicious. "He's not...*wasn't* an asthma demon."

"Well, he's running a bit of a temperature now, isn't he?" Self-Hatred watched Vicious stare intently at the burning demon. He was uncertain whether he had crossed a line with his caustic statement. "Lord Vicious, I know he had grown useful to you. I hope I—"

"Have you seen my footstool?" said Vicious.

"Your footstool? Oh, you mean Hideous. That pathetic, broken demon. I'm pretty sure I saw him being swept away in the flood." Self-Hatred left out the part about the smile on the demon's face and the middle finger he held shoulder high as he was carried off.

Vicious screamed a curse. He simmered at the thought of losing his trophy. "That worthless piece of garbage."

Self-Hatred said, "That he certainly was."

"How many have I lost?"

"I would estimate that you've lost eighty percent of your demons. And of those who remain, only a handful aren't severely injured. Those who were carried off will try later to return. How much later, who knows? The remaining demons will try to help them back in."

Vicious was stunned. A stronghold demolished in a moment. And his name was on this mess. He'd have to answer for this failure.

Self-Hatred knew Vicious wasn't well-versed in the intricacies of low-level warfare. But he had no idea that a demon of his ferocity and reputation could be *this* ignorant about such elementary matters. What did he think happened when someone turned to God?

Wasn't he the one always spouting off Scriptures like he was some kind of theologian? There was a big difference in quoting God's word and understanding it.

"All is not lost, Lord Vicious."

Vicious looked at him as though he had lost his mind.

Self-Hatred slowly stretched his arm left to right as he spoke. "*This* is why you called me."

Vicious's eyes bore into the demon. He contemplated the repercussions of ripping to pieces a demon who was so well-connected and highly esteemed among powerful principalities.

Self-Hatred read the demon's eyes. "Fortunately, Most Vicious, it would be quite premature of you to resort to violence just yet—when the fun is finally about to begin. My army—"

"Enough of your lies!" screamed Vicious. "Look around you. All is lost. You've been promising an army since the first day you showed up. You're a fake."

Self-Hatred looked at Vicious in his high-level eyes. "I am many things, Most Vicious. Fake is not one of them. Look at the woman."

He did.

Vicious went through a series of open-mouth expressions. "What is this?" he said, as armed long-haired soldiers poured out of and into the woman. Then he saw their faces. He looked at Self-Hatred in bewilderment. "I...don't understand. How can this be? The soldiers...they look like the woman."

"Lord Vicious, they are the woman," said Self-Hatred.

Lord Vicious wasn't a street-level tactician. But he was a strategist. He now saw it completely. "You convinced the woman to hate herself. This causes a civil war within her. Like an autoimmune disease. The body fighting itself. Like cancer cells fighting good cells. She's fighting herself."

"Exactly," said Self-Hatred.

Vicious grinned darkly. "You knew the fire and flood were coming. You hid your army."

"Guilty as charged, Lord Vicious. True salvation is quite a precarious and unpredictable thing. The fire and flood may instantly wipe out an entire stronghold." He snapped his finger. "Just like that. Or it may leave it standing. But I'm quite adept at outlasting a salvation event."

"You're expecting another attack, aren't you?" asked Vicious. "From angels this time."

"I suspect that will be the case," said Self-Hatred.

"And their superior numbers—"

Self-Hatred jumped into his own story. "Won't mean a thing. As long as the woman fights herself, they...can't...win. God doesn't force anyone to be free."

"When do you think the angels will attack?" asked Vicious, anxious to turn his loss into a victory.

Self-Hatred stared at the woman. Vicious followed the demon's eyes. They both stared at her. Then she said something to Josiah that answered their question.

***

"Josiah, I don't want to keep secrets from you any longer. I need to tell you something, but I'm afraid you'll," she hesitated, "think differently of me."

He took her hand. "Please. You can tell me anything. I will not judge you."

Chapter 66

She had told him all. Beginning from her failed child beauty pageants to the depression and voices. Myra wiped a tear from her eye, while looking sadly at the carpet.

She dared not look Josiah in his eyes. He'd see her fear of being rejected by him. And as unlikely as it was that he shared her desire to explore the possibility of a romantic relationship, she knew she did not want to be rejected by this man.

He said nothing for several moments. Several excruciating moments for Myra.

She had just shared the most intimate details of her life with Josiah. More than she had even shared with her therapist. She had known this could backfire on her. That it could push him away. Yet, she had also known that her heart would not allow her to keep such a secret from him. Not if...

And that's where it had gotten incredibly confusing. Only days ago, he was simply an irritating, religious nut. Beautiful, yes, but no less irritating and nutty. Now days later, it was impossible to deny that something had happened to her heart.

She was in his orbit. His gravity had captured her and was pulling her irresistibly toward him. Escape was impossible. It was also unwanted. But his silence had spoken. This relationship was purely project driven. It had served its purpose.

Yet, Myra found herself strangely at peace. For even though Josiah was not a part of her future, His God was. And not *his* God. God was *her* God. She had heard His voice. He had called her by name. She had heard Him call her His daughter.

"Myra," said Josiah.

She lifted her head and looked at him. In the deep ocean of her soul she was at peace. But she prepared for the crashing of waves against the rocks. "Yes, Josiah," she answered bravely.

He got on one knee in front of her. He put his hand on the side of her face and neck. It was large and warm and cupped her securely. His thumb caught and ended her tear. He said softly, "I will not leave you."

Myra heard the embarrassing low horn sound in her throat.

"I told you that you can tell me anything. I will never judge you harshly. I will never abandon you. I will never leave you."

Myra and Josiah both wondered at his words. *What exactly was he saying?*

Myra's throat went dry. She coughed lightly.

Josiah sprang to his feet. "I will get you some water." *Lord, my God, I am certainly not myself,* he thought.

He got both of them a bottle of water and drank half of his before he turned around to return to Myra. Maybe the break and water would help him think and speak more clearly. He brought her the water.

Myra stared at his face as he handed the bottle to her. She said nothing as she extended her hand to take it. He said, "Here, let me open it for you." He handed it to her and wondered why he could not say or do the simplest thing to her without making it seem like something more.

"Thank you, Josiah." She took a nervous swallow, trying to process the moment.

"Things will be different now, Myra. You have a new life. Old things have passed away. The devil no longer owns you."

"I do feel new."

"There will now be peace and joy," he said.

A few awkward moments passed.

"It's nice to have a friend like you," said Myra. *Well, someone had to say something!*

"It is also nice to have a friend like you." He had no idea what to say next. Apparently, neither did Myra. His phone rang. *Thank you, Jesus!* He didn't say it, but he felt his bones shouting it.

He looked at his phone with puzzlement and swiped. "Mama? Is everything blessed?" He listened. "A dream?" He looked at Myra and motioned with his finger. He stood and walked away a couple of steps. He abruptly stopped and slowly turned back around.

Whatever his mother had said made Josiah start stammering. Myra hoped everything was okay. She said as much with her eyes. His awkward stare registered surprise and slight panic and only heightened her concern.

"I—well, Mama—yes, I do know His eyes run to and fro—no, nothing is hidden from His sight. Yes, Mama, I know that without holiness no man shall see the Lord. Yes, Mama, the road is straight and narrow."

"She is there, is she not?" Mama demanded.

Josiah's eyes widened. He said nothing. He couldn't. He didn't know what to do.

"Boy, the woman is with you now."

"Mama—"

"You will put this woman on the phone, or I will wake up Papa. We will catch a flight and be there in one day to examine your soul."

Josiah's forehead was moist with perspiration. *Oh my God and King, how could You do this to me?* He said, "Mama, please do not wake Papa. Everything is holy."

"Boy, I will not discuss this with you till the second coming of Christ. If I hang up, do not call back. For you will see the face of your Mama and Papa in one day. The face of the prophetess and pastor. We will not come in peace. Put the female on the phone now."

Josiah slowly stretched out his arm. Myra looked surprised. "Mama wants to talk to you." The thought came to his mind to hurry instructions to Myra. What good would that do? He shook his head in defeat and handed Myra the phone and went to the bathroom. He was feeling sick.

Chapter 67

"Myra," answered Myra.

"I am Mama. Josiah is my boy. It is four o'clock in the morning, and I am on the phone talking to you. Do you know why I am on the phone talking to you at four o'clock in the morning?"

"No, Mrs..."

"It is not Mrs. Mama. Just Mama."

Mama? She wants me to call her Mama. Myra couldn't help but to be pleased and amused. "No, Mama," said Myra, as though each word was a complete sentence.

"I am talking to you at four o'clock in the morning because the Almighty told me that you are with my boy. Is he there to lay hands?"

Myra wanted to make a good impression. She thought of conversations she'd had with Josiah. She brightened. "Not yet. I think he's going to though. My roommate isn't here. So it's just the two of us. I'm ready. He has prepared me well." Myra added with feeling, "I really want this."

Mama gasped and clutched her chest and howled as she ran through the house. "Pa-paaaaa!"

Myra became alarmed. She went to the restroom and knocked. The toilet flushed. She bubbled her eyes. Things were getting really intimate, really quickly. The door opened. Josiah's eyes looked bad.

"I think you need to speak to your mom. Are you feeling okay?"

"I am better."

Myra looked at his expression. "You don't look better."

"I will be better," he said. He placed his ear to the phone and heard a lot of high volume talking. He couldn't make out what was being said, but he was familiar with the pattern. Mama and Papa were upset! "Myra, what did Mama say? What did you tell her?"

"Not much. She told me to call her Mama. I did. And she asked one question. That's all."

"What did she ask?"

"She asked did you come here to lay hands on me?"

Josiah's muscles weakened. His nausea returned. He placed his hands on both of her shoulders and squeezed lightly. "Myra, tell me. What did you answer?"

Myra didn't understand why Josiah was so tense. He seemed to be expecting the worst. Maybe it was a cultural or family thing. She was happy that she could relieve him of any worries.

"Relax, Josiah. I told her that you hadn't yet laid hands on me, but that we were alone. So I thought you would." Myra didn't know Josiah's insides were sinking to his feet as she spoke. She smiled. "I told her...Mama, that I'm ready. That you prepared me well. And that I really wanted it."

"That is what you told Mama?"

"Yep, that's what I told her." Myra's happy expression changed to match Josiah's. "Did I say something wrong? I thought you would lay hands on me to receive the Holy Spirit tonight while we were alone. You don't think I'm ready?"

Josiah broke out of his thoughts in a few moments and answered. "Yes, you are ready. But that is not what Mama was asking you."

"What was she asking?"

"She was asking you if I had come here with designs."

"Designs?"

"Without honor."

"Without honor?" Myra searched Josiah's face for an explanation. He arched an eyebrow. Myra's mouth dropped open. "You mean...?"

"In my culture, to lay hands on a woman is to..."

"Sex," said Myra, leaving her mouth open with an expression that was realizing in layers the comedy of the situation.

"Yes," said Josiah. "Mama asked you if I came here to have sex with you."

Myra smiled, then could hold it no longer. She burst out laughing. And laughing. And laughing.

"I am glad you can find amusement in my crucifixion."

"Oh my...oh...my...goodness," Myra laughed hard for several moments. "Designs," she laughed. "I guess I can see the laying hands business, but designs, Josiah?"

Josiah had never seen this side of Myra. He didn't know she had such laughter in her. It was quite appealing. A happy woman was ten thousand times better than a sad woman.

"Who came up with these sayings?" asked Myra. Her laughter had died down, but appeared to Josiah to be like a quenched forest fire waiting to flare up again.

"I do not know." As he looked at her, he found himself tempted to also see the comedy of the moment. But he was in a tight spot. If he didn't handle this correctly, he could very well be looking into the faces of his parents within a day or so—*Pastor Papa and Prophetess Mama!*

"Josiah, just explain to them what happened," Myra coaxed. "They'll understand."

"It is not that simple."

Myra shook her head. "Josiah, it is." She smiled.

"It is a process."

"What process?"

"You will see." He put the phone on speaker. They waited another five or so minutes listening to Mama and Papa energetically discuss which of them had failed most as a parent, and how Josiah's transgressions would affect the family and church.

"Are they for real?" asked Myra.

"This is part of the process," said Josiah.

"Boy, are you there?" asked Papa.

"I am here, Papa."

"And that is the problem. You are there, and you are not supposed to be there. This is a great tragedy. This offense must be properly dealt with. This is a church matter."

"Papa, I did not come here to lay hands. I came with honor. I came to help my friend."

"The woman said you are there to help yourself. The woman expects you to lay hands on her. Is she a dumb woman?"

"No, Papa, she is very intelligent."

"You are correct, she is not a dumb woman. For she is smart enough to know you have prepared her for the purpose of hands."

"Papa, that is not what she meant."

"The woman told Mama that she is expecting this and is looking forward to this sin."

"She is Delilah," Mama cried into the phone over Papa's voice.

"Your son prepared her for hands," said Papa. "This does not sound like Delilah. It sounds like Bathsheba. Josiah is King David. He is not Samson."

"Samson and Delilah? David and Bathsheba?" Myra said to Josiah. "I did go to church as a child. I know who these people are."

The process went on until Myra felt the last drop had been squeezed out of the comedy sponge. She broke into Papa's speech. "Papa, this is Myra. May I please speak to Mama?"

"What are you doing?" Josiah whispered, shaking his head at the indiscretion. "I will be instructed about this."

"This could go on forever," she whispered back. "Someone's got to stop this merry-go-round."

Papa was shocked that the young woman had interrupted him. He handed the phone to Mama. "Mama is here," declared Mama. Papa also had his ear to the phone.

"Mama, I have something to say."

"The woman is confessing her sin," Mama said to Papa.

"That is good," said Papa.

Myra had experienced enough of the process to know that she had to stay on track. Otherwise, Mama and Papa would go off on another tangent. "Josiah came to my home with honor. When you asked me whether he had come to lay hands on me, I thought you were asking if he was going to pray for me to receive the Holy Spirit. I did not know that the term in your culture meant physical intimacy. I apologize."

Mama and Papa were quiet.

Josiah looked at the phone. He looked at Myra.

"He is there for the Holy Spirit?" asked Mama.

Myra and Josiah looked at one another. She shrugged at him with an open palm. "It's not a lie," she whispered to him. "You would've prayed for me eventually, right?"

He nodded.

"Yes. Josiah led me to the Lord. I am a new person because of him."

Mama and Papa laughed in relief. Papa popped away from the phone and waved his arms over his head as he spoke. "Mama, I do not know why your rooster crows at midnight. Your facts are too early. You get me all riled up with bad data. I knew my son would not go to a woman's home without honor."

"Your words are on record with the Most High, Papa. You cannot put the echo back into your mouth." Mama turned her attention to Myra. "I must apologize for Papa and for calling you Delilah. This whole thing could have been avoided had Josiah moved his lips."

"It's understandable," said Myra.

"Now, we must hear of this conversion," said Mama.

Papa yelled from another room. "Has she been cleansed?"

"I don't know," Mama yelled back. "Did Josiah clean you up?"

Josiah's eyes widened. "Please, give me the phone, Myra."

She did.

He took it off speaker. "No, Mama." He began to whisper. "I do not believe she needs this. She has had a glorious transformation."

"Is this woman human?" asked Mama.

"Yes, Mama, but she—"

"Papa," Mama yelled out.

"Mama, really, I am here, and I see the work of the Lord in her," said Josiah. "I would know if she needed to be cleansed."

"Put the woman on the phone," said Mama. "Papa, Josiah's cake has no eggs. The woman has not been cleansed."

Josiah covered the phone. "Myra..." he searched for a way to tell her.

"What?"

"There is a custom we have in the church." She looked at him waiting for more. "The early church did it for everyone who came to the Lord."

"Did what?"

"They prayed for them."

"Okay," she said, wondering what was so different about that.

"It was a special kind of prayer."

"Okay."

"It was a prayer to make demons leave people." He waited for her response. He couldn't blame her if she was offended. In Africa, people knew demons were real. This was not the case in America.

"This special prayer is for people who have already come to God?"

"Yes. It is to make sure that the new Christian does not bring any demons with him from the old life into the new life." He looked apologetic. "I am s—"

Myra cut him off. "I want this prayer. Give me the phone."

Chapter 68

"What is this special prayer they're talking about?" asked Vicious. "Should we be concerned?"

Self-Hatred masked his surprise at the question. *Only if you're not suicidal,* he thought. "Yes," he answered simply.

"What's so special about it? Prayer is prayer. We deal with it all the time in the higher realms. The effects may not become bothersome for years—if ever."

"Of course, Lord Vicious, you are correct..." He paused until he could see Vicious was anxious for him to continue. "If you are speaking of intercession." He paused again. "I have no experience in the higher realms. But others more knowledgeable than I," *and you, you glorified moron,* he thought, "have remarked that the effects of intercessory prayer in high areas are usually invisible and indiscernible until—" Self-Hatred searched futilely for the right words. "I guess there's no better way to say it. Until all hell breaks loose."

This was a hazard Vicious understood. Situations at the higher levels required great amounts of persistent prayer from the saints to cause damage. Things would seemingly be going the way of darkness, even getting worse—or *better* if you were a demon—and then one more wretched child of God would lift up one more wretched prayer, or darkness forbid, a tear.

This line of thoughts revived memories of old failures and old wounds. Vicious unconsciously rubbed his burning butt. "Your sources have their facts straight. What's the difference in intercessory prayer and this prayer you're talking about?"

"Lord Vicious, this kind of prayer is called deliverance prayer."

"People pray for deliverance all the time," said Vicious, unimpressed.

"Yes, but that's petition and supplication. Asking God to do something and then waiting for Him to do it." Self-Hatred looked around as though he was expecting something. "This is not asking and waiting. It's commanding and taking."

"Commanding and taking? You can't command and take anything from the enemy."

Self-Hatred was unsure if his usual ability to mask his true feelings was up to the task. He looked at Vicious and thought, *My darkness, the more you open your brilliant strategy mouth, the dumber you get.*

Vicious stepped into Self-Hatred's space. "I don't like your face. You have something you want to say?"

Self-Hatred took a step backward. "My apologies, Lord Vicious, for my indiscretion. It's the stress."

Lord Vicious eyed him intently. "I understand. Stress can make you do terrible things." He stared silently at him until he was sure Self-Hatred understood his point exactly."

"Understood, Lord Vicious. We need to get back inside. Or at least, what's left of inside."

Lord Vicious didn't move. "Tell me of this deliverance prayer."

After the fire and the flood? thought Self-Hatred. *Oh, you are a fool.* "Deliverance prayer doesn't command God. It commands us."

"Commands us? That is ridiculous!"

"At your level, it's ridiculous. Prayers and armies of angels and special rules and God's sovereignty and all that jazz. But not at our level. At our level everything is dangerously simple. Some saint commands us to leave, and God unleashes the fury of heaven upon us. All they have to do is believe and speak. It's somewhere in that cursed book."

Vicious looked inside his vast reservoir of Scriptures. He'd never seen a need to memorize that Scripture, but he could faintly see it. "These signs shall follow those who believe. In my name shall they cast out demons. They are still doing that? I thought that ended when the apostles died."

"Yeah, well, some Christians do read and believe their Bibles. So, yeah, it's still being done."

"And that's what they're planning to do?" said Vicious, looking at Josiah and Myra and trying to come up with a strategy.

"Forget about strategy, Lord Vicious. There's no time for that. Once the gun barrel is pointed at you, the only strategy is to get out of the way of the bullet. We need—to get—inside."

"And what about your invincible army?" Vicious asked sarcastically.

"You did not mention there would be deliverance prayer."

"What about this army!" yelled Vicious. "Will they or will they not secure what is left? Will this or will this not be my last assignment?"

"I don't know."

Vicious let out a tirade of curses. Self-Hatred was sure the furious demon would dismember him and to hell with the consequences. Finally, Vicious said, "You go run and hide. I'm staying here. If this is to be my last battle, I will not be destroyed hunkered down under a desk.

Chapter 69

"You are crowding me, Papa." She put the phone on speaker.
"You want to be cleansed?" said Mama.

"Everything God has for me. I want it all," said Myra.

"She has no manners, but she has good sense," said Papa.

Myra's mouth dropped open. She looked at Josiah.

"You interrupted him when he was speaking. That is not something we do to our parents or elders or pastors."

Myra sighed. "You people have a lot of rules, Josiah."

"Are you sitting?" Mama asked.

Myra sat. "Yes."

"You are going to cleanse the woman over the phone, Mama?" said Papa. "Josiah can do this thing. He is there."

Mama said, "A minute ago he was there to lay hands, and you were calling a church meeting with the elders to take care of the matter. Now you want him to cleanse this woman? Anyway, you are the pastor. You know it is inappropriate for a man to cleanse a woman. It is your rule. Mama, will cleanse this woman."

Papa nodded as though this were his idea. "You must cleanse this woman," he ordered.

"You are sitting?" Mama asked again. "You need to be sitting?"

Myra looked at Josiah. "Yes, Mama." Myra whispered to Josiah, "Why is she so concerned about me sitting?"

"In the name of Jeeesus, Mama says come out!"

Myra was thrown to the floor.

Chapter 70

Lord Vicious listened to Myra and Josiah and the people on the phone with extreme interest. What was this cleansing? The woman had already been cleansed. He had a burnt butt as proof. And what was this thing Self-Hatred said about children of the enemy commanding demons and taking things from them? This scandal could not be true. Not at any level.

He suddenly felt a sense of unease. He turned in a full circle, surveying the wreckage of what used to be a stronghold. He saw no threats. Just a few damaged buildings still standing, but for the most part rubble. Rubble and terrified demons peering out at him from debris.

Cowards! he thought. If Bludgeon were here, he'd be standing right here by my side, weapons in both hands eager to fight. Another thought surfaced. What if Self-Hatred is not exaggerating? What if these low-level demons are hiding for good reason?

He spat this thought out of his mind. He was not a low-level, ditch-digging demon. He was a high-level dignitary. Special Deputy of the Council of Hatred of All Women. Even if this thing were true, it could not possibly apply to a demon of his stature.

Mama said, "In the name—"

Vicious's eyes riveted toward the sound of the voice coming from the phone. Fury pulsated from him. The thought of a woman's voice chasing him into a pile of rocks to hide like one of these low-levels made his chest rise with contempt.

"Come and get me, you putrid piece of—"

"—of Jeeeesus—"

Vicious snapped his head in every direction at the lights that popped out of nowhere. Hundreds. No thousands. He squinted and focused his eyes. They weren't lights. *They were Angels!*

He was surrounded by thousands of angels. There was no escape. He snatched out his two swords. "Sure could use you now, Bludgeon," he said, as he wondered at the stillness of the angels.

"—Mama says—"

"Weapons out!" yelled Jezrael. "Attack on her command."

On her command? Vicious was stunned.

"—come out!"

Now he was stunned and forced to fight for his life.

Chapter 71

"Mama, she is on the floor," said Josiah.

He had grown up seeing his parents cleanse many people. Falling down was common. But he had not expected Myra to fall. And he definitely had not expected her to flop around on the carpet like a fish out of water.

Thanks be unto the good Lord that Mama is—

An angel touched his phone.

"Mama? Mama, are you there?" He looked at Myra's bouncing body. He looked at his dead phone. "What is this madness? Lord, you cannot do this to me! No. No. No. No. No. I am a software engineer. I am not a deliverance minister. "

Josiah scanned the room, not knowing what he was looking for. A pillow! He hopped up and snatched one and put it under Myra's head. Her head slammed repeatedly against the pillow. He tried to calm her down by placing a hand on her shoulder. She jerked sideways. Her breast pressed hard against the back of his hand.

"Jeeesus!" he said, snatching his hand from the fire. "This is why Papa forbids this thing. It is totally inappropriate. Jesus, you have to do something here."

Jesus didn't do anything.

Josiah reached forth both hands as though he was going to hold her shoulders down to keep her from bouncing. He pulled his hands back and instead took her hand. She gripped him hard.

He felt utterly worthless. It was shameful. Mama would have made this devil behave. "Lord, make this devil behave," he pled.

Myra bounced more violently than before. Josiah looked at her face. Her eyes were shut tight. "Myra, can you hear me."

She kept bouncing.

Josiah looked at the ceiling and cried out, "Lord, are you going to help her? Why have you done this thing? I know this is You."

You help her.

Josiah continued to pray to the ceiling. For that is exactly how he felt. God was nowhere to be sensed. The only thing that came across loud and clear was that he was totally unprepared for this confrontation. The other was this troubling thought.

You help her.

Josiah answered God, but he pretended to be speaking to himself. "I may as well try to walk on water."

Peter walked on water.

"What is this?" Josiah said, loudly. "I am a software engineer."

You are a son of God. Now stop acting helpless and help her.

A realization came over Josiah that these corrective soft thoughts were the voice of the Holy Spirit. He was arguing with the Almighty! Fear swept over him. He looked down at Myra. Her eyes were still shut, but Josiah got the feeling that something was looking at him through her closed eyes. She started thrashing. Arms swinging. Legs kicking. And now a low growl coming from her closed mouth.

This caught Josiah off guard. He jumped back. A flash of holy anger hit him. He pointed and yelled, "In the name of God's holy Son Jesus, I am a son of God. You obey Papa and Mama in Africa. You will obey me in America. I bind you. Behave and stop this foolishness now!"

Everything stopped immediately.

Josiah's eyes had been wide with anger. Now they were wide with surprise. Myra's head slumped to the side. Her mouth was open. So were her eyes. But they stared straight ahead. She was so still that Josiah wondered whether the demon had killed her on the way out.

He looked at her belly and chest. He still couldn't tell whether she was breathing. He moved his head closer to her torso.

Dear Lord, what has happened here? he thought in panic.

He looked at Myra's death stare, trembling. What had he done? "Myra, are you there?" He meant this literally. For the body without the spirit was dead. And her spirit appeared to be gone.

"Myra, are you there?" he said, again, hoping against what he was seeing.

"You don't know what the hell you are doing!" barked a gruff voice.

Josiah scooted back and jumped to his feet. "Oh, Lord Jesus, this demon is still here!"

Chapter 72

I'm not going anywhere, you pathetic moron."

Josiah stared at Myra for an hour squeezed into several seconds. The demon playfully stared back. *What would Papa do?* thought Josiah.

"Well…?" the demon taunted.

Josiah felt himself withering by the moment under this evil spirit's mocking stare. What did you do once you commanded a demon to leave and he didn't obey you? Josiah's mind produced a hundred reasons why the demon was still there.

Maybe I don't pray enough.

Maybe I don't fast enough.

Maybe I have sin in my life.

Maybe I don't know enough Scripture.

Maybe God is mad at me.

Maybe I don't have enough power.

Maybe I don't have enough authority.

Maybe I enjoyed how Myra's breast felt pressed against my hand.

That's must be it. I'm not holy enough.

The list seemed to have no end.

He could tell by this demon's sneer that the demon knew that he knew he couldn't cast him out. Fear gripped Josiah. He had seen terrible confrontations between Papa and Mama and people with demons.

Papa and Mama always beat the demons, but sometimes it took them very long periods of time. Sometimes if things got tough, they would fast for days and pray for hours before going back into the battle. Plus, they had elders to help them.

Josiah couldn't leave to go pray and fast. He couldn't call for the elders. Whatever he did had to be done here and now—and alone.

Then it got even worse. There was nothing between him and this demon. Nothing could prevent this thing from jumping on him. He had seen Papa wrestle with people who had demons. He envisioned he and Myra entangled and rolling around on the floor. What if her roommate came in on that?

Lord God, please do not make me wrestle with Myra, Josiah begged.

"Leave me alone, and I'll leave you alone," said the demon.

That thing knows I'm scared, Josiah thought.

"It doesn't have to get nasty," threatened the demon.

Wait a minute. Why is this thing just lying there like that? thought Josiah. He looked at Myra's arms. They were pressed hard to her side. Her legs were straight and pressed together. She looked like she was...

She was!

Josiah's blood started circulating again. This thing couldn't hurt him. He had bound the demon, and the good Lord had heard him. Papa and Mama were not here. The elders were not here. But the Holy Spirit was here.

"You are tied up," said Josiah.

"I told you to leave me alone. Now I'm going to hurt you," said the demon.

"Heh," said Josiah. "You are like a tight cigar. The Lord has rolled you up. You will hurt no one."

"Leave me alone!" yelled the demon.

"I will not leave you alone," Josiah yelled back. "In the name of the mighty God Jesus Christ, come out of Myra."

Myra let out a long and terrible scream. Her head fell back onto the pillow. He had seen demons come out screaming many times. This was a good sign. Maybe this time the demon had really left.

Josiah wondered whether her scream had prompted someone to call the police. This matter needed to be resolved quickly. He knelt beside her on one knee. "Myra, are you okay? Is the demon gone."

"Yes," she said.

"Glory to God," said Josiah. He looked into her eyes. They didn't look like the eyes of someone who had just been delivered from a demon. They looked hard. And angry. "Demon, you are still there!"

"I'm not going anywhere!" Myra made a sound as though she would spit on Josiah.

"Demon, you will keep that spit in your mouth. In Jesus' name, come out!"

Another long scream and slumping of the head. Josiah tested to see if the demon was gone. He wasn't. This cycle went on repeatedly for over two hours. Josiah felt his faith weakening. *Lord, why won't this demon leave?* he prayed inside.

As though the demon could read his thoughts, he propped up on an elbow—he wasn't tied up any longer!—and looked at Josiah with all the confidence in the world, and said, "Because you can't cast us out. We have a right to be here."

Josiah looked at the demon in shock. Us? There's more than one demon in there?

Chapter 73

Lord Vicious had never been a low-level demon, fighting on the front lines for low value targets such as a sole woman. Someone had to do it. He just never thought he'd be among those doing it. This was nothing like the infrequent, but cataclysmic battles that took place in the heavens. Battles that determined the bondage of tens and hundreds of millions.

Nonetheless, as inglorious as it was fighting alongside ditch diggers for one female dog, Vicious surprisingly found himself appreciating and even admiring these low-levels. They had come out of their hiding places with a fury.

It was obvious they were going to lose this battle. Yet, they weren't fighting defensively. They were taking the fight to the treacherous angels like desperate, angry warriors who were defending their home from invaders. How could demons of such courage and ferocity have ever been under the command of Hideous?

But bravery was no match for the inevitable. To make matters worse, every so often that African would give a command, and one or more demons would suddenly find themselves in chains and being snatched away by an unseen force. Their terrible screams the last vaporous evidence of their surprising bravery and stubborn tenacity.

Now it appeared that inevitability was banging on his door.

Vicious crouched and circled, eyeballing the ten or so armed angels who had him surrounded. He was brave but not delusional. They were going to get him. And if by some miracle of darkness they

didn't, the hundreds of others who were closing in on this area would get him.

Then the unlikely miracle of darkness happened. Renewed fighting spontaneously broke out everywhere. The angels who had planned just moments before to make him a pin cushion were now fighting for their lives!

Vicious caught an approaching light from the corner of his eye. He turned. An angel coming right at him. Then another and another. He quickly scanned. Angels were passing by demons to get at him. *He was the objective.*

Vicious chose the fast approaching angel on his right. He'd dispatch of him and then get the one— He stopped in awe at the sight.

Winged demons descended from above with great shrieks upon the angels, biting and slashing and whipping them with their thick tails. Some spat a blinding substance onto the angels, while others swooped upon the surprised prey. Then a thunderous rumble and trembling of the ground introduced hordes of animal spirits that charged in from every direction.

A rhinoceros-like demon sank his long horn into the angel that Vicious had planned to take out first. Great gorilla spirits ran into groups of angels and beat and tossed them as though they were little children. Fiery serpent spirits filled the earth and hunted angels' legs like torpedoes hunting ships. Angels writhed on the ground in pain, nursing immediately discolored and swollen legs.

Vicious had participated in victorious battles. But he had never seen anything like this. This wasn't a fight. It was a massacre. Where had this mighty army come from?

"Protect the strongman!" said a thunderous voice.

The mysterious army surrounded Vicious.

Vicious looked around for the voice.

"Lord Vicious. Up here!"

Vicious looked. Someone was standing atop a structure, waving. It was Self-Hatred. Vicious was dumbfounded.

"My army," Self-Hatred proclaimed. "Your army."

Vicious looked around at the army in silence. There weren't words to describe this scene. This carnage of light.

"The woman," said Self-Hatred, knowing that Vicious had a hundred questions. "All that you see is her. The angels are fighting her army of self-hatred. As long as she hates herself, you are safe."

Vicious looked closer at the vast army. Spread out liberally among it was the woman. Demons who looked exactly like her, except for their darker hair and deeply grimaced face.

"This is why I have so many friends in high places," yelled Self-Hatred. "Casting out demons is one thing. Changing a person's beliefs is something entirely different. You are safe."

Chapter 74

How many ways could you tell a demon to leave? All Josiah was getting was a bunch of manifestations. But the demon was still here. And now this thing was saying there was more than one demon. What else could he do?

Talk to Myra.

Josiah doubtfully contemplated the thought. He hadn't considered that option. He hadn't known it was an option, and still didn't know. It was worth a try. He had tried everything else. "Myra, can you speak to me?"

"She doesn't want to speak to you."

"Devil, I was not talking to you. Shut up."

Myra's lips pressed tightly against one another.

"In the name of Jesus, let Myra speak to me."

Tears rolled out of both of her closed eyes.

"Stop interfering, demon. Let her open her eyes."

Myra's eyes opened. Her voice was full of woe. "Why won't it leave, Josiah? Why won't this thing leave me along? Where did it come from? Why did it choose me?"

Each question hit Josiah with the force of a penetrating projectile, burying deep within and exploding into a rupture of bloodied impotence. He had told her about the great God, and had convinced her to give her life to Him. And now when Satan was attacking her so terribly, Josiah had proven useless.

"I do not have the answer to these questions, Myra."

How cruel could life be? To experience such exhilarating joy and freedom only to have it snatched from her. The dam inside of her soul broke. She rolled over onto her side and clutched her chest. Josiah watched her body heave with desperate crying.

A memory came to Josiah. It was the boy with the stubborn demon in Mark 9. He recalled Jesus asking the father how long the boy had been afflicted before he cast the demon out.

Another memory. This time it was Mark 5. Jesus was casting out a really stubborn demon. (It was two thousand demons!) Jesus asked the demon his name before He cast them all out.

Josiah wondered about this. Papa never let a demon talk. Mama always interrogated them. They both successfully cast out demons. Both ways worked.

Josiah felt like the inmate on television who was locked in a cell and was reaching through the bars for the set of keys that was just out of reach. He pressed his face hard against the metal bars and pressed until he grabbed what he hoped were the right deliverance keys. He'd do whatever it took to get Myra free.

"Myra, the Lord has given me hope."

Myra's desperate cries continued.

"In the name of Jesus, who are you? I command you to tell me your name!"

Myra immediately stopped crying.

Chapter 75

The angel had only caught a glimpse of the rhinoceros demon before its horn caught him under one arm and burst through the flesh of his other arm. The beast violently shook the impaled angel in every direction before he was thrown free.

The angel landed grotesquely on a bunch of jagged rocks. His head slammed against one, stunning him. The blow to the head was not enough to quiet the raging pain that filled his upper body.

"Lord God," he said, weakly, wanting to stay in the fight. He looked down at his right hand. His clenched fist still firmly gripped the long sword. His dagger, however, was lost somewhere out there amidst the fighting.

Angels didn't die. But according to the rules of spiritual warfare, if one of these demons finished him off, he'd be taken off the battlefield—forever. Everything in him fought this horrid possibility. He was a ministering spirit, a captain of angels, sent forth to serve God by fighting battles for and with people. *That was his high calling!*

But here he was lying helplessly on the ground in a broken, bloodied, and half-conscious heap. If he were spotted, his direct service to people would be over.

The angel turned his woozy head to the left. Nothing but fighting. Swords and daggers swinging. Javelins and arrows and knives flying. Hand to hand combat. Grunts and cries and...

Amidst the fierce fighting was something odd. It was like a wide bowling lane sectioning off the chaos of war on both sides. At the end of the uncluttered path there was that rhinoceros demon staring at him with blazing red eyes. The beast repeatedly pushed the soil back with his hooves in preparation of his attack.

The angel's fighting instinct kicked in. His expression hardened as he gritted his teeth. He tried to arise. His broken and punctured body rose a few painful inches and fell back to the wet ground. All he could do was lie there and wait for the demon to finish his assault.

Jezrael thought of Aaron-Hur and Mishnak. They were safe.

He thought of Myra's likely future. She had submitted her life to God and had received eternal life. But she still had demons. She'd be like so many others who truly loved the Lord, but who would live in unnecessary bondage because the job was incomplete.

With great effort, he lifted his head and looked at the battlefield. He had never been a part of such a disaster. *And why were there demons that looked like Myra?* He looked at the rhinoceros. Somehow, he even saw Myra's face on this demon. It shook its big horned head and started running toward him.

Jezrael rested his head on the stone and stared toward heaven. A tear rolled down his holy face. *If only they would use their authority in Christ,* he thought, as he felt the demon almost upon him. "Creator, I am sorry for failing you. I am sorry for failing your daughter."

Chapter 76

Josiah was surprised at the immediate effect on Myra. He watched her lift herself to her hands and knees. He couldn't entirely see her face.

"What are you doing?" came the whisper from under Myra's hanging hair.

Was this Myra or the demon talking to him? Josiah asked tentatively, "Myra, is that you?"

The whispery, simmering answer came through clenched teeth. "What do you think?"

"Demon, it's you," Josiah said, with surprise.

"What an idiot," said the demon.

Josiah got distracted by the insult for a couple of seconds before recovering. "I command you in the name of Jesus to tell me your name."

The demon didn't answer.

"I said tell me your name," Josiah yelled. "I command you to talk to me."

"I'm not deaf," said the demon. "You don't have to yell."

"Demon, you don't tell me how to cast you out."

"You need someone to tell you what to do."

"I do not need a demon to tell me anything. I have the Holy Spirit."

"That's not all you have." The demon chuckled at his private joke.

"What do you mean by that, demon? What are you saying I have?"

"Bad breath."

Josiah was shocked at this demon's behavior.

"Smells like a dog's butt," the demon added.

Josiah blew into his cupped hand and smelled.

Myra lifted her head back as far as it would go and let out a loud laugh, and said, "What an absolute idiot."

Josiah recalled why Papa refused to let demons talk. He said the more time people spent talking to demons, the less time they have to cast them out. "Demons will distract you with their talk forever if you let them," is what Papa had said.

"Demon, I am not going to spend all night talking to you."

"I'm only doing what you told me to do," said the demon. "You commanded me to talk to you. Make up your mind, idiot."

"Shut up!" Josiah ordered. "Get up off that floor and sit on that chair."

Myra sat on the chair. "Would you like some tea?" asked the demon.

"I said shut up. You will talk only when I tell you to talk."

Myra smiled and used her pinched fingers to zip her lips.

"You will not think it is funny when you are walking through dry places," said Josiah. The demon made like it was going to speak. Josiah pointed his finger. "You speak when I tell you to speak. You say only what I tell you to say."

Myra again zipped her lips.

"We will see about your sense of humor," said Josiah. He lifted his hands and by faith looked past the ceiling into the very throne room of God. "Father, I ask you to help me overcome this stubborn demon. Send your mighty angels to help me."

Josiah went to the kitchen and grabbed a chair. He placed it in front of Myra backwards and straddled it. He pointed his finger and began his assault. "In the mighty name of Jesus—!"

Chapter 77

It happened almost simultaneously.

Jezrael heard it before he felt anything in his body.

"Father, I ask you to help me overcome this stubborn demon. Send your mighty angels to help me."

It was like vaporous gas catching hold of a pilot light. The flame of the reviving life of the Creator flashed through his entire body before erupting on all his flesh as a small blue flame. His eyes widened at the welcome sight of it.

The rhinoceros demon was only a few yards away and too overcome with fury to see the flame.

"In the mighty name of Jesus—!"

The rhinoceros demon aimed his formidable horn for the downed angel's belly. He stuck at the target and slung backwards.

Jezrael rolled out of the way as the horn went by him. He effortlessly leapt to his feet, relishing the feel of the power of the man of God's faith and authority pulsating through his body.

The demonic beast's small eyes couldn't widen at the three deep stabs of pain that had surprised and paralyzed his big, muscled body before he rolled over onto his side. He saw the figure come fully into view. It was that angel.

Jezrael looked at the gasping beast in his visible eye. The beast gurgled out, "You could not beat us...without the man's prayer and authority. You have nothing...to say?"

Jezrael answered by a thunderous strike to the demon's thick neck.

He didn't speak to demons.

Jezrael joined his energized brothers in battle. The tide turned. The angels pushed forward against the mysterious army of Myra. Then the battle slowly began to turn against them. The army of Myra was proving too strong—even for angels freshly anointed with power.

Chapter 78

I do not understand," said Josiah.

He had not meant to say this out loud. It was just that the battle had seemed to be going great. Demons were coming out. Myra felt them leaving her body. Victory was within reach. Then suddenly they hit a wall. The stubborn demon was not only still there. He was stronger than ever.

"I am still here, idiot of God."

Josiah looked at Myra with exasperation. He knew Myra was not the demon. But this thing had called him an idiot so many times that he wanted to wring its neck. It had even sang to him that he was an idiot.

"Josiah."

Josiah looked warily at Myra and said nothing.

"Why won't it leave?"

Josiah jumped at the opportunity to talk to her. "Myra, I do not know why he has not yet left, but I will not leave you in this condition."

"I want him gone," Myra said, pitifully.

"We will get him," said Josiah. Josiah thought about Allison. *Lord, please keep her away until Myra is free.*

"I know his name," said Myra.

Josiah's face lit up. "You do? You know his name? What is it?"

"Self-Hatred."

Josiah was underwhelmed. Self-Hatred? He was expecting something like *Great Chief of Darkness* or *Ninki Nanka* or *Tikoloshe* or *Leviathan*. "Self-Hatred?" he said. "An emotion? This is what the demon said?"

"No. I saw him."

"You saw this demon?"

"I saw fighting. He was arguing with an angel. The angel said, 'The Lord rebuke you.' The demon laughed at him and said, 'The Lord rebukes me, but she doesn't rebuke me.'"

"Shut up, you ugly dog!" said the demon. "You talk too much."

Myra doubled over in pain.

Josiah gasped. "Myra." His eyes narrowed. "Stop it. You demon of self-hate, come out of her!"

Myra moaned, "It hurts so bad, Josiah. Make it stop. Make it stop."

"Satan, I said come out of her!"

"I'm not Satan, you idiot."

"Self-Hatred, come out of her."

"Don't call me that."

"I will call you what I please. Come out of her, Self-Hatred."

"He doesn't like it when you call him by his name."

"Myra?"

Myra gritted her teeth and spoke through the spasm that was twisting her gut. "Use his name, Josiah. He doesn't like it when you use his name."

"What is wrong with your stomach?"

Myra cried out in pain and heavy breathing. She resembled a woman in labor. "I don't care," she groaned, "about the pain. Make him leave."

"Self-Hatred, I said come out of her," yelled Josiah.

After twenty minutes of Josiah using the demon's name and commanding him to come out, he finally got a response from him.

The demon laughed and said, "Make me, you idiot."

Chapter 79

L *ord, help me. I don't know what else to do. You said that if any us lacked wisdom, we could ask You for wisdom and You would give it. What am I to do here? I cannot yell at this demon all night. He's not listening to me anyway.*

Something came to Josiah's mind.

"Self-Hatred, I command you to let Myra speak."

Myra gasped for air and rolled over onto her side as though she had been holding her breath for several minutes.

"Help this precious woman, Lord Jesus," Josiah muttered. He waited until her breathing was normal. "Myra, you said when the angel challenged the demon, the demon said, 'The Lord rebukes me, but she doesn't rebuke me.' Maybe it is you who need to order this evil spirit to leave."

The words popped out of Self-Hatred's mouth. "Won't work. Won't work. Won't work." He cursed and seethed in fury at his inability to maintain discipline.

It was an embarrassing fact of spiritual warfare that just the legitimate threat of being cast out was often enough to compromise a demon's discipline, personality, and intelligence. Self-Hatred still carried heavy regrets and shame for involuntarily jumping up in the synagogue and challenging Jesus nearly two thousand years ago. Oh, those awful words still echoed accusingly in his dark mind.

Let us alone! What have we to do with You, Jesus of Nazareth? Did You come to destroy us? I know who You are—the Holy One of God!

"If I would have kept my big mouth shut, He would have left us alone. He didn't even know we were there." he said. "And it's in that cursed book for all the world to see!"

Josiah looked at Myra. "You crazy demon, I do not know what you are speaking of, and I do not care. Shut up. I do not want to talk to you. Let Myra speak."

In a few moments, Myra began to weep softly. "I think I know what it is."

"What?"

"I saw demons that look like me in this thing's army. The whole army is me. Even the demons that don't look like me are me."

Josiah sat down and rolled his fingers down his forehead and face. "Okay. Okay. Okay. The Lord is showing us something here."

Myra continued. "Somehow I'm fighting against myself. I'm helping this thing."

Before Josiah knew what he was doing, he pointed his finger at the demon in Myra and demanded, "In the mighty name of Jesus, how is Myra helping you."

Before Self-Hatred knew what he was doing, he blurted out, "She's ugly! Ugly! Ugly! Ugly!"

Josiah continued pointing for several seconds before slowly lowering it. Another round of going at it with this demon and listening to his insults weren't going to get them any closer to deliverance.

Myra broke out into heavy crying.

Josiah gave her time.

"I've always felt ugly."

She may as well have said she had always felt like a jumbo jet. Josiah would have changed his expression had he known how exaggerated and silly it was.

"It started when I was little. You saw Mom and my sisters. They're all way beyond beautiful. Mom used to put us in beauty contests. I won some. But then I stopped winning. I remember the day Mom said that it was a waste of time to enter me in beauty contests any longer because I didn't have a chance of winning."

"Your own mother said that? Oh, Myra."

Myra didn't bother to wipe away her tears. She had lived in secret pain for years. No more. The tears would fall. "She even said that I had grown out of my beauty. And that she was fortunate to still have two daughters with exceptional beauty."

Josiah's mouth went wide in shock.

"I'm not telling you this to make my mother look bad."

"I know this is not your purpose."

"It's just—I think that's where this evil spirit came from. I started hating myself. How I looked. And every time Mom said something negative, or Lauren, or Tina, or even Dad—and he doesn't even know what he's saying—their words...it was like I could literally feel their words enter me like arrows."

"I think you are right," said Josiah. "The demon must have an open door to enter. Your mother spoke death over you." He began to apologize. "I do not mean to—"

"It's okay. You're right," said Myra. "It was a toxic environment. It is a toxic environment."

"Well," said Josiah, turning the kitchen chair around to face Myra and sitting, "I think it is time to give this demon the Holy Ghost boot. I am going to cast this thing out of you, and this time he will go."

"Josiah, wait. I think I need to pray. Are there Scriptures that tell me how I should think of myself?"

"Yes. Many. The whole Bible—" He lifted his hand. "Wait, I will get my Bible." He hurried to his room and came back. "It says here in Philippians 4:8:, 'Finally, brethren, whatsoever things are true, whatsoever things are honest, whatsoever things are just, whatsoever things are pure, whatsoever things are lovely, whatsoever things are good report, if there be any virtue, and if there be any praise, think on these things."

Myra read the Scriptures herself. "This is what I need to do. Something is telling me I need to change the way I think."

Josiah looked at her in wonder. "Myra, this is Romans. 'And be not conformed to this world, but be transformed by the renewing of your mind.'" He smiled widely and shook his head. "Ha, the Holy Spirit is teaching you right here before my eyes."

Myra's abdominal muscles cramped until her knees almost bent. Nausea filled her gut. The demonic helmet clamped shut over her face and head at the same time the fat anxiety demon jumped back on her.

She fought to remain standing. *She had to stand!* But she wobbled. Josiah was instant. He held her arm and said, "Sit here, Myra."

She shook her head with closed eyes and pushed his arm away. "No, I need to stand. I need to resist this thing."

Josiah was reluctant to let go, but she kept pushing against his arm. He grimaced at her discomfort. Yet, he knew that sooner or later Myra would have to learn to stand alone with Jesus. Sooner was always better than later. He slowly let go, assuring himself that she was steady.

Myra didn't even know where to begin in her imagination of the new torment she now felt. And, really, it wasn't altogether new. She had felt something similar before. Like the very essence of who she was was being eaten away by a million bugs.

Now the army was smaller. Yet, the attack was more intense. Instead of a million tiny bites, she felt a thousand knives stabbing her soul and mind and everything she was. The pain wasn't physical, but it was no less real.

Myra willed herself to stand. She pushed her heavy, trembling arms upward. She lifted her face toward heaven and prayed with open eyes filled with tears, some of joy, some of pain, and said, "Lord Jesus, if You have accepted me, I am accepted. You have washed away everything about me that was ugly. All of my sins.

"You called me Your daughter. I am now in Your family. So, it no longer makes a difference how my family sees me."

Myra slowly went to the floor with her eyes wide and focused, as though she were looking at something fantastic. Joyous cries and laughter joined her tears.

"Myra, what do you see?"

"Oh God. Oh God. Oh God," Myra said.

"What is it?" said Josiah.

"Yes, yes, yes," Myra cried and laughed.

"Oh, Lord my God," said Josiah, crying himself.

Myra began to quote Scripture after Scripture. "Charm is deceptive, and beauty is fleeting; but a woman who fears the Lord is to be praised. The Lord does not look at the things people look at. People look at the outward appearance, but the Lord looks at the heart. I praise you because I am fearfully and wonderfully made. I know that fully well.

"Your beauty should not come from outward adornment, such as elaborate hairstyles and the wearing of gold jewelry or fine clothes. Rather, it should be that of your inner self, the unfading beauty of a gentle and quiet spirit, which is of great worth in God's sight."

"No! No! It's not true!" a growling voice said, shaking Myra's head violently. "I hate her! I hate all women!"

Josiah was about to move in on the demon. But just as suddenly as this demon had interrupted Myra, her face was now peaceful and smiling. Then her smile grew as wide as her face would allow. She pushed her outstretched hands farther upward, as though trying to reach something she was looking at. She began to laugh and cry.

Josiah watched silently. Finally, he could remain quiet no longer. "What do you see, Myra? Please tell me."

Her eyes stayed fixed above. She continued to laugh and cry and answered him. "I see the Lord. He's singing to me."

"What is He singing?"

"He's singing, 'You are altogether beautiful, my darling there is no flaw in you.'"

"The Lord God Almighty is singing the Song of Solomon to you?" Josiah muttered, in holy fear. He slowly sat down and bent over and buried his face in his hands. This was a holy moment. When it finally appeared appropriate to proceed, Josiah said, "Are you ready to continue?"

"Continue what?"

"Casting out the demon."

Myra beamed a lovely smile to him. "The demon left. They all left. I'm free, Josiah."

"He left? All of them? Just like that? Jesus ran them off!"

"It was His word. The truth ran them off, Josiah."

Josiah exulted. "You were quoting Scripture. One after the other."

"I don't know any Scriptures. I've never memorized a single one. I saw an angel. I knew he was an angel of truth. He touched my tongue with something hot and said, 'Speak the words of life.' They rolled up and out of my belly. When I heard them, I believed them. When I believed them, the demons left."

Josiah was too excited to sit. He jumped up and clapped his hands together. "Ha-haaa. Take that, devil!"

Myra lifted her palm toward Josiah for a high five. "That's right. Take that, devil."

They smacked palms and talked and talked and talked, like neither of them had to go to work in the morning.

Finally, Myra said, "There's one thing left that needs to be done. Two things, actually. No, three."

"What is that?"

"We need to tell your parents what happened?"

"That is a good thing for me."

"We need to have a sit-down with Allison. Get me off the hot seat."

"That is a good thing for you." Josiah waited. "And the third thing?" he asked, noting a hint of mischief in Myra's eyes.

"Ahh, the third thing," she said, having fun with the words. "The third thing is a clarification about something you said."

Chapter 80

Self-Hatred was shocked at this development. It was a rare occurrence. So rare that he'd heard about this type of thing happening, but he'd never seen it himself. *A slave delivered by nothing but the word of God.* It would take a long time and many victories to live this down.

And his behavior under pressure? He had talked like a parrot with diarrhea of the mouth. Shameful. Just shameful. Well, he sure wasn't telling anyone about this.

But the priority now wasn't the preservation of his reputation. It was the preservation of his life. The dark prison was no place for a demon like him. Motor mouth or not, he had a great future ahead of him—at least until the lake of fire.

I'm getting out of here. If Lord Vicious is still alive, he's on his own. Self-Hatred quickly scanned the battlefield. He didn't see Lord Vicious. What he did see was a one-way trip to the dark prison if he wasted one second more. His army of self-hate demons was being decimated.

Self-Hatred crawled stealthily on his elbows from one mortally wounded demon to another. He lifted himself to a knee beside a headless rhinoceros demon. He had to get out of there, but he couldn't be reckless. He had to wait until—

"You have washed away from me everything that was ugly."

The woman's words shot a jagged chill that tore through Self-Hatred's body. It froze his calculations and movements. It almost froze his heart. He crouched lower and stole a quick glance around the corpse.

Angels were everywhere. Some were doing mop-up jobs with what was left of his army. Others were looking among the vanquished to find demons like him who might be hiding. Maybe they wouldn't find him.

Self-Hatred smeared himself with the rhino demon's pool of blood and laid down on his belly. He positioned himself in an unnatural position. Maybe that would keep an angel's blade from making sure he was dead.

He waited.

"I praise you because I am fearfully and wonderfully made. I know that fully well."

That cursed woman's words entered his ears and began its diabolical work. His closed eyes popped wide open. Furious rage and irrational defiance filled him from head to toe. He jumped to his feet and left the concealment of the rhino carcass.

As the compromised demon shouted at the angels and gesticulated wildly, he strained with his whole heart to stop himself. "I am Self-Hatred. Cunning and shrewd. Are you here to destroy me before the time?"

Self-Hatred's suicidal adrenaline rush evaporated the moment the last word left his mouth. The eyes of a thousand angels fixed on him. An awkward second passed. He made eye contact with several of them.

Self-Hatred took off running. The ground was littered with the thick carnage of demonic beasts, some whole, but most in pieces. The terrified demon's footing repeatedly betrayed him as he zig-zagged and found himself on the ground in a foul soup of chopped up serpents. Nonetheless, fear propelled him closer to the rubble of the stronghold despite his clumsy running.

The buildings were close. He could hardly believe his good fortune to have made it this far. He saw an opening in the debris. He glanced over his shoulder just before he slid on his back through the hole.

Self-Hatred came out the other side, hopped to his feet and ran through the maze of large fallen stones. He leaned against a wall and tried to catch his breath as he wondered why the angels had not pursued him. It didn't make sense.

The demon clutched his chest and thought of his predicament. This was supposed to have been a routine mission. He cursed Lord Vicious and started making his way through the debris. He approached a piece of building to get a look outside. Why hadn't the angels pursued him?

He saw Lord Vicious crouched and hiding behind a large fallen demon just as he had done. Then the crouching demon jumped up out of his hiding place with two swords. He shouted at the angels, "No! No! It's not true! I hate her! I hate all women!"

In a flash, angels were all over the lofty demon. Self-Hatred could hardly believe the brutality and efficiency of the scene. To see such a high-level demon put up as much a fight as a side of beef on a butcher's block.

"If he went out like that, what kind of chance do I have," he said.

"None," said the truth angel behind him.

Self-Hatred turned around just in time for the sword of truth to enter his chest. The angel pushed until the sword's handle was flush against the demon's flesh. The last thing Self-Hatred heard before entering the dark prison was the Lord singing to Myra, "You are altogether beautiful, my darling there is no flaw in you."

Chapter 81

One Week Later

Josiah rang the doorbell. He fidgeted nervously and pulled the flowers from behind his back and smelled them. He hid them again before re-inspecting them, hiding them again, and closing his eyes and muttering a prayer.

Myra smiled as she watched the whole adorable thing through the peephole. She opened the door and was pleased at how utterly unsuccessful Josiah was at hiding that the holy man of God was floored by her beauty. "Josiah, so glad you could come."

"I would never miss your one-week salvation anniversary."

"Does your back hurt?" she asked.

"Oh," he smiled, presenting her the flowers. "I hope you like these flowers. I find them beautiful."

His words hung in the air. It was like an invisible interpreter was shouting, "What he is really saying is, 'I find *you* beautiful.'" Josiah cleared his throat and pulled his gaze momentarily from her lovely face.

Now it was Myra's turn to be surprised. She had seen the flowers through the peephole, but not what kind they were. "These are...lovely flowers, Josiah." She went to set the flowers down.

Josiah said, "May I come in?"

"Oh yeah, that's right. You don't live here any longer. Let me think about it for a sec. I did invite you. So, okay, you can come in."

"Thank you," he said, smiling. "Yesterday's favor is not today's obligation."

"Let me guess," she said. "An ancient African proverb."

"Not very ancient. Papa created it." Josiah looked at the kitchen table. The first word that came to mind was *romantic*. "It smells delicious in here."

"You like candles? I love candles," Myra said, as she rearranged the table to make room for the new flowers.

"They are very nice," he said, noticing there were two sets of tableware and not three. "May I wash my hands?"

"No, Josiah, you may not wash your hands. Yesterday's favor is not today's obligation."

He laughed. "Okay." He went to the restroom. When he returned, the lights were dimmed, and Myra was seated at the table. He sat down under her playful gaze. "Did you know you are glowing?" he said.

"I know I am glowing inside. I didn't know I was glowing outside. Would you like to pray over the food?" she asked.

"I would love to pray for us." *She said pray over the food, Josiah, not pray for us,* he thought. "May I take your hand?"

"Will you give it back?"

"Maybe," he joined the joke. He prayed and released her hand. "You see, I am a man of my word."

Myra began her presentation. "We have an avocado, tomato, and corn salad. The world's best mac and cheese. Greens. A little something you may recognize. Fresh, hot acacia bread."

"Is that goat?"

"It's not chicken."

"And for dessert, we have biskuti ya nazi."

"Biskuti ya nazi? Who told you about biskuti ya nazi?"

"The same person who told me about goat."

He pondered, then made a *No way!* Face. "Mama?"

"Mama," said Myra.

"You talked to Mama? What are you doing talking to Mama? No one told me you two are in conversation."

"Josiah, Mama is grown. I'm grown. We don't need to tell you we are in conversation."

"Papa is right. You are rude."

Myra chuckled. "Papa is right. I am rude."

"But you are a good rude. And anyway, we have goat. We have biskuti ya nazi. All is forgiven. It is under the blood."

"Dig in," said Myra.

"Where is Allison?"

"Not here."

There was something about the way she answered that slowed his scoop of macaroni. He grinned and continued. "I was under the impression that she would be here for the anniversary celebration."

"She was here."

He kept the grin as he continued to get his food. "That is quite clever."

"We thought so."

Josiah tasted the goat. "What? This is Mama's goat. She gave you her recipe? She gives no one her goat recipe. It is a great mystery. Like the holy Trinity."

"She gave it to me."

He dipped his bread into the goat gravy and ate. He bounced his finger at Myra. "I can see now that I am in great danger."

"Why lavender roses?" asked Myra.

"They are beautiful. I thought you would like them."

"Lavender?"

"They are the wrong color?"

She studied his face for the slightest sign that there was a smile behind the innocence. "Now, Josiah, you are a man of God. You can't lie."

"Now, Myra, you are a woman of God. You cannot manipulate. You are already rude. This combination might damn your soul forever. You have only been a Christian for one week. Why take a chance?"

She couldn't laugh at his joke. She needed to know about these flowers. The safe thing would be not to ask. But she'd never get to sleep not knowing his true feelings. "So, you don't know what lavender roses represent? You just picked them out because they're beautiful?" She was afraid of what the answer might be.

"Nooo, I didn't say that. The florist helped me. She knows a lot about flowers."

"A florist should know a lot about flowers, Josiah. How did she help you?"

"This bread is very good with the gravy. I am not saying it is not good without the gravy." A tiny grin began to betray him. "Some food is only good with gravy."

"How did she help you, Josiah?"

"Well, she is like you. She is a woman of many questions."

"What kind of questions did she ask you?"

"You know, florist questions. She was very inquisitive. Actually, I think these were not professional questions. I think this florist was nosy. She asked a lot of questions about you and I."

"About you and I?"

"Imagine that," he said.

Myra started feeling better. "And what did you tell her?"

"I thought that your assessment of the macaroni and cheese was biased. But now I agree. It is the best macaroni and cheese I have ever eaten."

Myra folded her hands together and leaned forward on her elbows.

Josiah patted his mouth with a napkin. "Oh, the florist." A little more of the grin appeared. "You never know about these florists. They ask you so many questions that it is easy to get confused. I can tell you this, whatever I told this woman got her all giddy. She congratulated me and insisted that these were the appropriate flowers."

Oh, really? Now why would that woman congratulate him? What did he tell her? Myra felt her own giddiness grow. But she didn't show it.

"Now I have a question," said Josiah. "When you asked me to join you and Allison for dinner—whom you conspired with to not be here for dinner—you said you would ask me for a clarification of something I said. I am assuming that whatever this clarification is, it is not for Allison to hear."

"That's brilliant, Mr. Spock."

"Thank you. That was a fine program. But Mama doesn't like it. She is sure Captain Kirk is a fornicator."

"You said I am beautiful. Do you really think I'm beautiful?"

Josiah turned his face sideways and narrowed his eyes at her.

"Don't you look at me like that, Josiah. You said it."

"I will admit—and I think the Lord will allow this since we have been through so much together—you are a beautiful woman." He paused. "Really beautiful." He paused again. "Exceptionally beautiful." He playfully bounced his finger at her. "But this is the first time I have ever told you this. I was thinking only of your soul."

Myra chuckled and shook her head. "That is not true. And you are no Mr. Spock. You're a Mr. Spock wannabe. The night Allison blackmailed you into moving in, you called me beautiful in your prayer."

"What prayer?"

"This prayer, 'Oh Lord, I cannot believe this. What have you gotten me into? I am holy and pure, and you make me move in with two beautiful women. This is insane. This is totally insane.'"

"I remember praying something similar to that, but not the part about beautiful women. And, anyway, how can you remember my whole prayer correctly?"

"How can I not remember it? You called me beautiful."

Josiah smiled. He went back to that bouncing finger. "You keep saying that. Even if I did say that, how do you know I was speaking of you?"

Myra reached over and pushed his hand to the table.

"You are trying to smash my hand into my macaroni and cheese," he said.

"Because there were only two women in the apartment," said Myra.

"How can we say this? There could have been other women in other rooms."

"Just admit it, Josiah."

"Admit what?"

She smiled. "You have designs on me."

"What? Designs on you? You have designs on me."

"Don't try to shift this."

"Shifting? *I* am shifting? You kissed me."

Myra's face went plain. "Excuse me. But I am sure you have me mixed up with someone else. Maybe one of your software engineering babes."

"No, I am quite certain it was you who assaulted me."

"Assault? Josiah, what are you fantasizing about?"

He smiled. "Fantasy huh? I could press charges. The night we were at Barnes and Noble. You remember it?"

"Yes."

"Then you are almost locked up. You were sick. Or, in retrospect, you appeared to be sick. I now doubt your condition."

"I was sick."

"That is for a jury to decide, not me. Anyway, you appeared to be about to pass out. 'Oh, Josiah, I feel very heavy.' You remember saying that?"

"I did feel heavy. I felt like I was going to drop."

"Here's what I think," he said. "You were trying to get yourself into my arms. That's where the heaviness came from. Your heart was heavy that you were not in my arms. I carried you, as any man of God would. You appeared to be in distress. The next thing I know your lips were on my neck."

Myra burst out laughing. "I'm sorry, Josiah, but you are lying. That did not happen. You're mixing your imagination with reality."

"I felt...your lips...on my neck."

Mischief was on Myra's face again. "You did?"

"I did."

"Were they soft"

"They were."

"Were they moist?"

"They were."

"You being a holy man of God and all, did you move your neck away from my soft, moist lips?"

"I most certainly did not. I was gathering evidence that you had designs on me."

Myra burst out laughing again. "Oh, you are so full of it. That's not a sin to say that, is it?"

"No. But if it were, the Lord is good. He would have mercy on you because He knows you are a woman under the influence of designs."

Myra went into another round of laughter. She reared her back and said, "Aaahhh, Josiah! What am I going to do with you?"

He smirked and said, "I am sure this is not the first time you have asked yourself this question."

"Okay, you're holding on to the Spock thing even though your cover is blown sky high."

"Is it?"

"Blown," she said. "You have shown way more interest in me than any pupil-student or preacher man-disciple relationship. You drop hints here and there. You moved out a week ago and you have asked me out every day since you've been gone."

"You asked me here tonight."

"Yes, one night," she said. "You pray for me and you somehow find a way to include how beautiful and precious I am in every prayer. Even when you pray over our food."

"I think that is an exaggeration," he said.

"Really?" said Myra. "Tonight—"Josiah prepared to keep from smiling—"'Dear God, I thank you for this evening with your beautiful and precious daughter. Your beautiful and precious daughter has been through so much and has been treated so badly. But you have brought this beautiful woman, this lovely flower out of a very dark place.'"

Josiah could hold his laughter in no longer. "Okay, you can stop."

"Are you sure? Because I can go on. Josiah, you never even got around to praying for the food. It was just precious this and beautiful that. Everything you're eating is unblessed."

"You have a very good memory."

"Yes, I do."

"Did I really call you a lovely flower?"

"Yes." There was a pause as they looked into one another's eyes. "That was nice," said Myra.

"You are nice," he said, without a hint of levity. "You are beautiful. And you are precious."

Myra's eyes were instantly moist.

Josiah saw this. "Let's eat the rest of this delicious food, even though you caused it to not be blessed. Afterwards, we can have coffee and biskuti ya nazi—and talk." He could see that she wanted to talk now. "I promise to not leave until all your questions are answered."

Lord, please make Your plan clear to us, he prayed inside. *I do not want to make a mistake. I do not want anyone to get hurt.*

Chapter 82

They sat in the living room.

Myra ate one of the macaroons and drank some coffee. She enjoyed neither. Her stomach was in knots. It had been in knots ever since Josiah suggested they eat rather than continue their talk.

Sure, he had promised that all would be clear before he left for the evening. But she felt his suggestion was to buy time. He liked her, but how much? She didn't think he knew the answer. At least not deep inside. He was still figuring this out. That's what was so unsettling. The big question mark hanging over this whole thing.

Josiah drank the last of his coffee and sat the cup down. "Papa and Mama have been married forever. Forty-three years. My grandparents and uncles and aunts have all been married for many, many years. It is a mark of the blessing of the Lord and of submission to His will. It is very important to us."

"Why are you telling me this?"

Josiah took in a deep breath and exhaled. "It is something I desire."

What is this man saying? she thought.

"I am a man of commitment, Myra."

She still didn't know what he was saying, or how she should respond.

"I do not make a commitment unless I am fully resolved to follow through."

"Josiah, this is excruciating. Let me help you out. You like me. A lot. I'm precious and beautiful. But you are unsure of your feelings for me. I appreciate your honesty. And just for the record, Josiah, this isn't Africa, but we have customs, too. We generally date before marriage. Not that it does any good, but that's how it's done here."

Tears rolled freely down her face. Yet, she found herself surprisingly calm despite her pain. She belonged to God, and she was truly beautiful because she was beautiful in His sight. Everything was going to be fine.

"Oh, no, Myra that's—"

"Would you hand me my purse, please? It's over there," she pointed. "I need some tissue."

Josiah went to the purse, unsnapped and opened it, put his hands on the packet of tissue, turned half-way to Myra, and froze. He stared at the wall with wide eyes and a wide mouth.

"Did you just go into my purse?"

"Oh, dear God in heaven," he said.

Myra said, "Mama has talked to me about this. You have designs on me."

Josiah laughed and laughed and laughed. "Beautiful...precious...lovely flower, I told you that all would be clear before I left your home. Yes, I most certainly have designs on you."

The End

Please Write A Review!

If you liked the story, please leave a review on Amazon.
It helps potential readers, and it helps the book qualify for special marketing
and promotion programs.

Get Free Spiritual Warfare Short Story!

Join my email family and get one of my free short spiritual warfare stories here: https://dl.bookfunnel.com/ajx91tx3ku.

Contact Me

Here's my contact info: ericmhillauthor@yahoo.com.

Other Books by the Author

SPIRITUAL WARFARE NOVELS
The Fire Series Box Set
Bones of Fire (The Fire Series Book One)
Trial By Fire (The Fire Series Book Two)
Saints On Fire (The Fire Series Book Three)

The Demon Strongholds Series Box Set
The Spirit Of Fear (Demon Strongholds Series Book One)
The Spirit Of Rejection (Demon Strongholds Series Book Two)
The Spirit of Ugly (Demon Strongholds Series Book Three)

OTHER NOVELS
The Runaway: Beginnings (Out of Darkness Series Book One)
The Runaway: Endings (Out of Darkness Series Book Two)
The Great Crime Spike
Finding Angel

NONFICTION
Deliverance from Demons and Diseases
What Preachers Never Tell You About Tithes & Offerings
You Can Receive Answers to Your Prayers